"I don't know what came over me."

Des reached out and took her hand in his, and she didn't pull back. Though their potential business relationship deemed everything romantic inappropriate, this man created such amazing feelings inside her....

"The same thing that came over me the minute I saw you," he said, closing the distance between them with one step.

"Why is that?" Jessica whispered, her heart playing a beat in her ears.

"The same reason I can't help but do this," he said, a second before she found herself pulled into his strong arms, his mouth claiming hers, his tongue sliding past her lips.

Perhaps she should have objected, should have pushed him away. But how could she? With his kiss, Des made love to her in a way most men wouldn't do with their entire bodies.

And she melted...lost in the moment and the man.

Books by Lisa Renee Jones

Silhouette Nocturne

*The Beast Within #28
*Beast of Desire #36

*The Knights of White

LISA RENEE JONES

is an author of paranormal and contemporary romance fiction. Having always lived in Austin, Texas, Lisa will soon be making a new home in New York. Before becoming a writer, Lisa worked as a corporate executive, often taking the red-eye flight out of town and flying home just in time to make a Little League ball game. Her award-winning company LRJ Staffing Services had offices in Texas and Nashville. The firm was recognized by *Entrepreneur* magazine in 1998 as one of the top-ten growing businesses owned by women.

Now Lisa has the joy of filling her days with the stories playing in her head, and turning them into novels she hopes you enjoy!

You can visit her at www.lisareneejones.com.

BEAST
OF DESIRE

LISA RENEE JONES

To Diego for being my "Des" and never letting me give up

SILHOUETTE BOOKS

ISBN-13: 978-0-373-61783-8
ISBN-10:   0-373-61783-6

BEAST OF DESIRE

www.silhouettenocturne.com

Printed in U.S.A.

Dear Reader,

Writing the KNIGHTS OF WHITE series has been such a fun experience for me. The idea that real heroes exist, ones who are willing to sacrifice for all that is good and all that they love, is the ultimate fantasy.

When I wrote *The Beast Within,* Des was already showing his rowdy self and demanding his own story. He was strong-willed then, and nothing changed when he got his own book! I had the joy of falling in love with Des, and I knew it was going to require a special woman to make me let him go! I simply wanted to keep him for myself. But Jessica convinced me that she was, indeed, the woman worthy of Des.

Beast of Desire most certainly is a story about passion and forgiveness, but most of all, it's a story about love conquering all.

I hope you enjoy!

Lisa

Legend of the Beasts

Sentenced to an eternity on earth for killing his brother Abel, Cain became angry and sought the good graces—and powers—of the underworld. By doing so, it is said that he was granted magical powers and given leave from the physical plane. But his gifts came with a price. Cain now rules an army of beasts who walk the earth, stealing souls and delivering them to the underworld.

Though Cain was allowed to get away with his actions, over time, the scale of good and evil began to tilt. The Angel Raphael, the healer of the earth, was given the duty of balancing the scale again. To do this, he assigned Salvador, his most trusted companion, the duty of saving those souls worthy of serving good against evil. These unique men are given back their souls and enlisted in an elite army...The Knights of White.

Prologue

Deep in meditation, Jag, leader of the Knights of White, sat cross-legged, his dark hair pulled back at the neck, his body draped in the earthly color of forest-green. Directly in front of Jag, dressed in the same attire, sat his mentor, Salvador.

Shaped as a perfect circle, the simple room had unnaturally white walls and white padded floors. Incense burned, as did candles and healing herbs.

It had been several months now since Jag had found his mate, and she had balanced the darkness of the Beast within him with her pureness. And since then, Jag had been gifted with magical powers to guide and protect his Knights of White.

Jag's eyes fluttered and then snapped open, the vision he'd experienced damn near twisting his gut in knots. A vision of his second-in-charge, Des, turning from White Knight to Darkland Beast. Of the man he knew as a friend becoming an enemy.

"What is this that you have shown me?"

Salvador's light green, almost fluorescent eyes darkened with truth, his long, dark hair secured at his neck. "You know he walks too closely to the darkness."

Jag inhaled, defeated by this reality. "I have to save him."

"He will have to save himself. Even now, as we speak, the wheels are in motion to give him a choice between Beast and man." Salvador's voice firmed. "You may guide but not interfere. Des's choices and his destiny will be of his own making. He must choose—darkness or light."

Chapter 1

A sexy eighties song filtered through the air of the elite Padre Island Men's Club, a lush brunette atop an oval stage, swaying to the beat.

Dim lights added flavor to a room designed for sin and seduction, dancers scattered at various other locations throughout the room, working the music and the men. In the far corners the walls were lined with couches for those who wanted to remain discreet, while private shows were available for those willing to pay the price.

Preferring both his entertainment and his women full of excitement, Des had chosen to sit front and center, at the edge of the stage. Here he had a perfect view of the dancer who called herself "Veronica" as she seduced the audience with her curvy hips and inviting, full breasts.

Beside him, two of his fellow Knights of White, Rinehart and Rock, each nursed a beer. Des preferred the bigger bite of tequila. He was immortal, after all. It wasn't as if the stuff was going to kill him. Even getting a buzz, for their kind, was nearly impossible.

"Veronica" eased closer, kneeling in front of Des as she sang the words of the song. Then she turned the song into a question. "Do you think I'm a nasty girl?" she whispered.

"I don't *think, mi hermosa,*" Des murmured in a low voice, his hungry eyes taking in her naked body, her pebbled nipples. *"I know."*

She'd been quite the feast two weekends before. A hot Mexican mama who matched his heritage and did a good job of trying to match his lust. But as good as that night had been, he wouldn't be repeating it. He never allowed himself to repeat. Repeat performances invited questions about his past, about his life, that he didn't welcome.

Talk, no. Sex, yes.

Besides, tonight was about Rock, not him. The kid had it bad for their Healer, Marisol, which meant he was out of luck. Healers were considered off-limits, forbidden physical pleasure, a rule Marisol took seriously despite her own obvious desire for Rock. In other words, the consequences of following her desire would be some deep trouble. Of course, helping the kid was no easy task. Rock really was as stubborn as a rock, though Des doubted that's what the name meant to the kid. How ironic he'd chosen his immortal name to be something so fitting. They all chose one name to define their existence within the Knights, something special to them and them alone, leaving behind their past—or at least trying to forget what once was.

With Rinehart as an accomplice, Des had convinced the kid to join them for a night out, with one agenda in mind…hooking Rock up with a woman. This particular dancer's flavor of "nasty" was exactly the kind of distraction Rock needed.

Des drew a C-note from his pocket and leaned toward the stage. The Knights had money and he didn't mind using his. They'd all been given healthy trust funds after completing their training; money to live on. He'd been smart and invested his money well, though he didn't share that little bit of information with the others. If they were smart, they had as well. An eternity of living demanded funds. Besides, Des would be damned if the lack of money would ever make him feel beneath anyone again. He'd been there, done that, was never doing it again.

Motioning the woman forward, Des whispered in her ear. She leaned back and smiled, waiting patiently for her reward. Sliding his fingers up her thigh, he placed the money under her garter. She stood and walked toward the stairs in a sexy strut.

"Tell me you didn't," Rock said, running a hand over his short, sandy brown hair, a muscle in his jaw jumping.

Des eyed Rinehart, an ex-military man who sat arms crossed, cowboy hat pulled low over his buzzcut, shadowing his eyes. "Tell me you did," he said. Eyes that were normally cold and calculating now twinkled with mischief.

"Come on, Rock," Des said. "You know you have to."

Each Knight possessed a soul, but each had also been touched by a Beast. Each had turned into a demon later saved by Salvador, a recruiter for the Knights. Now, they lived with that Beast inside, some more than others, forced to fight their primal urges. To control the urges, they needed to put them to use. To burn them out. A task best achieved in war or sex.

But Rock was so hung up on Marisol he took risks he couldn't afford to take. He let himself live on the edge. "She knows, man." Des lowered his voice for Rock's ears only. "Marisol knows you have no choice. And you both know Healers are off-limits. As in, you're not going there, so stop thinking you are. You're wound tight. You need this. It's a woman or the battlefield, and since the Beasts are remarkably quiet right now, I'd say it's the woman."

Veronica appeared floor level, her body working in a sultry rhythm meant for Rock's exclusive pleasure. Yet, the younger Knight started to complain. "Des, man, I told you, no. I—" Veronica straddled him and Rock lost his words.

Rinehart laughed and held up his beer in a mock salute of Des. "May Rock's pleasure be our sanity."

"Hell, yeah," Des said, laughing at the truth of the statement. "I'd say that calls for another drink."

Raising his hand to flag a waitress, Des spotted their new security specialist, Max, in the doorway. Des grimaced at the unexpected visitor. He didn't like Max, and he didn't know why. Something was off with the guy.

Taking advantage of his position of observation, Des sized Max up, trying to put his finger on what it was. The newcomer appeared normal enough. As normal as an immortal who fought demons could come off. Des sized Max up as he often did, trying to figure out the newcomer. His brown hair, a bit longer than Des's own, touched his shoulders. The biker getup Max favored of leather jacket and matching pants had to be hot as hell, though, in the current hundred-degree Texas heat. That was exactly why Des stuck to jeans and a T-shirt. Simple. Easygoing. But nothing about Max was simple.

Des's eyes locked with Max's and they stared at one another, a standoff of sorts. Rinehart turned, following Des's gaze, but he didn't comment on Max's appearance. Rock didn't notice Des's distraction at all. Veronica had him standing at attention.

Des wasn't about to be the first to break eye contact. A topless waitress did the job for him, stopping in front of Max, and giving both Knights an excuse to change focus.

"What's Max doing here?" Des asked, shooting Rinehart a suspicious look.

"Guess he was thirsty," Rinehart replied with a nonchalant shrug, adjusting his gaze as if he were checking out Rock's private dancer, which was bullshit.

Des knew damn well Rinehart wasn't checking out the dancer. He was in avoidance mode. "You invited him." It wasn't a question; more a statement of disbelief.

"You might make your dislike a little less obvious," Rinehart commented, sidestepping a direct answer.

"I don't trust him," Des said. "The guy shows up out of the blue one day and he's a Knight, no training needed. He's already trained. By who? And where?" He shook his head. "Makes no sense."

"Jag trusts him," Rinehart offered.

Des ground his teeth and wished for another tequila. "Right. I forgot."

Rinehart snorted. "You're just pissy because Jag won't tell you Max's story. For once, you're like the rest of us. You're being told things on a need-to-know basis, and apparently, you don't need to know."

Des shot Rinehart a "go to hell" look. "Drink your damn light beer and shut up. If I want your opinion, I'll ask for it."

Rinehart tilted his beer back, but not before he fixed Des in a far too perceptive stare and let out a bark of laughter. They both knew Rinehart had hit the nail on the head with his assessment, but probably not for the reasons Rinehart thought. Jag's recent closeness to the Knights' creator, Salvador, was part of being their leader, a part of the new powers he'd been gifted when he'd found his mate. Des understood that.

Yet Des's exclusion from Jag's inner circle bothered him and not because he wanted to have his damn hand held. He worried about what Salvador had told Jag about him. Des knew full well he walked a little too closely to his Beast. Jag had always worried that Des embraced his Beast too readily. Des argued it allowed him control over his darker side. But maybe Salvador knew just how close to that dark side Des felt some days.

Max appeared beside the table, snapping Des out of his reverie. "Looks like they'll let anyone in this place these days," Des said, grinning as he acted as if joking, though they both knew he wasn't.

Grabbing a chair from an empty table, Max turned it so that his arms rested on the back, legs straddling the seat. "You're afraid I'll steal some of the attention," Max said, with a half smile.

Max enjoyed egging Des on. In some ways, Des enjoyed it, too. Kept things interesting. He sort of liked disliking Max. Gave him somewhere to put all the tension when he wasn't on the battlefield or in bed. "Hey," Des said, giving a nod. "If you can earn it, take it." A hint of challenge laced his tone, subtle but evident, by intention. "How'd you even know we were here?"

"I told him," Rinehart admitted, grinning, the look in his eyes daring Des to give him crap about it.

And Des wanted to. His hand itched to reach up and smack Rinehart's big-ass cowboy hat right off his head. Instead he said, "I'd say you owe me a tequila, cowboy."

Des shifted his gaze to Max, about to tell him he was buying the next round after Rinehart paid up, but before he could get the words out, his cell phone rang. He frowned when he noted the number.

He glanced up at Rinehart. "It's Jag."

All three of the Knights were instantly on alert. Jag wouldn't call to simply say hello. Des stood and started walking, punching the button to answer the call while he worked his way to the back of the room where it was quieter. An unnecessary attempt to find quiet considering the call lasted all of sixty seconds. Jag's instructions were short and to the point.

"Duty calls," Des reported to Max and Rinehart when he returned to the table. "We need to hightail it back to Brownsville."

Rinehart's brows dipped, his expression registering concern. "Any idea why?"

"Nope," he said, not elaborating because the truth

was, when he'd opened his mouth to ask, he'd been met with a dial tone.

Rinehart and Max were already standing. "He didn't give you any idea?" Max probed, as if he thought Des was hiding something.

Des grimaced. "What did I say, Maxwell? He said nothing."

"Max. The name is Max."

Waving off the words, Des had nothing else to say to the guy. Max set his teeth on edge. The man had a dark edge that cut like a knife. Once during battle, Des had even thought he'd seen a glimpse of red in Max's eyes. That, along with the secrets Max kept, rang a bell in Des's head. Max was trouble. His secret was trouble. Maybe Jag didn't tell Des about Max's history because it was so damn dirty, Des might flip out.

Des eyed Rock, noting how well Veronica had taken him into oblivion. Letting out a heavy sigh, he accepted defeat. Rock wouldn't be finding satisfaction after all, and they'd all feel the pain of his bad mood tomorrow.

He exchanged a look with Rinehart and held up two fingers an inch apart. "We were so close to getting him taken care of."

"Another week of his grumpy ass," Rinehart said, shaking his head. In a defeated tone, he added, "I'll get him."

The waitress appeared with Des's drink and he grabbed the shot glass from the tray, downed the contents and returned it to the tray. He shoved money into her tip glass. "Thanks, sweetheart."

But the drink did nothing to calm the rush of adrenaline already shooting through his blood. The low hum of edginess that had started taking form with Max's entrance turned to an outright scream. He reached deep, in a way he'd taught himself years before, pushing away the discomfort, wrapping himself in control. He inhaled and let it out as a smile touched his lips.

He needed to funnel his Beast. Trouble was brewing, and Des couldn't wait to introduce himself.

Des brought his motorcycle to a stop in front of the main house on the Jaguar Ranch, a fifteen-thousand-square-foot property where the Knights of White both lived and trained. Oh, they did other things here, such as horse breeding, but only for the purpose of hiding their true operation from the rest of the world.

As Des approached the house, he found Jag standing on the porch with his wife, Karen, by his side, the two making a striking couple. At well over six feet, Jag's muscular body towered over Karen's petite frame, his long, dark hair contrasting with her blond hair, his dark skin against her fair. She was the first of her kind, a mate to a Knight of White. Perhaps *one of a kind.* None of them expected they would find a mate. It was unheard of before Karen. And the situation that had brought her to Jag had been a complicated and emotional one. Karen had been Jag's wife in her prior life as well, killed by the Beasts as Jag had watched. No doubt, finding each other again, so many years later, had been destiny.

Karen spotted Des, waving at him. She kissed Jag's cheek and headed inside the house. Des liked Karen, and he was happy Jag had found her again. Himself, he didn't expect to be anything but alone in his life. In the nearly hundred years he'd lived, that was how it had been. The way he saw it, that was how it was supposed to be, too.

Des stopped at the bottom of the porch steps and rested his foot on the second step from the top, his elbow on his knee. A jumbo-size mosquito—the only way they made them in Texas—landed on his arm and he brushed it away. The night was hot and the air thick, bringing the giant bugs out in armies.

"What's going down?" Des asked, prodding Jag when his leader didn't immediately speak.

Jag crossed one booted foot over the other, leaning against one of the white pillars framing the steps, the porch light illuminating his features.

A smile touched Jag's lips for the briefest of moments. "I expected you'd make it back before the others."

Des narrowed his gaze on Jag, trying to read between the lines. "Which means you planned it that way."

"It worked out for the best," Jag commented, reaching up and running his hand over his goatee. He took several long seconds, stroking it, seeming to think about his words. Finally, he said, "You're one of the few people I've ever told about the day I became a Knight." He fixed Des in a direct look. "Just you and Karen and she lived through it."

Des nodded. The secrets they'd shared made Jag's recent silence harder to swallow. "As I've shared things with you I have with no other."

"I know you have," Jag agreed, taking a seat on the top step of the porch. "I trust you, Des. I trust you as no other Knight." A moment of silence. "I trust you as a friend."

Des didn't know what to say to that. It had always been that way. He and Jag had been close, though they'd never used the word *friend*. His chest tightened with an unfamiliar emotion. He tried not to let such things inside, where they could hurt. But it was too late. It was there, ripe, alive. Maybe he should be happy for that. The Beast didn't completely own him or he'd feel nothing.

"I'd like to think we are," Des said simply, adding nothing more because Jag appeared to have a point he was working on revealing.

"That's why I'm putting a sensitive task in your hands."

Des sat down, following Jag's lead, certain something big was about to be exposed. "I'm listening."

"A museum has announced the discovery of the long-sought-after Journal of Solomon, which legend says contains a map to a treasure box. In the box is said to be a list of angelic bloodlines. In short, these bloodlines are magical, and will be considered a threat to the underworld. Those on this list will hold special gifts capable of battling evil. They will be in danger, hunted by our enemies."

"Legend." Des said the word in a flat tone. "We don't know if any of this is real."

"It's real," Jag assured him. "And so is the danger to the people who are part of those bloodlines." Des nodded his agreement. Jag continued, "The box does have a form of protection. It will self-destruct if evil touches it. But we both know the Darklands won't let that deter them. They'll find a way around that."

In the back of Des's mind, he wondered what that meant about him. Could he touch it? How much darkness had eroded his soul? He wasn't sure he wanted to find out. Shoving the thought aside until later, he asked, "Can't Salvador tell us where the list is buried? He does have the upstairs connection." They all knew Salvador spoke directly to the Archangel Raphael.

"Even if he knew, which I don't think he does, he can't interfere. You know that."

"Right," Des said dryly. "The rules."

Jag ignored his comment. The abstract rules were often a source of frustration for Des and they both knew it. "This is going to be your show," he said. "Take Rinehart, Rock and Max with you and get that journal."

"You're not going?" Des asked, surprised.

"I want Karen by my side. I'm not risking her becoming some sort of leverage in all of this. And taking her isn't an option. She's not leaving Eva while she's adjusting to the ranch anyway."

Karen's sister, Eva, had been claimed by a Beast and saved by Salvador, the only female Knight in existence. Normally, the Darklands killed the women, recruited the men. But Eva had been leverage used against Karen to get to Jag. Though she'd transitioned well, she was still learning and changing, adjusting daily to her new life.

Des nodded his understanding. "I'll find the journal." That brought him to another subject. "I need men I trust to do this right. Max—"

Jag interrupted. "I trust him," he said, giving Des a direct look. "He'll be important to you, Des. *Trust me,* even if you don't him."

Though Des considered objecting further, he decided against it. Instead, he gave Jag another quick nod. "I do." And he did, but he didn't trust Max.

"Besides," Jag said, pushing to his feet, Des following, "Max could hack into Fort Knox. You'll need his skills to get into the museum. Speed will be imperative. The journal is scheduled to arrive at the museum sometime this week, and there is a charity black-tie event soon after to unveil it to the public. I imagine the chaos of the party will be a good time to extract the journal, if not sooner."

The sound of Max's motorcycle engine roared loudly behind him. Immediately after came the crunch of gravel beneath the tires of Rinehart's F-150 pickup.

"Consider this handled," Des said, assuring Jag he'd come through.

"I'm counting on it," Jag said. "I'll leave you to your team."

Jag went into the house as Des turned to find Max approaching. "What's the story?" he asked as he stopped at the bottom of the steps.

Rinehart and Rock joined them before Des had a chance to answer, not that he was going to anyway. He was still fighting uneasiness about Max, despite Jag's assurances. Nevertheless, Jag had a point about his skills. Max had installed a new security system on the property that was as state-of-the-art as it came, yet still discreet enough that it didn't invite questions.

"Pack up, boys and girls," Des said to all three of them, rubbing his hands together and grinning. "We're going to the Big D, and yes, I do mean Dallas. We have us a treasure hunt to go on." He eyed Max. "Whatever you need to work your technology magic, bring it along." Again to all of them. "We're pressed for time. Meet me at the van in fifteen minutes. I'll fill you in on the road."

As Des headed for the front door, he didn't feel like laughing anymore. Something stirred inside him, a feeling of destiny. A premonition of some life-changing event.

Chapter 2

Sitting in her corner office at the Dallas World Museum, a place she normally considered her comfort zone, Jessica Montgomery decided she was definitely, irrevocably, in hell.

It didn't matter that she had her favorite candle lit, the room scented with its warm, cinnamon flavor. Nor did it matter that she was surrounded by pictures of all her favorite destinations. Or that her favorite burgundy wingback chair sat nearby, on its cushion a history book open to the last page she had read.

What mattered was the man who had just charged into her office unannounced. "What is this I hear about someone trying to steal the journal?"

Jessica blinked up at her father, his presence taking her off guard. Ever since the journal had been found a week before, he'd been a wreck, worried over its safety, his mood uncharacteristically edgy. Her father was a senator well respected in the community, his dark hair as perfectly groomed as his three-piece black suit. He rarely allowed sharpness in his tone. Yet, there was no mistaking the sharpness of his voice and mood, now.

And Jessica understood why. Her mother had died while hunting for that journal. Though her father had sworn off the world that Jessica inhabited, the one obsessed with history, he still held his wife's work close to his heart. Finding that journal had been her dream, its safety the safety of her memory.

Jessica kept her response soft, reassuring her father without reserve. "The journal is in a vault and it's safe. Besides, the creeps who tried to steal it were after a decoy. They were never close to the real journal."

"You're certain it's safe? Who would want to steal it?"

"Yes," she said, lying to make him feel better. She had been fighting the feeling that the journal was still in jeopardy. Which was silly. Security at the museum was equal to a maximum-level prison. "I watched them lock it up myself. As for who would want to take it—we both know the journal is a valuable piece of history, not to mention a religious artifact that could impact religious beliefs. These things make it a target to many."

He eased into a chair, a breath sliding from his mouth. "You've actually seen it with your own eyes?"

A smile touched the corners of Jessica's lips. "Oh, yes. Not up close, the way I want to, but I've seen it." It was impossible to hide the thrill she felt over the journal. She'd grown up hearing her mother talk about this discovery. The journal held ancient history but also evolved into a part of her present life story.

Senator Montgomery eyed his daughter. "So like your mother," he said. "You get as excited over history as a kid does candy."

For almost a year after her mother's death, she'd taken a job working for her father. Grief had turned to blame, and he'd turned the pursuit of history into the enemy. He'd loved history, loved his wife's work— even traveled with her often. That was until she had encouraged him to run for the Senate, swearing she'd let her team do the fieldwork. And she had—until the journal. It had become an obsession, and she had trusted no one else to hunt for it, acting as if it were a life-or-death discovery. Upon losing his wife, the love of his life, her father feared Jessica would get the same kind of obsession over history and that she, too, would be taken from him. She'd agreed to a brief departure from the museum because he'd needed her close, and at the same time, being around it had kept the pain of losing her mother alive. But staying away for long had been impossible.

"I love it here," she admitted.

Something dark flashed in his eyes. "I wish I could be happy about that."

Jessica knew he feared she would become obsessed over her work as her mother had. Jessica worried because at times her father seemed irrational about her work. He agonized that Jessica's job would somehow lead to her demise, as he claimed her mother's had.

Kate Montgomery had died of breast cancer that might have been cured if it had been caught early enough. She'd missed her checkups and been diagnosed late, a fact her father blamed on her fixation on the journal. His wife had spent the last two years of her life at a dig site in Mexico, away from those who loved her, claiming an urgency for finding that journal as the reason that no one but her understood.

"I still can't believe you kept funding Mom's team, Daddy." Her father had turned bitter upon her mother's death, and Jessica had assumed he'd ended the search team's efforts to find the journal. Now she knew otherwise.

"I feared your mother would turn over in her grave if I did otherwise." His tone and expression were serious, as if he believed his words. "I better go." He pushed to his feet.

Jessica stood as well, intending to give him a hug. Her intercom buzzed and she made a frustrated sound. Her father leaned over the desk and kissed her cheek. "See you this weekend."

Jessica sank down to her chair and hit the button on her phone. The voice of the receptionist, a sweet older woman named Rebecca, filled the air. "There's a Mr. Smith to see you, with Smith Systems. He says he has a possible donation to the museum."

Jessica frowned. Usually people didn't drop by to make a donation. Feeling a tad giddy with stress, she asked, "Did you tell him we aren't Goodwill?" Her assistant, Michael Wright, would be proud of her for actually cracking a joke. His favorite word to describe her was *uptight*.

Rebecca didn't say anything. Apparently, she didn't get the intended humor. Jessica sighed. Maybe she wasn't meant to tell jokes.

A male voice murmured something in the background,

and for some reason, Jessica felt an odd shiver race down her spine. That was weird. She heard the voice again and felt all warm inside. God. She was losing it. She'd barely heard the guy's voice and she was wondering what he looked like. That was what she got for living a darn-near celibate life these days. Since her father had taken office, she seemed to draw men with agendas, and it had gotten old. Despite her recent man boycott, this stranger had her imagination all fired up. Was he as sexy as he sounded?

Rebecca whispered into the phone, pulling Jessica from her reverie. "I'm pretty sure you'll want to see Mr. Smith."

Jessica almost laughed. If Rebecca knew where Jessica's mind had been, she would laugh, too, this time for sure. But curiosity over how this visitor looked wasn't enough to justify seeing him in the middle of a busy day. The chance that a walk-in was worth her time was slim.

"I'm completely buried with the party organization. Hold on and let me look at my calendar. Can he schedule next week? Better yet, can I call him?"

The man's voice again. Another chill down her spine. Then Rebecca. "He says he has an appointment."

A light went on in her head. Her boss, Greg Ward, had mentioned this days ago—some referral from one of their directors—and promised her more detail that he'd never given to her.

Truth be told, the breast-cancer charity event she was coordinating was a few days away, and she'd forgotten to follow up, busy with the planning. The event had been a condition of her father donating the journal to the museum. She hoped the insurance people would allow the journal to be shown that night.

Debating, Jessica pondered bowing out of the meeting.

If she turned this guy away and he was important, Greg Ward could hang her with the board. He'd taken her job when she'd departed over her mother's death. Now, he resented her return, even though she now reported to him, and did everything within his reach to undermine her.

She sighed, resigned to taking the meeting. "Tell Mr. Smith I'll be right down."

Jessica pushed to her feet. Time to meet the man behind the sexy voice.

But first, she detoured to her boss's office, hoping to get a file on her visitor. A stop that proved fruitless, as Greg's assistant had nothing to give her. Since Greg had yet to arrive at work, Jessica was forced to wing her meeting, feeling completely unprepared. She hated being unprepared.

The elevator dinged to signal Jessica's arrival on the lobby level of the museum *exactly* ten minutes after the announcement of her visitor. She knew this because of her recent obsession with her Cartier watch, or rather with a memory of the way it had been given to her. The watch, her thirtieth birthday gift from her father, had been delivered by courier. He'd been upset over her return to the museum and mourning her mother, but his actions had still hurt.

All her sad thoughts slipped away as she exited the elevator. The sound of a deep, sultry laugh fluttered along her nerve endings, igniting a silent charge. It was the man she'd heard over the intercom. Her visitor.

Standing a few feet away, she sized him up, taking in the appeal that went beyond his voice.

Tall and dark, he was striking, even from a distance. Chin-length brown hair, streaked with auburn, framed a square jaw and high cheekbones. His clothes were well fitted and clung to a body meant to tease and please a woman. Tailored black slacks emphasized his long, muscular legs. Broad shoulders tapered to a thin waist and, no doubt, a rippling set of abdominals.

Not only was he the first man she'd reacted to in a heck of a long time, he was also quite possibly the sexiest man she'd ever laid eyes on.

But it wasn't merely his looks that washed over her in a tidal wave of awareness. Nor his air of utter confidence. It was the mixture of danger and daring she found all too appealing.

As if he felt her eyes on him, he turned in her direction, taking a casual stance, resting his elbow on the horseshoe-shaped desk. She started walking toward him, conscious of the attention he placed upon her.

Despite his cool exterior, there was nothing casual about the way his hot stare swept her body, taking in her fitted crème-colored skirt and matching blouse with such absorption she'd have sworn he saw right through them. Her limbs heated with the touch of his eyes. Even more so when their gazes locked. A sizzle darted through the air and mutual attraction flowered into instant, shared awareness.

She stopped at the desk, trying to muster up a smile as cool and professional as her image demanded. Not at all how she felt at the moment. "Hi," she said, offering her hand. "I'm Jessica Montgomery."

Straightening to his full height, he towered over her five feet five inches. Jessica guessed him to be at least six foot three.

"Nice to meet you, Ms. Montgomery," he said, his

voice rich and deep, with just enough of a Hispanic accent to be sexy.

His hand closed around hers and heat skittered up her arm. Good gosh, what was wrong with her? Men did not get to her this way. "Nice to meet you, Mr...." Her words trailed off. What had Rebecca said his name was?

"Desmond Smith," he said, a twinkle in his eyes, as if he knew what she'd been thinking and found it amusing. "I love watching people's faces when they hear my last name. They always look confused. In case you're wondering—and I know you are—I'm adopted."

With his dark-chocolate eyes and milk-chocolate skin, she did expect something more exotic. Her cheeks warmed. "Smith's a good, strong family name rich with history," she countered, realizing he still held her hand, and snatching it back, suddenly self-conscious of Rebecca's watchful gaze.

He smiled. "It is. A fine history, too. Right now though, I'd like to talk about Texas history."

Perking up at that, Jessica asked, "I understand you have a donation to discuss?"

A hint of a smile on his face said he was amused. The scar above his full top lip simply said sexy. "*Possible* donation," he corrected, retrieving a slim silver case from his pocket and offering her a business card.

Jessica accepted it and read, "Smith Systems." Her gaze lifted, her eyes narrowing on him. She didn't miss the connection between his name and the company name. "Forgive me for not being more prepared, but what exactly does Smith Systems do?"

"Oil is the company's main bread and butter," he commented. "I run the philanthropy division focused on

Native American and Mexican history. In short, we fund expeditions to find lost history. Recently, we've been privileged with some big finds, though I admit one particular item is exciting to me."

"Really?" she asked, with genuine interest. New finds were exciting to her, too. They didn't have a Native American collection at all, and their Mexican-history wing was pathetic, especially for a Texas museum. Maybe a sit-down meeting would be worth her time. "What would that be?"

"The Treaty of Council Springs." He narrowed his eyes on her. "Do you know it?"

This was a test. If she didn't know the history that he held close to his heart, the museum wouldn't be getting that treaty for display. Fortunately, it was a test she could pass.

"Signed in 1846 with a Comanche chief, it placed the Native Americans under United States protection," she said, silently thankful she'd been reading up on Native American history. One book picked up by chance had led to several more. Unbelievable how good the timing now appeared.

He smiled, seeming pleased with her knowledge, his demeanor playful and light. "Do you know his name?"

"Yes," she said, finding herself smiling back at him. "Buffalo Hump."

"Buffalo Hump?" Rebecca said. The receptionist inserted herself into the conversation for the first time since Jessica's arrival, though she'd clearly been listening in. "What kind of name is that?"

Jessica and her visitor laughed, their gazes catching at the similar response, her stomach fluttering with the connection. Yet, it felt comfortable. Charged with attraction, yes, but still amazingly comfortable. Not something she usually felt with a stranger.

"Buffalo Hump was a mighty warrior and a brave leader," her visitor told Rebecca.

"A vicious one, too," Jessica added. "But then so were his enemies."

"A name like that would make anyone want to fight," Rebecca commented dryly, but before she could go on, her reception panel buzzed and she had to answer a call.

That left Jessica and the sexy visitor one-on-one. "I apologize, Mr. Smith," she said. "I shouldn't have kept you standing here this long. How about I buy you a cup of coffee? There's a café on the second floor."

"On one condition," he said, his voice laced with flirtation, his eyes filled with mischief.

She tilted her head to study him, not sure what she expected him to say, but more than a little eager to know. "Which is?"

"That you call me Des," he said, his voice holding an intimate quality. As if he'd offered her more than his name.

"Okay, *Des*," she said, her chest tight with an odd sensation she didn't remember ever feeling before. Something about this man really got to her. "But only if you call me Jessica."

"Jessica it is," he said. "Let's go have that cup of coffee and talk about how we might make a little history, you and I."

His words were innocent enough, but the look in his eyes said he was talking about more than the treaty. Jessica decided she was okay with that, too. After all, he was only in town a few days. That meant he was dangerously attractive but still safe.

Mr. Smith—*Des*—represented a distraction that fit her every need.

Chapter 3

So far so good on his cover story, Des thought as they arrived in the museum café and ordered drinks, chatting flirtatiously. The party would facilitate a cover to extract the journal. That meant getting inside and prepared well in advance. The knowledge he learned from Jessica would help ensure they had all bases covered.

Max had expertly crafted his cover. Des had been provided with every imaginable resource to prepare in advance for this meeting. That was except for the surname fiasco, which had forced Des to come up with the stupid last-name joke to avoid suspicion and make his cover work. Aside from that, Des was almost impressed with Max at this point. He was most certainly impressed with Jessica.

They claimed a table in the café and sat across from

one another. Des watched as Jessica adjusted her skirt, trying to keep his eyes from skimming those sexy, long legs beneath sheer hose. She sipped her mocha. Her skin was lovely, pale. Her face heart-shaped, angelic. Lips full, kissable. "Hmmm. They make a darn good cup of java."

He'd ordered the same, sharing in her confessed chocolate addiction. Sampling his coffee, he gave a thumbs-up. "Not bad for a museum coffee shop."

They laughed and shared small talk, but there was nothing small about how this woman affected him. For the first time since becoming a Knight, he was completely blown away by a female.

He wanted to share a lot more than coffee with this woman, had wanted to since he'd started scouting the museum a few days before. Since the moment he'd set eyes on her.

"How many museums have you talked to about your collection?" she asked.

He used his drink to offer a delayed response but the truth was he was mesmerized by her eyes. Light blue. A blue more tantalizing, more compelling than any he'd seen before. So light they were almost translucent.

"You're the first on a list of five I have immediate interest in," he said, taking a sip of his coffee.

"Up to this point, our museum has been more natural history. Unlike most Texas museums, we certainly aren't known for our local history collection. What made us draw your attention?"

Sharp-witted woman. He liked it. She was quick to feel him out, to get to the point. "One of your board members and I have a mutual acquaintance. Apparently, this board member, Mr. Waymon, has recently married into the Native American culture."

She nodded. "I know Ralph Waymon well, actually, and his new wife seems quite nice."

"I'm told his bride may have an interest in growing the museum's collection toward all things Texas. Of course Mexican culture is directly related to Native American culture, and my collection would offer both." He gave her a sly smile. "Frankly, I'm being a bit selfish. I want my collection to shine. With your limited collections in these areas, I feel it gives mine a chance to stand out."

A slow smile slid onto her ruby-colored lips. He wanted to kiss that painted-on color off. "Ralph had mentioned her interest to me, though just in passing so far. We hadn't talked in detail. This sounds like an exciting match-up."

"I think it might be," he said, working toward his primary goal. "Any chance we could take a tour? I'd like to get a feel for what you have on display."

Someone cleared his throat. Then a male voice said, "Jessica."

Jessica turned as Des fixed his gaze over her head. A man stood in the doorway, tall and broad, his blond hair and clothes conservative. His expression tense.

"Can I see you a minute?" The man framed his words as a request but it came out as an order.

Jessica turned to Des. "That's my boss, Greg Ward. You'll want to meet him at some point. Can you excuse me a moment?"

"Of course," Des said.

He watched her go to her boss. Watched them

talking. The man's expression was harsh, his brows furrowed. His exterior seemed all business, but Des sensed something beyond that. Something sinister. Was he under the control of the Beasts? He'd have access to the journal.

This could be trouble.

Not just for the Knights either. For Jessica. The thought of her being in danger stiffened his spine. Protectiveness surged within. He didn't know why. He only knew he had to keep her close. To ensure her safety.

A sudden wave of emotion swept over him. *Jessica.* Impossible as it seemed, he was sure he was feeling her emotions. It was as if she was funneling them through him. And she was upset. He couldn't see her face clearly, but her body language backed up his instincts, her arms crossed defensively in front of her body.

He had to force himself to stay in the chair rather than go to her side. His entire reaction to Jessica was like nothing he'd ever experienced. Even lying to her about why he was here was twisting his gut in knots. Which was nuts. This was necessary. This was about good conquering evil. It wasn't as if he could say, "I'm a demon hunter. Now give me the journal."

Jessica started back toward him, her hand raking through her long silky hair. He wondered if it was as soft as it looked. Wondered what it would feel like against his skin. Wondered what it smelled like.

She slid into her chair, forcing a fake smile. "Where were we?"

"Don't do that," he said.

"Do what?" she asked, confusion darting across her heart-shaped face.

"Pretend nothing is wrong. You're upset. Admit it."

She drew a deep breath and let it out. "It's that obvious?" she asked, looking disappointed in herself. "I thought I was fairly good at putting on a happy face."

"Not with me." He wanted to make her smile, this time for real, and resorted to old faithful—jokes. "Want me to go kick his ass for you?"

She rewarded him with a slow smile that turned to a laugh. "That would be nice, but no. If you go to jail, I'll never see that collection of yours."

"Are you sure?" Des asked, realizing he wasn't completely joking. If he found out that man had done anything to hurt Jessica, he'd make him sorry he had. "I will if you want."

Jessica took a sip of her coffee. "No, but thank you. I don't think a man has ever offered to 'kick someone's ass' for me before."

Interesting. Why not? A woman such as Jessica deserved to have a man who'd do anything for her. He studied her a moment, noting the way her teeth worried that sexy bottom lip of hers.

His gaze slid to her slender fingers as she wrapped them around the mug, and he wondered what it would feel like to have them touch him. What it would be like to touch her. They were the only ones in the tiny café, and he swore he could almost hear her heart beating. The sweet scent of honeysuckle floated in the air, warming him with her presence. Deep inside, he felt his Beast stir, hungry to find out if she tasted as good as she smelled.

"Did I get you in trouble?" he asked, trying to nudge her to tell him what Greg had wanted. Any hint that might tell him if her boss was working with the Beasts.

"Oh, no," she said quickly, waving off the idea. "Greg's just stressed about the charity event coming up this weekend." She held up a finger. "Which reminds me. Did you get an invitation? I'd love for you to come. You can tour the museum during the party. There will be lots of great food and entertainment."

"I received an invitation," he said. "Will you be there?"

"I'll be there." Her voice said it wouldn't be a pleasure for her.

"Then I'll be there, too."

"Good." Her eyes twinkled with sincerity. With interest beyond him joining the guest list.

"I do have a problem, though. My flight leaves early the next morning. I'd prefer to do the tour now so I can go ahead and put my thoughts together on the donation."

Her teeth went back to her bottom lip, and he knew she wanted to say no. "I need to take care of a few rather urgent matters," she said. "Maybe later this afternoon?"

He pushed his cup aside and leaned forward, resting his hands in front of him, eyes locked with hers. "I have a better idea. Have dinner with me. We can take a tour before we leave."

Surprise flashed across her face. "That's probably not a good idea," she said, her voice cautious. But her eyes, her eyes were warm with interest.

"Do it anyway, Jessica," Des urged, his voice low, his body raging with the possibilities of having her alone, to himself.

He told himself this dinner was about the journal and about her safety. Keeping her close while he got what he needed and protected her from the Beasts at the same time. But it was more than that, and he knew it. He wanted to know this woman, as he had never wanted to know another. It was crazy. Nuts. There was no future for them. Nothing but maybe a night of hot passion, and that would be wrong under the circumstances, beneath a veil of lies.

They sat there, eyes locked, heat simmering between them, as electric as a live charge. Silently, he willed her to answer the way he wanted her to, willed her to want him the way he wanted her. Holding his breath, he waited.

Finally, she responded. "All right, then. Seven o'clock it is."

And with her words, Des decided he could breathe again.

A few minutes after her sexy potential donor departed, Jessica stepped into Michael's office and waited for him to finish a phone call.

To say that Des had taken her by storm was an understatement. Why she'd said yes to dinner when she really had no time for anything but preparing for the party, she didn't know. Especially considering the blow Greg had just delivered.

Michael ended his call and Jessica gave him the news. "The caterer has food poisoning."

He gave her a blank stare, as if he couldn't have heard right. "Excuse me?"

He'd been with the museum for five years, and they'd become fast friends. His immaculate dress and manner went well beyond metrosexual. Not a wrinkle could be found in his blue-and-white pinstriped shirt or his per-

fectly fitted blue slacks. His tie matched the color of the
stripe in his shirt to perfection.

"What do you mean the caterer has food poisoning?" he asked. "As in, the person coordinating the
party?"

She sank into the chair directly in front of his desk.
"I wish it were so simple. The entire staff has it. As in,
so sick several people have been hospitalized."

"Wait." He set his pencil down with a precise thud.
"You're telling me the people responsible for *providing
food* to our guests have *food poisoning*."

"Right." Her lips pursed. "And even if they recover
in time for the event, they don't know what caused it.
What if they give our guests food poisoning?"

"The party is Saturday!"

"I know. Believe me, I know. The good news is the
owner feels horrible and has offered to do everything
he can to help, including working the event himself.
He's available to meet with our replacement service
and help pull it all together."

"Unbelievable. Truly unbelievable. And everything
was going so well. Beautifully, in fact." He straightened,
clearly ready to dig in to finding a solution. Michael
never dwelled on the negative. "Okay, then. What
options do we have?" He grabbed the phone book. "I
better start making calls now. No doubt we'll pay a
hefty fee and settle for tasteless, premade nonsense to
pull off a last-minute miracle." He grimaced. "We're
really going to be settling on the quality of food. There's
no way around it."

"No need for calls." She slid a card across the desk.
"Greg says he lined up a new company himself. He

assures me they have already talked to our current provider and are pooling resources."

Michael ran a hand over his clean-shaven jaw and cast her a dark blue, disbelieving look. "What am I missing here? So Mr. 'Never lifts a finger' lined up a new service on his own?"

"I'm sure he wants to tell the board he saved the day. Besides, he didn't offer to do the work. He came in, gave me this and left for some meeting. It's all on us to fix this."

Agreement flashed in his eyes. "That sounds like the Greg I know." He snagged the card. "We have a tiny window of time to deal with this. Is he even sure this place can handle something of this magnitude so quickly?"

"He insists they can, and in fact are already in action. Of course, he wants us to deal with the arrangements."

Michael snorted. "All the glory and none of the hard work. So fitting of Greg. I have to tell you, those months you were gone were hell. I had no buffer to bear his obnoxiousness."

She gave him a fake smile. "So glad I can be a buffer for you, though I must remind you I endured those days *with* you. Your phone calls were many."

"You know you loved staying in touch with this place. Speaking of needing a buffer," he added, "I saw your father charge past the reception desk earlier. I assume you got the brunt of his frustration?"

"Oh, yes," Jessica agreed. "I'd barely escaped a bunch of insurance people who showed up to protect their investment in the journal when he appeared. And he was livid, of course." Her voice softened as she thought of his reasons. "But then, I don't blame him.

He's worried about the journal. It's so a part of my mother to him."

"And to you, too," Michael said, his expression knowing. "No amount of insurance money would replace the sentimental value it represents. Or the history for that matter."

"Exactly," she said and sighed, her shoulders slumping a bit. "The idea that someone tried to steal the journal is unsettling."

"*Tried* is the operative word here. The journal is secure inside the museum. You know that."

She smiled at him. "You're right, of course. That's what I told my father, too."

"Why do I sense a *but?*"

"I don't know. I've got this strange sense of unease."

"Who wouldn't, considering the crisis at hand?" He indicated the business card. "I'll deal with the new catering service. You take care of whatever else you need to."

"Thank you." Jessica pushed to her feet, reaching for the lightheartedness she didn't feel. "You really are the perfect man for me."

He gave her a bright, white smile. "Watch out, now. If I don't find a man soon, I might just go straight."

She laughed, though it held an empty quality and she knew it. This party was important to her. Too important to allow it to go sour. It was about more than her job. It was about raising money to fight the illness that had taken her mother's life, and about celebrating her mother's life's work.

Jessica squared her shoulders. The party would be a success. She wouldn't allow it to go any other way. But even as she played those positive words in her head, a flutter of warning settled in her stomach. A really bad feeling that refused to be ignored.

A feeling that grew worse as her day continued.

Segundo sat in the comfort of a hotel room, an expensive leather chair framing his long, muscular body. Watching. With a glass of expensive merlot in hand, he watched two female servants pleasure the human male. As executive director of the museum housing the Journal of Şolomon, Greg Ward was proving to be a perfect target for manipulation. A perfect tool to lead him to the power he thirsted for. To lead him to the bloodlines so he could destroy them, and then be rewarded for his great achievement.

As Adrian's second-in-charge, Segundo had perks, of course. He had his own army of demon foot soldiers, not to mention a multitude of pleasures at his beck and call. But it wasn't enough. He wanted more. He wanted what his master, Adrian, possessed. He wanted to wield the magic Adrian held within him. And he wanted the favor of Cain, King of the Beasts in the Underworld.

Segundo thought of the failed attempt to steal the journal, and anger became a flame burning hot. He threw his glass against the headboard.

The glass shattered and Greg bolted upright to a sitting position. "What are you doing?! You scared the hell out of me."

"You'll soon see hell if you aren't careful." He ground his teeth together. "What progress have you made at the museum?"

"Nothing to worry about," Greg assured him. "Everything is going as planned. The catering company is out. My men will be in."

"How can you be certain the caterer will be replaced with your friend's company?"

One of the women sat up and started pawing over Greg, her hands caressing his body. Greg glanced at her, a smile playing on his lips. "I'm the boss," he said, as if he were talking to the woman. Then, he looked at Segundo. "They'll do what I say they do."

Segundo's body thrummed with excitement at how close he was to success. So much so, he could almost forget his irritation over the human's misplaced arrogance.

"How can I be sure you'll do as you promised?" Greg asked, his words laced with cockiness, with demand.

Segundo would have shoved the human's words down his throat and made him choke on them if he weren't amused by the question. A slow, evil smile slid onto his lips. Him? Keep a promise? Never. Soon enough, Greg would know this all too well.

Segundo's eyes traveled from one woman to the next before he fixed Greg in a hard stare. "You're in bed with your proof. They will do anything you ask of them, but they do it because I say so. Once you convert, you will own such power. Then, and only then, you will drink of their blood and control their minds."

Greed flashed in Greg's dark eyes. "Let me get this straight. I'll be able to make any human do anything I say? Give me anything I want?"

Segundo narrowed his gaze on the man. He needed to be clear with Greg, to be sure he knew who was in charge. Segundo had shown nothing but his human mask to this point. It was long past time Greg got to know his "Beast."

Willing his primal side to show, Segundo's adrenaline surged with the rush of transition to his natural form. He was stronger this way. Better. His face was now half Beast, ugly and distorted. His teeth grew long and one eye glowed yellowish-red. Greg gasped and shoved back against the headboard, his own eyes going wide. The two women laughed.

"I warn you, Greg Ward," Segundo told him. "If you fail me, you will regret it. I'll do more than watch you burn in hell. I'll burn every inch of your body, piece by piece." He let the words linger. "And I will laugh as you cry out for mercy that will never come."

With those words, Segundo stormed to the connecting room and slammed the door behind him. Two of his Beasts stood at the window overlooking the hotel. Both operated surveillance equipment, both cloaked in human form, wearing human clothing.

He had ten men in his Servidor Unit ONE, all loyal to him, not Adrian. Not that any Beast felt loyalty to Adrian. Most simply feared his magic, his pure evil, enough to obey him.

U1 snarled and straightened, switching his attention from the telescope he was looking through to Segundo. "One of the Knights just started up the stairs leading to the museum."

Segundo cursed under his breath and stomped toward U1, then shoved him aside to look through the telescope. He fixed his gaze on the Knight entering the building, and ground his teeth. He knew this one. Knew him all too well. He was the "Second" among the Knights, Segundo's equal.

He leaned back, ignoring the view, thinking. Frustration eased with a realization, a slow smile turning up his lips. How damn appropriate was this? He'd take out the "Second" of the Knights *and* steal the journal. Cain would be pleased. Adrian would fall, for sure.

Without warning, flames erupted in the room and Adrian appeared. He wore their battle gear—a black vinyl-like uniform that couldn't be touched by a blade. His dark blond hair was free around his shoulders, his black eyes tinged with red around the rims, a sign he was feeling impatient. That he was ready to inflict pain.

Segundo stood at attention. He might aspire to take Adrian's power, but he was no fool. Right now, his master could kill him with a flash of magic.

U1 and U2 stood at attention, their beastly side showing—their faces now half animal, half human. The Beast side bore one larger eye, longer hair, gruesome facial features. The display of their Beast side reflected submission.

Segundo had earned the right to hide his beast any time Adrian did not show his, one of the rewards Adrian offered his second-in-charge. One day he'd have Adrian's power. He'd have the ability to orb in fire. To bring a Beast to his knees with a mere wave of his hand. Soon, he silently vowed. Very soon.

"Where is my journal?" Adrian demanded.

"You will have the journal," Segundo proclaimed. He knew how Adrian worked. If he showed even a hair of doubt, of insecurity, Adrian would pull him from this job. "I will not fail you."

Adrian disappeared and reappeared directly in front of Segundo, his hands by his sides, fingers spread, a charge of power crackling from his fingertips.

Segundo's heart kicked up a beat, and he reached deep and warned himself to calm down. Behind him, U1 and U2 were oozing fear, damn near screaming it aloud. And damn it, Adrian fed off fear.

Segundo had to focus Adrian on himself to avoid an explosive situation, to keep his men from Adrian's wrath. Shielding his unit from Adrian helped retain their loyalty.

"All who get in the way, they will die," Segundo declared.

Adrian's eyes narrowed, the red glint darkening. "Do not fail me, Segundo."

Segundo's eyes met Adrian's glare, showing none of the fear he felt, pressing his hatred to the surface. Hatred was a thing Adrian understood, even encouraged. "I will not fail you, Master."

For several seconds, those red eyes fixed on him and Segundo didn't dare blink. Then Adrian's hands lifted, fingers splayed wide at U1 and U2, electricity spilling from the tips as he shocked their bodies.

Segundo didn't dare move, didn't dare protest. When his Beasts fell to the ground, brought to their knees by pain, Adrian released them.

"If you fail me, you will watch each Beast in your unit suffer. But you, my Second, will feel far more pain than all of theirs combined."

Fire consumed Adrian as he spoke the final word and disappeared. Segundo didn't move at first, frozen in his stance, anger burning a hole in his gut.

He whirled on his Beasts, frustrated to see them still on their knees. Adrian might cause him pain, but Segundo didn't dare allow his master the reward of seeing him crumble.

"Get up!" he shouted. "Act like the Beasts that you are!" He fixed them both in a hard stare as they pushed to their feet. "Now get back to work. We have Knights to kill and a journal to steal."

Chapter 4

Des watched as the receptionist packed her things into her briefcase for the night. He'd been in the lobby a good thirty minutes waiting for Jessica, ready to take her on their dinner date.

"I can't believe she isn't answering her pages." Rebecca stared at him a thoughtful moment before rounding the desk. "Come on." She motioned toward the elevator. "We'll go find her."

"That would be wonderful," Des commented, offering her an appreciative smile.

Before they could depart, Jessica rounded the corner, looking frazzled. Her hair was a bit wild, as if she'd been running her fingers through it, her lipstick gone, her eyes tired. And still, she was the most beautiful woman Des had ever seen.

"I'm so sorry," Jessica said, her eyes meeting his, the

impact intense. "I was in an area where I couldn't hear the intercom. A security guard found me and told me Rebecca was paging me."

Des felt their shared look in an unexplainable way. Potent and all-consuming, her emotions wrapped around him as they had earlier that day, claiming him as if they were his own. He sensed her need for support, for comfort. The need to give her these things went well beyond simple good manners and he couldn't begin to understand why.

He cast her a warm look, his voice soft and full of concern. "Don't worry on my behalf." He glanced at Rebecca. "Thanks for taking such good care of me. Will I see you at the party, then?"

Rebecca beamed. "I was more than happy to help, and yes, I'll be at the party."

"Ready for the tour?" Jessica asked.

"I am," Des said. "Unless you need to take care of other things first? I can wait, if you like."

"Actually, getting away from it all for a bit will do me good."

"If you're sure," he said. "I'm looking forward to it."

They started walking toward the elevator and arrived just as the doors opened. A slim, immaculately dressed, blond man appeared, relief washing over his aristocratic features as his gaze settled on Jessica.

"Oh, thank God, I found you." He held up a folder. "We need to review the new menu for the party."

A look of distress flashed across Jessica's face and she glanced at Des. He didn't give her time to speak. Didn't want her to fret another second on his behalf.

"Why don't I go pick up food and bring it back," he

suggested. "You can review what you need to while I'm gone. Then we can talk a little business while we eat. No rule says the tour has to be right this minute."

Jessica looked torn. "I… No. Your donation is valued. I don't want you to feel you're not important."

"I don't," he said. "It's clear my trip was poorly timed."

"I'm sorry," the man from the elevator said, stepping into the hall beside them. "I didn't mean to interrupt." He smiled at Des and offered his hand. "I'm Michael Wright."

Des accepted his hand, sensing Michael to be trustworthy. "Des Smith. Nice to meet you, Michael, and you're not interrupting. In fact, I'd be happy to pick up some food for you as well."

Michael's eyes filled with approval. "That's quite generous of you."

"Too generous," Jessica inserted. "I'm sure the menu is fine, Michael. I trust you."

Des reached out and gently touched her shoulder, drawing her gaze. "Look at the menu so you can put your mind at ease." Not giving her time to argue, he addressed Michael again. "Can you suggest a good place to pick up takeout?"

"Right this way," Michael said, hurrying toward the reception desk. Des followed but not without noting the cute way Jessica glowered at Michael's back.

"Two blocks on the left," Michael said, writing a name down on the paper. "It's called Cura's Bar, and it has a little of everything. Jess loves the grilled chicken salad with salsa, no dressing. Actually, I'll write it out, and you can just hand it to the hostess."

Des accepted the paper. "Excellent. I'll be back in a

few minutes. How do I get back inside the museum when I return?"

Jessica motioned him forward. "I'll walk you to the door and introduce you to Larry, the head of our night-time patrol."

Des offered Michael a nod and then fell into step beside Jessica.

"You really don't have to do this," she said.

"I don't mind," he said, drawing to a halt a few steps from the guard post. "Besides, I have a motive. I don't want your divided attention. I want you all to myself."

And he did. He wanted her alone, naked and beneath him. To touch her, and kiss, to make slow love to her. To take her in a way he'd not dared take more than physical fulfillment from a woman since becoming a Knight. But he dared now. He couldn't seem to help himself. Jessica had called to more than his primal nature. He wanted more than sex. She'd managed to awaken the man. A detail that scared the hell out of Des, because he'd long ago learned to control his Beast—it was the man in him who'd once gotten him killed in his human life. A thought he pushed away as he stepped outside, his instincts suddenly going on alert.

Des sensed the enemies in the shadows, lurking some-where nearby, waiting to attack. The walk to the restau-rant took a dark path that crossed two deserted parking lots.

The microphone discreetly placed behind his ear allowed for instant communication with his team. "I have company."

"Copy that," Max said. "We've got your back."

"No," Des said, rejecting the support. "Watch the

museum. We can't risk anything happening to that journal."

Rock interjected, "You're unarmed."

"Hold your positions." The idea of Jessica being prey to the Beasts bothered him more than it should. "And stay alert."

Approaching the first parking lot, Des noted the rows and rows of vehicles offering plenty of cover for the Beasts. His feet crunched on glass as he moved beneath a broken streetlight.

The instant he passed the first car, his peripheral view caught movement to his left. He turned as the dark shape charged at him—a Beast in primal form, his face half animal, half man. A saber sliced through the air, and Des ducked within an instant of losing his head, but not without the blade slicing into his hand. The cut would heal in a few hours with the unique abilities of the Knights. Losing his head would be death.

He rotated around to kick a second attacker, throwing the big Beast to the ground with the force of the blow. His first attacker sliced a blade at him. Des leaned to the left, to the right, dodging the sword, wishing for his own.

As if in answer to that wish, Rock charged forward, appearing from the shadows. "Des!"

He looked up as a blade flew through the air. He caught it by the hilt and wasted no time putting it to use. While Rock took on the other Beast, Des matched blades with the one he'd kicked to the ground.

The Beasts wore their standard armor suits, damn near impossible to damage. Not that they bled anyway. They had no blood, no souls. But they could feel pain and Des wanted to inflict some.

With a well-practiced move, Des knocked the Beast's sword from his hand, and followed up by slicing his blade through his attacker's neck. The Beast's head tumbled to the ground. Mere seconds later, the body exploded into flames, burning to ash. The armor and weapons belonging to the Beast disappeared, products of dark magic.

Des turned to find Rock victorious as well. "You don't follow orders well," Des snarled. The kid had a knack for being impulsive, and one day it was going to get him killed.

"You're welcome," Rock spat back. He shoved his weapon into the casing that hung off his belt beneath a jacket the hot night made unnecessary.

Des tossed Rock the sword he'd used in battle. "You're bleeding like a stuck pig," Rock noted, eyeing Des's hand. "You need Marisol."

Rock was right. He needed their Healer's assistance if he was going back into that museum. She could heal him instantly. Marisol and Jag were the only two in their operation who could orb from place to place. Times like these, Des wished like hell he could orb.

Des hit his mic. "Max."

"I'm here."

"Any trouble at the museum?"

"We're clear here. Looks like the Beasts simply want to clear their path to the journal by killing us off. Or rather, killing you. Someone thought you were a problem."

"I was an easy target. See if you can get Marisol to flash over to the van."

"How bad are you hurt?"

"Too bad to walk into the museum without Jessica

insisting I need a doctor. Tell Marisol to bring bandages, too. I need an excuse for the blood all over my shirt." No one would know he was healed beneath a bandage. "I'll tell Jessica someone had car trouble, and my efforts to help backfired."

"Copy that," Max said.

Des eyed Rock and reached in his pants pocket with his good hand. "I need you to go get the food so I won't bleed all over the restaurant. Order me something, too. She expects me to eat with her."

Rock inclined his head in agreement and started to turn away. "Rock," Des called after the young Knight, waiting until he knew he had his full attention. "Thanks, man. For once, I'm glad you didn't listen to me."

Des didn't wait for a response. He took off running, making his way back to Max's location, cutting left to the alley. When he arrived at the surveillance van, he yanked the rear doors open, not bothering to announce himself— Max could see his approach with his equipment.

As expected, Marisol was inside waiting for him. The minute she saw the blood dripping from his wound, she tossed him a towel. Des wrapped it around his cut, slowing the blood flow enough to allow him to pull the doors shut behind him. He couldn't have Marisol working her healing powers with an audience.

With long brunette hair, green eyes all healers possessed and a feisty personality, Marisol was as beautiful as she was devoted to the care of the Knights. Unlike the Beasts, Knights could bleed to death. Granted, it would take damn near draining them dry, but it could happen.

Once he was seated on a bench, he unwrapped the

towel and held his hand out to Marisol. She placed her palm over his and a bright light splayed across his injury. A second later, his wound was healed.

He made a fist and tested for full use. "Good as new."

Marisol tore open the bandage. "You do have quite a lot of blood on your shirt. It's a shame you don't have a way to switch it out."

"I'd have to explain why I changed, if I did that. I better stick to the plan and say I helped a stranded motorist and got hurt." He looked over Marisol's shoulder to where Max sat at a computer. "Any more trouble?"

"Nothing," Max said. "They were after you. That strikes me as odd."

"It has to be because I'm the closest to the journal," Des said. "I'm inside now. And I told you, I'm pretty damn certain that Jessica's boss is working for the Darklands. My instincts are never wrong and they are screaming about that little pipsqueak of a man. He'd have access to the vault so he's the perfect target for the Beasts. You tagged him, right?"

"His cell, his car, his apartment. If he breathes, I have it recorded. But we need the same access to that vault that the Beasts have, if your suspicions are right."

"I know. I told you before. I'll get Jessica's security card." He grimaced and then murmured under his breath, "I wish I could just tell her what's going on."

Marisol narrowed her gaze on him, her expression probing. After a moment, she said, "Lying to her is bothering you." It wasn't a question.

As the leader of this mission, Des had to make tough choices that protected humanity as a whole, not choices to protect one woman's feelings. He didn't need

Marisol going back to Jag and suggesting his decision-making ability was compromised. Because, damn it, that wasn't true. He'd made a mistake over a woman in his human life, and been betrayed. He would never be that foolish again.

"Her cooperation would simplify things, that's all," he explained to Marisol, despite the fact that she hadn't asked. "The Darklands have a willing helper in her boss, Greg. I'm sure of it."

"There's no way to know how she'd react to the truth," Marisol commented.

Des gave her a nod. "I know." And he did. That didn't mean he had to like it.

Max focused on the immediate problem: how to get Jessica's security card, which was attached to her key ring. "Jessica needs her card to log her exit," he commented. "You need a way to get her and her card outside that building." He considered a moment. "What if I make sure she has a flat tire and needs a ride home?"

"That works," Des said, thinking about how much more complicated this night was getting with each passing second. Taking her home, to her apartment, represented temptation.

"All done," Marisol said, finishing up with the bandage.

"Thanks," Des said absently, his mind on Jessica and trying to figure out *why* she affected him so intensely.

"Incoming," Max announced, a second before the doors flew open and Rock appeared.

Rock and Marisol locked gazes, and Des rolled his eyes. He didn't have time for their tormented looks of an impossible love.

Des maneuvered out of the van and grabbed the restaurant bags from Rock's hands, not even bothering to try and snap him out of his Marisol fixation. It was time to get back to his assignment, back to lying to Jessica.

A duty that was twisting his gut into knots.

Chapter 5

The minute Jessica saw the blood on his sleeve and the bandage on his hand, her eyes went wide. "Oh my God! What happened?"

"It's nothing," Des said, handing Michael one of the bags. "A lady had car trouble and I caught my hand on a piece of metal. The restaurant hostess found a bandage."

"Oh, was it Monica?" Michael asked, as they walked toward the elevator. "Tall brunette with really good taste in footwear."

Jessica noted the funny look Des cast in Michael's direction, and she wondered if he picked up on her friend's feminine tendencies. If he had, he didn't seem bothered, and she was pleased about that.

"I think so, yes," Des said. "'Monica' sounds right."

Michael clucked his tongue on the roof of his mouth.

"I knew we shouldn't have let you get the food," he said, as if he hadn't been the one to push Des toward the restaurant.

Jessica and Des both looked at him as if he were insane. "What?" Michael asked innocently as they stopped on his floor. He stepped into the hallway and held the elevator, addressing Des. "Thanks for dinner."

"No problem," Des said. "Enjoy."

The door started to shut and Michael stuck his hand inside to stall it again, concern on his face as he eyed Des's hand. "You should get a tetanus shot."

"I've been on plenty of dig sites," Des said, laughing. "Thanks for the concern, but believe me, I'm covered."

"All right, then," Michael said, releasing the door and waving at Jessica, his eyes twinkling with mischief. He'd been giving her a hard time about finally showing an interest in a man.

As the elevator moved on, she found herself sharing a laugh with Des, their eyes locking in a sizzling stare. She'd never felt this kind of warmth with a man. This instant, overwhelming attraction that made her want to fall into his arms. Her reaction to Des seemed to intensify with each contact, with each passing second. She didn't even know what to do with something this potent. It was almost, well, almost more fantasy than reality.

Certainly, she'd heard of people feeling such potent reactions to strangers, but she had really thought it only possible in fairy-tale romance novels. Not real life. Certainly, not *her* life. The men in her life had been more interested in her father than her.

Before she could begin to conjure words, the doors

opened to her floor. "This is where my office is. I figured we could eat in there. If that's okay with you?"

"Of course," Des said. "Sounds perfect."

They stopped at a soda machine in the hall, and then Jessica led Des into her office.

"It smells good in here," Des commented.

"Thanks. I have a thing for candles." Jessica motioned toward the corner and her favorite chair, a matching one beside it. "We can sit there."

He settled into a seat and began pulling the food out of the bag. As Jessica claimed her position beside him, the room took on a more intimate quality. Funny how she'd never noticed how close the two chairs were before.

"I feel bad about you getting hurt," she said, accepting the container of salsa that Des handed her, her eyes lingering on his bandage.

"I'm fine but if you feel really bad, you can make it up to me."

"How's that?" she asked, warming with the heated look he cast her way.

"Let me take you out to a real dinner tomorrow night."

A smile touched her lips. "Aren't you jumping the gun?" she asked. "We haven't even made it through this dinner."

He opened his box to display a burger. "This is takeout. Not to be confused with a dinner date. And in case there's any confusion over my intent tonight, that's what tonight was supposed to be."

A shiver of excitement raced up her spine. For so long, Jessica had shut out the opposite sex. After a few too many money-grubbers and political movers who wanted a piece of her father, it all seemed like too much work.

"Mixing work and pleasure is never smart," she said.

"Neither is ignoring opportunity," he countered. "I'll ask again before the night is out."

She laughed at that and dumped salsa on her salad. "Well. Dinner or takeout, I'm glad to have the food. I'm beyond starving."

He tore open a ketchup packet and then dabbed some on several fries. "Sounds like I planned my trip in the middle of crazy times for you."

"You don't know the half of it," she said, taking a bite of chicken. "Earlier today you commented on how stressed I seemed. You know, right after my boss interrupted us."

He nodded.

"I tried to hide it, but you were right. I'd just found out the caterer for the party has food poisoning. Or rather, the entire staff has food poisoning. We had to get a new service with the event almost upon us."

He frowned. "Huh."

"What does that mean?"

"That's just a little odd. The entire staff?" He grabbed a fry and ate it. "What are the chances?"

Uneasiness churned in her stomach and she set her fork down. She'd thought of this before and tried to put her mind at ease. "Right," she said flatly, making a mental note to check out the catering company again. "What are the chances?"

Des reached out and touched her arm for the briefest of moments. "I'm sorry," he offered gently. "I really said something wrong, didn't I?"

She glanced at him, finding herself lost in the depths of those dark eyes. Why did her skin tingle where he touched her? What was it about this man that drew her like a magnet, charged her with a powerful reaction? And how could she feel this excited, this aroused, and still feel warm in a comfortable kind of way? Safe even. *Safe.* It was such an unusual word to come to mind.

Delicately, she cleared her throat and reached for her voice. Talking to Des about the museum security issues wasn't an option, even if he did feel "safe." There were rules and policies to follow.

"I guess planning this party is getting the better of me," she managed to say. "It's important to me. It's, well, it's about my mother."

She eyed her food, feeling the intensity of his stare. Her lashes lifted, and in his gaze she found genuine interest in what she had to say, to share. Yet, he didn't press her, didn't ask questions. The way he let her decide what to share and what to keep inside somehow encouraged her to talk. Oddly, she almost felt as if her mother was in the room, urging her forward, pressing her to share her work.

She continued, "My mother's research was responsible for the donation we hope to unveil that night—the Journal of Solomon."

"I saw something about that on the news," he mentioned. "Actually, that's what struck me as odd about the catering situation. Didn't someone try to steal the journal?"

She made a frustrated sound. "I don't know how the media got word of that, but yes, there was an attempted theft. Attempted and failed, thank God. It's locked away nice and safe now, and hopefully the insurance company will still let it be displayed at the party." Her voice softened. "That journal was my mother's life's work, her passion. If anything happened to it, my father would be destroyed. She died of breast cancer while they were excavating the final dig site where it was eventually found. He saw the exploration through to the end, because he honored her compulsion to find the book, even if he didn't understand it."

"Which is why the party is a breast-cancer charity event," Des commented.

"Yes," Jessica said. "It was a condition of the donation my father set up."

"I get the feeling your mother's death was recent?" He spoke the words in a low voice, as if he wasn't sure he should ask the question.

She inhaled and reached for her fork, thinking about that for a few moments as she took a bite of her food. "More than a year, but I think the fact that the journal is here, right around the corner, waiting to be explored, has opened up the wound a bit. I mean, she not only lived to make that discovery, she died for it." She shook her head sadly. "But she will never actually see the contents."

He swallowed a bite of his burger and reached for his drink. "Your father fulfilled her dream. That means something."

"Yes," she said a bit sadly. "I suppose that's true." A sizzle of excitement formed inside her. "I'm looking forward to learning more about the contents. My mother had specific ideas about what was inside. She was obsessed over that journal. I feel driven to see this through for her."

"*Obsessed* is a strong word."

"An appropriate word," Jessica assured him. "That journal became everything to her. She was like a bull charging forward after a prize."

"That really isn't that uncommon," Des said, taking a drink of his soda. "There are plenty of people who spend lifetimes hunting a piece of history for whatever their personal reasons. Sometimes they feel like it will rewrite history, or that it will change the world. In other cases, I think it's just that drive to touch a past era one feels connected to."

True enough, but it had been her mother's urgency to find the journal that bothered Jessica. As if a clock had been ticking. She couldn't help but wonder if her mother knew about her cancer and hadn't told them. Regardless, Des's understanding of her mother's motivations amazed her. If only her father could have shared that understanding as well.

"She was intrigued by the idea that it held some of Solomon's greatest secrets," Jessica said, thinking about what had driven her mother to search so hard. "Secrets with biblical importance."

"I'm a bit of a biblical scholar myself," Des admitted. "Are you speaking of the map said to be inside?"

She smiled. "You know the story?"

He inclined his head. "It's been a while since I read it, but if I remember correctly, the legend says that Solomon guarded a list of bloodlines said to be descendants of angels. The journal is said to hold a map leading to that list."

"Exactly," Jessica agreed. "And that list is enclosed inside a magical box of diamonds and gold said to self-destruct if evil touches it. A box Solomon asked his son, Prince Menelik, to hide in a faraway land, away from his enemies." She brushed crumbs off her hands. "It's an intriguing story, but, of course, how much of it is pure myth?" She shrugged. "That's what I hope to find out. I try to keep an open mind like my mother always did."

Leaning back a bit, he paused, a fry halfway to his mouth. "Do you believe in angels, Jessica?"

The way he asked the question had her doing a double take. Seriousness laced his tone. "My mother always said I had a guardian watching over me," she commented, a smile playing on her lips as she thought of the bedtime promises of angels from her mother.

For a moment, Des sat perfectly still. Then he laughed and popped the fry in his mouth, obviously dismissing the subject. "So what other secrets did Solomon hide in the journal?"

"To be honest, I don't know if there are any secrets at all. Everything we just said could be a big fairy tale. But my mother believed in the journal, and now we know it's real." She paused, frowning, almost thinking she could smell her mother's perfume.

"Something wrong?"

"No," she said quickly, and continued discussing what her mother had thought to be in the journal. "Sorry. Where was I? Oh yes. The secrets in the journal. My mother would have decoded the content with more ease than most. For her entire career, she studied Solomon, his writing, his way of life."

"Surely members of her team have insight into her work?"

She took a sip of her drink. "To some degree and they'll assist of course. But you'd be surprised how guarded my mother was over her beliefs regarding that journal. I've promised the museum that I'd try to get my mother's personal diaries to help. Of course, my father is clinging to them. He seems to feel letting them go is letting her go. He hasn't even let me read them. Not yet, but I will soon. I think he only gave up the journal to keep it safe."

She picked at her salad a minute, thinking. "I wonder how the world would respond to a list of people said to be descendants of angels?"

"Probably get the attention of a few demons," he commented.

"Let's not even go there," she said, her eyes going wide. "I'd like to think any demons hanging around in Solomon's time were long ago cast to hell."

They began a debate about how that information might be received in today's times. Would the angelic bloodlines be like royalty or treated as outcasts? Des's obvious and genuine interest in her mother's research led them into a long conversation that went well beyond finishing their food.

A knock on the open door sounded before Michael popped his head around the corner. "I'm headed out. It's just you two and security."

"Night, Michael," Jessica said, and Des murmured something similar. As Michael disappeared into the hall, she glanced at the clock. "Oh my gosh. It's nine o'clock and I haven't even taken you on the tour." Her cheeks warmed as she darted to her feet. "We didn't even talk about your potential donation, let alone take the tour. We should do that now. I'm so sorry."

Des pushed to his feet beside her, turned to face her. "Don't apologize. I enjoy talking with you. It's... calming."

"Calming?" She laughed. "What an odd choice of words." She tilted her chin up to study his expression, trying to understand his meaning, and their eyes locked and held. Her hand went to her stomach, to the flutter of awareness beyond her control.

"I don't normally talk so much," she said, thinking of how shut off she'd been from the rest of the world, wondering what it was about Des that had encouraged communication. "I don't know what came over me."

He reached out and took her hand in his, and she didn't pull back. Though their potential business relationship deemed anything romantic inappropriate, this man created such amazing feelings inside her.

"The same thing that came over me the minute I saw you," he said. "The same thing that kept me hanging on every word."

He closed the distance between them with one step, their bodies all but touching.

"Why is that?" she whispered, her heart playing a beat in her ears, her blood pumping liquid heat through her veins.

"The same reason I can't help but do this," he said, a second before she found herself pulled into his strong arms, his mouth claiming hers, his tongue sliding past her lips.

Perhaps she should have objected, should have pushed him away. But how could she? The kiss drugged her with passion and pleasure, pulling her into a spell of sensual heat. With that kiss, Des made love to her in a way most men couldn't do with their entire bodies.

No. She didn't object. She didn't even consider it. Instead, she did just the opposite. For once in her life, she let the prim and proper Jessica slide away.

And she melted.... Lost in the moment and the man.

Holding her, touching her, exploring the sweet flavor so uniquely Jessica, Des found himself losing his sense of time, losing reality. In a far corner of his mind, his reaction to Jessica registered as too intense, too all consuming. This wasn't a normal attraction. Whatever was happening here wasn't his normal raging lust, driven by the Beast inside that demanded sexual gratification. Yet, the Beast in him still stirred to life, screaming for this woman, for Jessica.

With extreme effort, Des shackled every ounce of willpower he owned and eased his lips from hers, eased back enough to look into her beautiful blue eyes. His chest tightened with the impact of their connection, and he heard her intake of breath. She, too, felt what he did.

And he knew in that moment, knew from the potency of emotions that rushed through him, that the destiny he'd felt calling him before he'd left the ranch involved Jessica.

Everything inside him screamed to take her, to throw her down on the desk and find his way inside her. To make love to her, and claim what was his. *His?* Holy shit, what was happening to him? Since when did he try to claim a woman? Any woman. Certainly not one as pure and sweet as this one. She was everything he was not. Everything that he could never have.

Abruptly, he stepped away from her, afraid he might lose control if he didn't. "Sorry about that," he found himself saying, scrubbing his jaw. "I couldn't seem to help myself."

She laughed, nervous, hugging herself. "I thought you said I was calming?"

"It appears you have quite a few effects on me," he said, feeling the burn of desire threatening again. "And if we don't get out of this tiny office soon, I'm going to kiss you again."

She bit her bottom lip, and he felt his cock throb in reaction. He needed space to get himself under control and he needed it fast. Fortunately, she moved, walking behind her desk and grabbing her keys, a white card dangling from them. The security card he needed.

"We can take that tour now if you like?"

"It's late." Once she was outside of the building, he could snag her keys. "Maybe we should do it tomorrow. If you would have time?"

Her brows dipped. "You seemed pretty urgent about the tour earlier today. I don't mind staying to show you around."

"That'll take a good long while if we do it right. It's important, but tomorrow will be fine. I'll be in town several days." He gave her a direct look, sensing she feared he was backing out of not just the tour, but the donation. "In all honesty, taking you to dinner was the only thing urgent. I hope we can try again tomorrow night."

Relief flooded her features. "Dinner sounds nice."

"Excellent," he said, feeling satisfaction way beyond simple duty. Whatever Jessica was doing to him, she was doing it in a big way. "How about I walk you to your car?"

A few minutes later, Des was beside Jessica, crossing the well-lit parking lot of the museum. He followed her to her dark blue Volkswagen Bug, thinking the vehicle distinctly feminine. How perfect for Jessica, who embodied softness and beauty.

Jessica pulled her keys from her purse and hit her security button a moment before she came to an abrupt halt. "Oh, no. No! My tire is flat." She leaned against her car, deflated by her discovery. "This is so fitting in a day full of nothing but trouble." He was about to object to being included in that list, but she seemed to realize what she had said and backtracked, adding, "Except you, of course. You aren't part of the trouble. Sorry. I've just had a bad day."

Des kneeled next to the tire, hating this charade he had to play with her. "It's not salvageable," he said. "Looks like a nail did more than punch a hole, it tore a couple inches of the rubber." He pushed to his feet and walked to stand in front of her, unable to stop himself from touching her. His fingers brushed a wayward strand of hair from her eyes. "Why don't I drive you home. Then tomorrow I'll have it repaired for you. I can even give you a ride to work—maybe we can do the tour early in the morning?"

She let out a breath. "I don't want to impose."

"You aren't," he said, and though this was all part of his cover, he enjoyed the idea of taking care of her. It had been a lifetime since a woman had sparked such desires, such protectiveness. A part of him already rebelled at the idea of leaving her. "And by your lunch hour, I'll have your tire repaired."

"You're sure it's no trouble?"

"None at all," he said, claiming her keys and sliding them into his pocket before closing his hand around hers. "Leave everything to me. I'm parked out front."

She looked up at him, trust brimming from her beautiful eyes. And as Des led her toward the street, he prayed for a way to be deserving of this woman. For a way to make truth out of lies.

Greg parked under the Highway 635 bridge in the deserted section of the downtown warehouse district, darkness surrounding him, thick and heavy. As instructed, he flashed his headlights two times and unlocked his doors. And then he waited, seconds passing like minutes.

Despite his commitment to his actions, to finally changing his life and not settling for being a nobody, nerves tore him up inside. But he was tired of having nothing. Tired of working his ass off and having prima donnas like Jessica steal his spotlight. But this time, he was turning the tables. As much as he hated her coming back, Jessica's return had become his impetus to fight back.

Abruptly, the passenger door opened, and Greg barely contained an instinct to jump, his hand jerking off the steering wheel before he smacked it back down. He'd seen no one approach, heard no one move before a man he knew only as Black Dog slid into the passenger seat. He wore black from head to toe, his square jaw covered in stubble, nose flat. He looked mean, like he'd kill you if you blinked wrong.

Black Dog led a team called the Hell Hounds who were known for making problems disappear...for a price. A team Greg had dug long and hard to discover, one that would do dirty work no one else would touch. But the Hell Hounds didn't take just any job. Greg had paid, and paid well, for their trust.

Not waiting to be asked, Greg handed over the envelope containing a large portion of his savings.

Black Dog eyed the contents. "We're in business."

"Tonight?" Greg asked, excitement beginning to expand in his chest.

The man inclined his head and handed him a key. "Check the lockbox at dawn." He said nothing more, simply opened the door and disappeared into the darkness. Gone.

Greg sat there, a smile sliding onto his lips. By morning, Senator Montgomery would be all over the news, his home broken into, his late wife's diaries stolen. The world would know of the theft, as would Segundo. And if Greg was right, and those diaries held the information he suspected they did, Segundo would know that Greg held them captive, that their content offered him leverage to make demands.

Because even if the journal led its holder to the list of bloodlines, deciphering the genealogy in present day would be no easy task. Jessica's mother had researched Solomon's life for years. Her diaries would surely hold her thoughts on tracking angelic genealogy and that would be worth gold to the demon Segundo.

By dawn, Greg would have the ammunition to ensure Segundo couldn't kill him without risking the loss of those diaries. Greg would make Segundo keep his promise to turn him into a powerful demon. He'd give Segundo the Journal of Solomon—but not without making those diaries his trump card to receive his immortality.

Greg would have his power. Segundo would not stop him, nor would anyone else.

Chapter 6

Des unlocked the door to Jessica's apartment and discreetly pocketed her keys. She lived in one of the new hotel-style high-rises that had indoor entry and a doorman. Des stepped aside to allow her to enter her home, willing himself to walk away with a mere kiss good-night. Knowing he wouldn't if she offered more.

"Would you like to come in for a few minutes?" Jessica asked, as if reading his mind.

He pressed his palm into the doorjamb over her head, fighting the urge to touch her. "Do you want me to come in?"

She wet her lips, nervous. Sexy. "I wouldn't have asked if I didn't."

Aroused, tempted, drawn into the heat of lust and desire, Des stared at her, inhaling her sweet scent. A scent laced with innocence and soft female desire. Stay.

Go. An internal war battled inside his head, inside his body. He had the keys, so he couldn't use that as an excuse to stay.

"Come in," she said, easing the door open and stepping inside the apartment, flipping on the light.

Without a conscious decision to do so, he stepped forward, into temptation, into her world. A place he had no right to enter under false pretenses. His desire, his need and want for this woman wasn't false though, he reminded himself, justifying his actions.

To the left of the door, Jessica hung her purse on a coatrack before walking into her living room, which appeared to be a larger version of her office: two high-back chairs, a fluffy couch with big pillows, various pieces of art and history.

Jessica drew a deep breath as she faced him. "I want you to know, I don't invite men to my apartment, no matter what the circumstances."

"But you invited me?" he asked, pleased with her confession.

"I did. And don't ask why. I can't answer that."

"Fair enough," he said. "I won't push you, Jessica." He meant the statement in every way possible. He wouldn't push her for answers, nor would he push her for more than she offered, no matter how much he wanted it.

The look in her eyes said she appreciated his declaration. "How about a glass of wine?" she asked. "I'd suggest coffee but I'm not sure my nerves could stand the caffeine."

"Wine would be nice," he murmured, the room surrounding him with the same warmth Jessica made him feel. Unfamiliar in nature, its presence, that warmth stole into his mind, into his limbs.

She turned and headed into the kitchen, and suddenly he needed to tell her the truth. It was as if one of the Archangels had whispered in his ear, as if Raphael had told him the truth would set him free.

He charged after Jessica, flipping the earpiece off so no one could hear their conversation. He found her facing the counter, reaching into an overhead cabinet.

Des didn't hesitate in the doorway, barely glancing at the gleaming white stove and refrigerator or check-ered tile. He approached Jessica, his intention to talk to her somehow lost, if only temporarily.

Closing in on her from behind, he framed her body. His arms caged her in front of him, his palms pressing on the counter. "Jessica," he whispered.

She sucked in a breath and then shivered, and he knew she felt this craziness as much as he did, this burn that seemed to demand they come together. He nuzzled her hair, the silky strands caressing his cheek, the floral scent teasing his nostrils.

She leaned back a bit, as if trying to absorb his presence, and her hand went to his cheek. The softness of the touch both soothed him and set him on fire. The primal part of him responded, the Beast screaming with hunger, screaming to take her. To pull her lush backside against his throbbing cock.

But the man inside, the Knight born of honor, fought for control, warned him to take this slow. His desire for Jessica went beyond the sexual side of his Beast. Deep in his soul, he felt this woman was part of him. How or why, he didn't know. But if he, like Jag, had a mate, he was beginning to think Jessica was his.

And he had to tell her about the journal, in such a way that she'd accept what he had to say, and be willing to help. But he also needed to confirm this connection was true, that she felt what he did. Because that connection would help him win her trust and her support in finding that list of bloodlines.

"I know we just met," he whispered near her ear, his hand sliding to her stomach. "But there's something between us. More than simple attraction."

"Yes," she whispered, rotating around to face him, her hands settling on his chest, their thighs touching.

Suddenly they were kissing. Crazy, hot kissing. Hands everywhere, exploring, touching, tasting. Des couldn't get enough of her, and from the way she worked to free his buttons, the way she shoved his shirt over his shoulders, he knew she felt the same way.

Her soft hands caressed his bare skin, his chest, his arms, his back. His mind burned with images of her naked body pressed to his. Sugar and spice laced his tongue, her kiss drugging him into searing heat. Somehow, though, he still managed to separate his lips from hers long enough to pull her blouse over her head.

But before he could press her close—to hold her, to feel their bodies pressed together—their eyes locked. They stared at one another, the air crackling with electricity, with the charge of their attraction, with the heat of their emotions.

He reached out and ran a finger down her cheek, the pale beauty of her skin beyond comparison. But it was the look in her eyes, so innocent, so trusting, that damn near stole his breath. And he knew he had to tell her the truth. Had to tell her before he forgot himself again, before he made love to her with the poison of lies between them.

"Jessica—"

She touched her fingers to his lips. "Don't. I can tell you are trying to talk yourself out of this. Don't. No guilt. I want this. For once in my life, I don't want to think. I just want to act."

As if to seal her words, she lifted to her toes and pressed her lips to his. She used the momentary distraction on his part to unhook the front of her bra and shrug out of it. His gaze dropped to her breasts. High and full, they beckoned for his touch, for his mouth, the nipples plump and rosy-red. The Beast in him raged to life as he watched them pucker and tighten into hard peaks.

Logic and restraint faded. He lifted her to the counter, pressing her legs apart, her skirt riding high as he stepped between them. One hand slid into her hair, angling her head, positioning her mouth for the on-slaught of his kiss. His tongue slid past her lips, parting them as he found her sweetness. Tasting her as a starving man would food. Hungry beyond any hunger he'd ever felt in his life.

Plain and simple, Des was on fire now, his cock hard, his body pumping out adrenaline, burning through lust like rocket fuel. He had to have Jessica. Had to claim her. His fingers skimmed her shoulders, her back, made a trail upward, over her knees, then her thigh-high hose.

Her tongue slid along his, a soft sound of pleasure filling the air, her hands moving almost frantically through his hair. As if she anticipated his next move as much as he did.

He inched his palms to the top of her legs, stroking the silk covering her mound. He could feel the heat radiating through the material, and he shoved it aside, his finger sliding along the slick proof of her arousal. A low growl formed in his throat, arousal pressing against his restraint. She was so wet. So ready. He filtered his passion into deepening their kiss, devouring her mouth. Fighting his burn to yank her panties off and take her, to bury himself deep inside her body.

Something amazing happened then. Jessica sighed into his mouth, the sound tracing his nerve endings, a fine mist of silky coolness. And with it, he calmed. Passion still burned, but man, not Beast, ruled. He hadn't even known that was possible anymore.

Jessica drew back ever so slightly, her lips lingering a breath from his, teasing him with their warm caress. He felt her as he could only feel himself. Felt her emotions, her desire…her trust.

Suddenly, taking Jessica became less important than pleasing her. He began a slow seduction, learning what made her moan, what made her cry out. Driven to pleasure her, he yearned to feel her shiver with orgasm. His fingers teased her swollen nub, explored her sensitive core. Des lost himself in Jessica, in the sweetness of her surrender.

Abruptly, a shrill ringing of a nearby telephone filled the air, ending Des's departure from reality, the fade into fantasy. His head turned to the sound, his actions stilled. A burst of awareness raked through his mind, over his nerves, shaking him with realization. He'd been completely, utterly lost in Jessica. Him. Des. Not the Beast.

For the first time since he'd become a Knight, the man

had prevailed, and it scared him. He knew what to do with the Beast. He had barely a clue of how to handle the man.

"Ignore it," Jessica said of the insistent ringing, pulling his mouth back to hers, fingers pressed to his face.

It was too late to slide back into oblivion. The phone had reminded him why he couldn't do this. Why he had to talk to Jessica. His hands settled on her thighs as he reached for the control needed to pull away from her altogether. But somehow, he couldn't stop touching her, couldn't bear the separation.

He inhaled and moved, reaching for the cordless phone where it hung on the wall. "It could be important," he said.

Confusion flashed in her eyes and she shoved her legs together, tugging at her skirt. "All right then," she said, accepting the phone and murmuring into the receiver. "Hello.

"What's wrong? Are you okay?"

Des didn't have to hear the other end of the conversation to know there was trouble. Discreetly, he flipped his headset back on, ignoring the murmured curse of reprimand from Max.

"I'll be right there," Jessica promised whomever she was talking with. She ended the call and spoke to Des. "Can you please take me to my father's house?"

He glanced down to see her fingers trembling where she still held the phone. Before he could ask what was wrong, she started to get down from the counter.

Des eased closer to Jessica, helping her to the floor, acting without thought, instinct pushing him to protect her despite the warnings going off in his head.

The more the man surfaced, the more the danger of the past arose. The more he lost the Beast that allowed him to focus in battle, that allowed him to defeat his enemy, the more he began to feel. And emotions got a man killed.

Knowing this did him no good. Still, Des found himself comforting Jessica. "I'll take you anywhere you need to go," he assured her as he took the cordless from her and set it on the counter behind her, his attentive gaze never leaving her face. She was rattled, without a doubt. He softened his tone. "Are you okay?"

She nodded but her expression said she wasn't okay at all. "Remember I told you about the diaries my mother kept?"

Des felt his gut tighten. "Yes," he said cautiously. "I remember."

"My father read something in one of them that's upset him. He doesn't get like this normally, though, so whatever it is must be disturbing in some big way." She hesitated. "Are you sure you don't mind driving me? I can catch a cab."

"I don't mind," Des said. His hands moved up and down her shoulders. This need to protect and defend that she brought out in him defied all he had done to stay focused on his duty as a Knight. To never let a personal attachment impact his decision-making, as he once had in the past.

A few minutes later, as he stepped outside and glanced to the full moon overhead, he thought of his purpose. The sky above, the sprinkling of stars always reminded him there was something bigger than himself out there. Something bigger than this internal war he fought over Jessica.

Des ground his teeth. A few weeks from now he'd be back at the ranch and Jessica would be here. If he did his job right, the people on that list would be safe.

She walked toward his rental car, a Porsche 911 meant to enhance Des's role as a rich donor. This thing with Jessica was a facade he'd somehow become sucked into. And it was dangerous.

Resolve formed as he opened the door for her, avoiding eye contact. He had a job to do. Duty to obey. His gaze shifted to her long, sexy legs, and he turned away, inhaling at the tightness in his groin. Damn it, he had to get a grip on himself.

Once she was settled, Des walked past the trunk of the vehicle to the driver's side. "Package at your six o'clock," he murmured into his microphone as he dropped Jessica's keys and security pass by the curb.

Duty before desire, he reminded himself as he yanked open his door and slid into the Porsche. But as he shut himself inside with Jessica, the sweet scent of woman surrounded him, and both Beast and man united for perhaps the first time ever...desiring the same thing—Jessica.

But if he claimed her—if he allowed Beast and man to become lost in Jessica—would he lose the man? Would the Beast destroy the woman the man simply wished to cherish?

Chapter 7

The ride to her father's house had been in blessed silence. Des seemed to know she needed time to compose herself, and Jessica appreciated his intuitive understanding. Because truth be told, her emotions were twisted in wild disarray.

Her world had started spinning out of control today and it hadn't stopped yet. Tonight she'd almost had sex with a man she'd only just met. As out of character as that was for her, if her father had not called, she would have gone through with it. Des got to her in a way that defied reason. Somehow, she felt as if she'd known him forever, not a day.

Which was exactly why, when she pointed out her father's house, Jessica sensed tension in Des. It was an odd sensation, coldness replacing the warmth she'd felt in him before. She'd never been so sensitive to a man's moods. Never been so sensitive to a man's touch.

He glanced out the window at the towering white mansion. Huge brick walls surrounded the exterior, a steel gate entry. "Who exactly *is* your father?"

Oh, how she hated telling the men in her life this piece of information. Hated seeing the spark of added interest when they found out. "Senator Montgomery," she said flatly.

But there was no spark of awareness in Des when she made her announcement. In fact, his coolness became an arctic chill. She hit a security button on the gated entry and pointed out a side garage.

Once he had maneuvered the car inside the space she'd indicated, she turned to him. "Des?"

Slowly, his gaze went to hers, the lit parking area giving her a clear view of his guarded features. "Yes?"

"Is there a problem with my father?" she asked, thinking this was really a first for her. Always before, men had salivated to get to know her father. She sensed Des would rather bolt in the other direction. "Conflicting political views maybe?"

"I have no conflict with your father."

"Something is wrong, Des. I—" She stopped herself, rattled by what had almost come from her mouth. *I know you.* That was what she'd been about to say. But she didn't know him. They'd only just met. Besides, forcing him to meet her father so soon was a bad decision on her part. He had every right to be uncomfortable.

"You what?" he prodded.

"If this makes you feel awkward, I can have my father drive me home."

He softened before her eyes, his fingers trailing along her jaw. "I'm not leaving without you."

She suppressed a shiver, his touch impacting her in a potent way. Just as his words did. They held a possessive quality that couldn't be missed. She'd never thought she was one to want a dominant male, but Des had a damn sexy way of playing that role. Not that she'd let him take the lead completely.

Thinking of their time back in her apartment, she hid a secret smile. The tug-of-war for power with Des could be an exciting game. She hadn't done "exciting" in far too long, and she realized she needed the escape he offered.

"All right then," she said, reaching for her door. "Let's go inside."

Jessica led Des along a paved sidewalk lined with manicured shrubs to the kitchen, at the back of the house. She stepped inside, silver-and-white decor sparkling around her, Des on her heels. Big open counters with shiny tile had once accommodated her parents' love of cooking together.

Inside the door, her father waited. His Dockers pants and button-down shirt looked crisp and fresh, but his face was weary and tired. She rushed to him and gave him a hug.

"What's got you so fired up, Dad?" she asked, leaning back to look at him.

His eyes were filled with concern. "You," he said. "I'm worried about you." His gaze lifted over her shoulder and caught on Des.

"Oh. I'm sorry." She stepped to her father's side. "This is Des Smith. He runs the philanthropy department of his family business. Mexican culture is his special interest."

Her father's eyes sharpened with disapproval. "Wonderful." His hands flew in the air and then smacked his legs. "You're dating another history chaser. I'll never get you out of that world at this rate."

Jessica was just plain stunned by her father's words. Even more so by the rude way he looked Des up and down. "Daddy! What is wrong with you?" She turned to Des. "I'm so very sorry."

"Don't apologize for me, Jessica," her father said, eyeing Des, speaking to him, not Jessica. "I want your new man to know how I feel."

Oh my God, she was going to crawl under a rock and die. "He's not my new man! We just met."

Her father kept talking to Des as if she had never spoken. "I don't want her living in the past when she could be living for today. Her mother obsessed over history and now she's dead."

"Obviously, I've upset you," Des said. "My coming here was a bad idea."

"It was a bad idea," Senator Montgomery said. He looked at Jessica. "We have family business to attend to. I'll wait for you in the den." He turned and walked away, not sparing Des another look.

Stunned by her father's behavior, Jessica stared after him a moment, before turning to Des and taking a step toward him. "Des—"

"I should leave," he said, hands up as if blocking her progress. "We both know I don't belong here."

His statement took her off guard because she had the sense it went beyond her father's bad behavior, beyond this moment. The darkness in his eyes held a quality that touched her deep inside. A dark past showed itself in his reaction. A past that had somehow impacted how he was responding to her father's comments.

Cautiously, she took another step in his direction, stopping so close she could reach out and touch him. "I invited you and you do belong. He's upset and not thinking like himself. This is not how he behaves. Please. Will you wait for me? I really want you to."

He stared at her, his dark eyes half-veiled, probing. Seconds passed, and then finally he spoke. "I'll be outside."

Reluctantly, she nodded. At least he wasn't leaving altogether. Not that she could blame him, considering her father's behavior.

Impulsively, she darted forward and kissed his cheek. "I'm sorry for how he acted. And I promise I won't be long." She eased back and looked into his eyes, feeling her chest tighten with the connection.

Slowly, she inched away from him, not expecting a response. She turned and rushed after her father, intending full well to reprimand him. He might be upset, but treating Des rudely had been uncalled for.

She found him sitting on the brown leather sofa in his den, the empty fireplace the focus of his attention. Jessica sat down next to him, sadly remembering what was lost, thinking of the many times she'd found her parents sitting side by side on this same sofa, reading.

Several seconds passed, silence lingering between father and daughter. "What was that all about?" she asked.

"I won't apologize for wanting to keep you safe," he said.

For an intelligent man, he wasn't acting rationally. "Des isn't putting me in danger.

He didn't respond. "Dad," Jessica said softly, preparing to reason with him, "Mom died of cancer. *Of cancer.* Her career did not kill her. Her work did not kill her, and even if it did, my job is much different from hers." She sighed. "And you loved her excitement over her work, anyway."

Grudgingly, he admitted, "I did until that journal turned from years of intrigue to downright obsession. In the end, it changed her."

"Which means you supported her and her work for thirty-seven years. Don't you think you are simply angry and in pain right now, looking for her work as a place of blame for your loss?"

"Don't blame my grief," he snapped.

He never snapped. "What's wrong with you tonight?"

He gave her a direct look. "Not tonight. All day. Did you know that your mother predicted the journal would be a target for theft?"

"No," Jessica said. "But, as we discussed, it's logical it would be targeted. It's an amazing discovery."

"I understand the importance of the discovery, but that isn't what I am talking about. Your mother believed she had to find that journal to *protect* it. That she had some personal obligation to ensure it didn't fall into the wrong hands."

"She wrote about protecting the journal?" Jessica asked. "In her diaries?"

"Yes," he concurred, turning to her, his brows dipped, forehead crinkled. "But I'm not sure you are hearing what I am saying to you. She didn't think some common thief would steal the journal. She wrote about a belief that *demons* would come for it, that they would want the map inside it."

Good grief, he was really distressed here. He'd taken the loss of her mother hard, but she'd thought he was doing better. "I doubt she meant demons literally," Jessica countered. "Humans can be dangerous beasts. Greedy ones, too."

He shook his head, his movements a bit jerky. "You wouldn't convince your mother of that. She believed demons walk the earth. She believed it with all her heart. I often thought she was losing her mind that last year of her life."

There was something he wasn't saying. There had to be. "What is this about, Dad?" Jessica prodded. "You're really concerning me."

"That attempted theft was a wake-up call. If there was the tiniest truth in your mother's beliefs, placing the journal at your work location was insane. It puts you in danger. I can't lose you to that journal, too."

A thud on the roof drew their attention. Both Jessica and her father looked up. Tension shot through her body. "What was that?" she whispered.

The sound came again, barely there, but Jessica heard it. She pushed to her feet. Her instincts screamed with warning, her heart beat double-time. "Call 911," she said.

Her father darted toward the phone and Jessica headed to the door. "Where are you going?!" he yelled after her, picking up the phone. "The line is cut." He dug in a drawer and mumbled, "I need my cell." Then he shouted after her again, "Come back, Jessica. It's too dangerous."

She didn't stop, ignoring his warning. "Des is outside, unprotected."

* * *

Deep down, Des was still the slave who'd fallen for his rich Spaniard master's daughter. What a damn fool he'd been, thinking Arabella had loved him. Well, he wouldn't be a fool again. Never again.

He leaned against the Porsche, one foot on the bumper. No doubt an owner of such a car wouldn't dare scuff it up, but right now, money and all the things that came with it, pretty much bit his ass.

He'd spent close to a hundred years distancing himself from the feelings he'd felt this night. Oh, tonight wasn't about money, but once again, the powerful father disapproved of Des. How fitting that Jessica's father was a senator. Arabella's had been a high-ranking military officer.

Memories of how Arabella had turned on him when her father had disapproved of their relationship rushed at him. Reminded him of the many reasons he and Jessica didn't fit together. Just as Des and Arabella had been of two different worlds, so were he and Jessica.

The brush of a warning touched his mind, pulling him out of his personal bashing. He stiffened, instantly on alert. The sensation increased. Abruptly, Des pushed off the car, his instincts prickling. "I've got trouble," Des said into his mic.

Max sounded in his headset. "Beasts?"

Des hit the clicker to open the trunk, reached inside to arm himself, then hiding the weapons at various locations on his body. He skipped the guns. They made unnecessary noise.

"Humans, I think." He scanned the area and cursed under his breath. With his exceptional night vision, he spotted two intruders about to enter the attic window. "Someone's on the roof."

"Backup headed your way."

But Des barely heard Max's words. He was already running. He climbed a tree at the side of the house and was on the roof in a matter of seconds. *Jessica.* Concern for her drove him into action, his Beast threatening to take control. With supreme effort, Des shackled his primal side. Killing humans was forbidden, and the Beast within him wouldn't care about breaking the rules.

Still, nothing in those rules said Des couldn't cause bodily harm. Doing so wouldn't be hard. Even with his Beast in check, Des was far stronger than any human male. He tossed a knife into the shoulder of one man, and made sure it went deep. The man crumpled over in pain.

The second intruder turned on Des, thinking he could face off with him. Des grabbed the man by the shoulders and tossed him over the edge of the short side of the roof. The fall wouldn't kill him, but he'd feel significant pain.

Des followed, jumping to the ground with animal-like agility, landing on his feet. He didn't stop to deal with the man. He wasn't moving but Des could hear his low breathing. There was only one thing on Des's mind now—getting to Jessica.

As if on cue, she called out. "Des!"

He took off toward the sound, rounding the corner of the house a second too late. One of the intruders stood close to Jessica, a gun pointed at her head.

Des didn't give himself time to think. He reacted. His blade moved through the air with rocket speed and cannon force, digging deep into the man's hand in the exact spot that would keep him from pulling the trigger. A screech of pain filled the air and the gun slammed to the ground. Des reached Jessica's side a second after she'd retrieved the gun and turned it on her attacker.

He cast Jessica a surprised look; he would have expected her to cower, not fight.

"Where'd you learn to do that?" she asked, obviously as surprised by his skills as he was by the way she'd grabbed the gun rather than shivering in fear.

"There's a lot about me you don't know, Jessica," he said, having no intention of saying more. Now wasn't the time or place.

The man on the ground moaned, blood spurting from his hand, drawing their attention. Des reached down and yanked the knife from the man's hand, wiping the blood on the intruder's shirt before sticking it inside his waistband.

"Get up!" he blurted. "Get up now. And I suggest you use your shirt to wrap around your hand and stop the bleeding."

The man struggled to his feet and started to remove his shirt. Des shoved him at the door. "Not here. Inside," he ordered, wanting the protection of secure walls around Jessica.

"Keep the gun on him," he told her, bolting the door once they were inside.

"Better yet. Hand the gun over to me, sweetheart." The voice came from the kitchen doorway leading to the rest of the house. He smiled. "Name's Black Dog and I'm in charge now."

A huge man stood there, both tall and broad, dressed like the other intruders in head-to-toe black.

He held a gun to Senator Montgomery's head. Two additional men joined him, each pointing a gun in Des and Jessica's direction.

Jessica remained calm, again surprising Des. Her hand shook a bit but she had her weapon aimed at the man. "Let him go."

Des fought the urge to grab her and push her behind him. Bullets wouldn't kill him but they would Jessica. His focus went to Black Dog since he claimed to be in charge. Des asked, "What is it you want?"

"You can start by dropping your weapons."

Des inhaled and let it out, debating his next move, his sworn oath not to kill a human weighing on his mind. The most important thing right now was getting Jessica and the senator out of here alive.

"Do it," Black Dog yelled. "Do it or I'll shoot the senator. I won't kill him but I'll cause him some real pain."

Des cut Jessica a cautious sideways look. "Do it, Jessica. Drop the gun."

"Do as they say, sweetheart," the Senator called.

Des felt her hesitation, her concern over obeying what had been ordered, but the gun fell to the ground.

"Now, kick it over here," Black Dog said.

Jessica kicked the gun to him.

Black Dog pinned Des in a hard stare. "Now your knives."

Making a good showing of dumping his weapons, Des kept a select few. If they wanted to search him, he'd use that as an opportunity to take them all down.

As Des tossed the final blade he was willing to give up onto the ground, Max spoke into his headset. "We're in position to move when you give us a go."

At least he had some support, but too little. It was now evident they were grossly undermanned. If his team was here, they weren't at the museum.

Des held his hands out to his sides. "You've got our weapons. Back to my original question. What is it you want?"

The senator spoke up then. "They want my wife's diaries."

"That's right," Black Dog said. "The senator's going to open the vault or his daughter will die." He motioned to one of his men.

"If you kill her I'll never open that safe," the senator spat, anger in his voice.

"Then I'll simply wound her," Black Dog said. "One painful bullet hole after the other." He motioned toward Jessica. "Get the girl."

Des pulled her behind him. "You touch her and you die." He said the words and meant them, his vow forgotten.

The approaching man stopped in his tracks, Des's deadly presence obviously having an impact. He'd lost his soul once before while fighting for a woman. *Arabella.* She hadn't deserved his sacrifice. He knew that now. She'd been ruthless and cold, using him for sex, but pretending it was more.

With a clarity he wouldn't have thought possible, he now recognized the differences between the two women. He'd felt Jessica's pureness, even tasted it on her lips.

She was the one worthy of protection this night. Regardless of his vow to protect humanity, these men were not worthy of sanctuary. If Des had to kill them to save Jessica, he'd face the consequences.

Des waited for his enemies' next move, prepared to do whatever was necessary to defend Jessica.

Black Dog laughed, a hint of uneasiness in the sound. He tried to hide it, but it was there. Des heard it, and he felt the man's discomfort.

"You're an arrogant bastard," Black Dog said. "I'd make you eat that arrogance if I had time. But judging from the way the senator is shaking in his shoes, I've made my point." He motioned to his men. "Bring them to the den."

Des pulled Jessica to his side, taking her hand. Their gazes locked for a quick moment, and he noted the appreciation in her expression, the hint of admiration and respect. It warmed him in a way he'd never experienced before. No woman had ever looked at him as if he were a hero. But Jessica did. He didn't know what to make of that.

He cut his gaze from hers, comforted by having her close, ready to defend her if needed, ready to spill human blood if it meant saving her life.

Once they were in the den, the two gunmen framed Des and Jessica, weapons pointed at their heads. The senator stood beside a corner safe built into the wall, and clicked the combination, one turn at a time.

When the safe opened, Black Dog shoved the senator aside and grabbed the notebooks. He smiled and eyed his men. "Tie them up. We leave in exactly two minutes."

Des didn't fight as they tied him up, confident he could easily free himself, confident his people would get those diaries. He'd already given Max a go for a takedown upon the intruders' exit.

"*Buena suerte*," Des said to Black Dog as he headed for the door.

The man frowned. "What's that supposed to mean?"

"It means *good luck*," Des supplied. "You're gonna need it."

Chapter 8

"Is everyone okay?" Des asked.

Jessica sat on the floor, her father by her side, Des across from her. Their legs were stretched in front of them, bound, their arms tied at their backs.

"Yes," she said. "I'm fine."

Her father murmured the same and added, "Better, if we get those diaries back."

Des freed his hands and started to work the ropes at his feet. Jessica stared in shock. "How do you know how to do all of this stuff?"

"You some sort of Special Forces, son?" the senator asked.

Des eyed Jessica's father. "Just resourceful, sir," he said, pushing to his feet and moving behind her to free her hands. "Your daughter is very brave. You should be proud."

She laughed, but not with humor. "More like pissed. I knew why they were here." She glanced at her father, her expression grim. "I knew they came for Mom's diaries."

"I hate that I called you here tonight. I mean, *holy hell,* I wanted to warn you about danger, and I led you right into it."

Her father never cursed. Nor did he show the emotion he had tonight. His gentle manner had, in fact, been what served him best in the public eye.

"It'll work out," she assured him, thankful Des had been here. Thinking back, Jessica realized her instincts to bring him along had been strong. Compelling, even. She looked up and murmured a silent thank you. Someone up there had been looking out for her when Des had invited her to dinner.

The bite of the rope on her hands eased and she let out a sigh. Though she didn't understand how Des had gotten loose, she didn't care. Thank God he had, or who knew how long they'd have been stuck here, waiting for help.

Once Jessica was free, she took care of untying her father. As soon as he was able, the senator grabbed his mobile phone off the floor. "They caught me right as I went for my cell. I only needed another few seconds." He punched in the numbers and called for help. When he ended the call, he stared at Des. "I don't want my daughter in this kind of danger."

"And you're telling me this why?" Des asked, his tone as sharp as the look in his black eyes.

"Tonight is an example of why she needs out of that museum. Out of that entire world."

Jessica felt as if her heart was going to explode out of her chest. "Why are you acting like Des is to blame? He might well have saved our lives." Her mother's diaries were gone, probably lost forever and her father was acting out of his mind. "Damn it, Dad. I told you those diaries would be safer in the museum."

The senator's eyes went wide at Jessica's rare disrespect. "Don't you talk to me like that."

The pain that crossed his face laced his voice, delivering instant guilt. Her tone softened. "I'm sorry, Dad. We're both upset."

Sirens sounded outside. "I'm going to meet them out front," Des murmured.

She watched him depart, fighting the urge to follow. The minute he was out of hearing distance, she turned her attention on her father. "I like Des, Dad. Please cut him some slack."

"Your mother is the one who got you involved in the museum. I had hoped you would see how it affected her life and leave it behind. This man is simply going to stir your interest the same way your mother did."

Her chest tightened, a whirlwind of feelings spinning inside. "I left the museum to please you and I was miserable. I love what I do."

Unbidden tears were pinching the backs of her eyes. She hadn't allowed herself to cry since the funeral, determined to be strong for her father. But this had been a tough day, even in a year that had been an emotional train wreck.

Her father continued, "You never bring men home but that man is here. I don't know how long you've known him, but it doesn't matter. The fact that he is here says you're serious about him." He drew a breath, his lips forming a grim line. "Besides, the real issue is that I don't want you working at the museum anymore. That world has done nothing but bring pain to this family. Tonight proves that once again."

Slowly she exhaled, understanding seeping into her mind. He was desperate, grabbing at anything to keep her safe. She went to him then, wrapping him in an embrace. "You aren't going to lose me, Dad."

His arms closed around her in a bear hug before he leaned back to look at her. "I *can't* lose you, too," he whispered, his eyes bloodshot, as if he, too, was fighting tears.

"You won't," she promised. "But you can't save me from living, either. And why would you want to?"

"Senator Montgomery?"

Jessica glanced up to see a police officer in the doorway. She looked back at her father. "You might not be able to save me, Dad, but maybe they can save Mom's work. It was part of who she was and what made her special."

He gave her a sad smile and nodded before greeting the police officer. Jessica watched him, wishing she could take away his pain. She'd never experienced the deep love he'd shared with her mother, but she'd seen the way they'd lit each other's eyes, the way they'd made each other happy.

She could only imagine his loss, and the pain of losing the one you cherished most. The one you felt in your heart to be your soul mate. Seeing him hurt was almost enough to make her never want to love. *Almost.* A memory of her parents strolling together hand in hand flashed through her mind. She smiled despite the tingle beginning again in her eyes, happy that they'd shared those times.

No one could walk away from that kind of love. But could they survive the other's death? And would her father ever be the same? Jessica's thoughts went to Des, and she wondered about herself—would she ever be the same after meeting him? Something about him called to her on a level she didn't quite understand. She wasn't sure what to do about it—only that there was no turning back now. She had to see where this thing with him was going, where her desire for Des would lead her.

Two hours later, the crowd had finally begun to break up. Jessica stood at the back door of the house, a foot away from Des. A plainclothes detective stood with him, drilling him with the same questions she'd heard asked several times before.

"And where exactly did you get the knife?"

Des shoved his hands on his hips. "For the third time, I took it from the attacker."

The detective studied him a moment. "How'd you manage that?"

Jessica had had enough at that point. She stomped forward and stood at Des's arm. "Detective. I've heard him explain his martial-arts training several times to several people. If you have any more questions, I suggest you direct them to my father." Why was everyone so damn determined to make Des the enemy?

The detective's face reddened but he flipped shut his notebook. "I'll be in touch, Mr. Smith."

Jessica turned to Des, ready to find some peace and

quiet. "Do I dare ask you to drive me home after everything I've put you through?"

His gaze swept her neck, her lips, her face, and she felt her limbs heat in response. "I consider it my duty to see you home safely." His voice held none of the warmth in his eyes.

Heat turned to a chill. "Duty?" she asked, shocked by how much she didn't care for that choice of word. She felt alone. Yes. And it hurt.

Alone had never hurt before but tonight it did. Tonight, a year of being tough appeared to be crashing in. "Never mind." The words were clipped. "Thanks for everything. I'll get an officer to drive me."

She started to turn away but Des grabbed her arm, stepping close, his gaze pinning hers. "Jessica."

Her name came out as a raspy whisper, and nothing but silence followed. He didn't have to say more. The raw need in his expression spoke beyond any words he might have offered. She didn't know this man, *yet she did.* She understood him on some unexplainable level, as she sensed he understood her.

Without question, he needed her as much as she did him. Would that need last beyond tonight? She didn't know. Right now, she didn't care. She simply wanted to get lost in this man's arms.

"Take me home, Des," she whispered.

Des stood beside Jessica in the elevator of her apartment building, every nerve ending in his body alive with her presence. The depth of his desire for this woman touched him inside and out. It pressed him beyond logic and reason, controlling his decisions and overcoming the turmoil of his thoughts, of his concerns. Of the many reasons to turn and walk away from Jessica. His team had already copied her security pass and keys, and had slipped them inside the Porsche at the mansion. Staying would ignite temptation.

But he didn't walk away. He couldn't.

The door to the elevator opened, and Des motioned Jessica forward, careful not to touch her.

While he worked the key to Jessica's apartment, he drew a breath. *Damn it.* Why was he putting himself through this? Jessica stirred the past in his mind.

He shoved the door open and allowed her a path inside her home. Desperate, Des grabbed the pain of the past and twisted it into anger, clinging to it, using it to shield himself from his interest in this woman.

As if she'd read his thoughts, she turned at that moment, fixing him in a brilliant stare, the long dark strands of her hair a contrast to the light blue of her eyes. His anger melted away, lost in the soft touch of her gaze.

"Thank you for everything you did tonight," she said, her tone laced with sincerity. Her face flickered with distress and then softened as she focused on Des again. "It was difficult to lose my mother's diaries, but it could have turned out much worse if you hadn't been there. I really think they might have hurt me. To prove to my father they meant business."

Guilt engulfed Des at her words. His men had stripped the intruders of the diaries before they'd ever left the property. As much as he wanted to tell Jessica they were safe, wanted to tell her everything that was going on, he'd seen how emotional she and her father had been back at that house. He couldn't risk telling her and having her decide he was the enemy. He had to claim the journal before the Beasts.

"Don't thank me," he said, his voice low, running a rough hand through his hair and discreetly turning off the mic, tuning out his men. They'd heard more of his personal life than they should as it was. Then he added, "I don't want your gratitude." Silently, he added, *I don't deserve your gratitude.*

Her eyes lingered on his, warming. Her voice lifted with challenge, a hint of seduction playing along the edges of each word. "Then *what do* you want?"

Lord help him, he wanted her and he wanted her in a bad way. His gaze traveled over the soft curves of her hips beneath the fabric of her skirt, clinging to all the right places, before returning his attention to the ivory perfection of her face. "More than I can have," he answered, the truth washing over him like a tidal wave. One night would never sate the yearning this woman had created.

She took a step closer, tempting him with her nearness, teasing him. His nostrils flared, the scent of her arousal now mixed with her perfume, insinuating into his senses, driving him wild. The softer side of Jessica had fled, replaced by a sensual woman who seemed intent on pushing him over the edge.

"My mother used to say you could have anything you want." She paused. "*If* you want it bad enough."

Oh, he wanted her bad enough all right. That was the problem. He wanted her too much. He followed her lead, reaching deeper into the realm of temptation. Every word, every moment ushering him to the place of no return. "What do *you* want, Jessica?"

"I want you," she whispered and took the final step that put them within reaching distance. One lift of her hand and she would touch him, and without question, his barely contained control would unravel.

Desperate to find his willpower, Des leaned against the door, pressing his hands against the surface, forcing himself not to reach for her. Adding space, no matter how minute, as an obstacle.

He used words to further his position, to aid his battle toward resistance. "You think you want me tonight. But in the morning, with all the craziness of tonight behind you, you may well think differently." He paused, letting his words linger in the air, and then added, "You can't turn back time."

"Des." She said the word as if it were a plea for understanding, her voice husky, seductive. "I don't need you to save my virtue. My decision to invite you here came before that call from my father."

He remembered all too well what had happened before that call. And he remembered how pleased he'd been to hear it was out of character for her to invite a man to her apartment. Not that he'd needed her to tell him that. He knew women. He knew Jessica better than most, it seemed.

"A lot has happened since then," he reminded her, when he really wanted to replay the earlier scene, wanted to grab her and kiss her.

Her reply came slowly, her gaze scrutinizing, probing. Uncertainty flashed in her eyes and she took a step backwards. "Clearly, you're trying to talk me out of this."

Des felt a wave of emotion, of Jessica's emotion, of her insecurity and pain, barely holding back a reaction. He was intuitive, all the Knights were. But this went beyond that. In this moment, and several times before, he'd felt Jessica's feelings as his own. This had been a rough evening for her and she yearned for comfort.

He made a decision then. He simply couldn't bear her pain. Screw keeping his hands to himself.

Des reached for her, pulling her against his body, enclosing her in his arms. Everything inside him screamed to protect this woman in all ways possible. It had back in that house and it did now. He couldn't stand the idea of hurting her.

"I was trying to talk myself out of this," he confessed, one hand framing her face. "You've been through a lot. I don't want to take advantage of you."

"You're not," she said. Her lashes fluttered and lifted, a hint of trepidation in her tone. "I really need you tonight, Des."

Requiring no further convincing, Des slid his fingers into the silky strands of her hair, his mouth claiming hers. She melted into him, arms lacing behind his neck, the hard peaks of her nipples grazing his chest. A low growl escaped his throat, passion rising, claiming, taking away his sense of present or past. There was only Jessica.

She kissed him with hungry strokes of her tongue, meeting his need with her own, setting off a firestorm of yearning in him. He couldn't kiss her deeply enough, couldn't get her close enough.

They kissed, nipped, tasted. Soft sighs of pleasure slid from her lips, the sexy sound driving his desire higher, hotter. His cock thickened, his hand finding the curve of her bottom, molding her hips to his. She wrapped her leg around his calf, her hands traveling to his hair, his face, his shoulders.

He was losing coherent thought, ready to take her here, now. Ready to find his way inside her wet heat, to find the satisfaction he couldn't with any other woman. He knew this, knew it with every ounce of his existence.

But not here, not like this. He tore his mouth from hers, acting with what little rationale he had left. She stared up at him, a question in her passion-filled eyes.

"Where's the bedroom?" he asked, determined to make love to her like a man, not a Beast. Not on the floor in front of her door.

She took his hand and started to guide him. The Beast in him demanded action. This time Des didn't argue. He grabbed Jessica and picked her up with ease. She gasped as if surprised but didn't complain.

She pointed him down a hallway and quickly went to work on the buttons on the front of his shirt. Good. He wanted to be rid of all barriers, to be skin to skin.

He found the bedroom, not bothering with a light. The curtains were drawn, but the full moon and an abundance of stars shone through and illuminated the room. Anticipation tightened his gut as he settled her on the bed. He shoved his shirt off even as he settled on the mattress above her, the temptation to remove his clothes overshadowed by the need to feel her beneath him.

She spread her legs, welcoming him as he settled between her thighs as if he belonged there. Her hands caressing his bare chest, his arms, his shoulders. Her mouth reached for his, commanding him to please her the moment he was able, the kiss deep, hot, full of passion.

There was no question, she wanted what he did, and despite the demand whispered in her kiss, neither dominated the other. A fire had been lit between them, perhaps from the moment they'd met. A fire that now burned with furious force. A fire that ignited some strange bond. *Mate.* The word screamed in his head and he tried to reject it. Primal heat pulsed through his veins, the Beast clawing at his mind, pressing him to claim her. It wanted more than satisfaction. It wanted to taste her. It wanted to feel her blood on its tongue.

He pulled back, his forehead pressed to hers. His breathing was heavy as he remembered Jag speaking of finding his mate. Of how the Beast screamed for him to claim her. Of marking Karen with his teeth and bonding them for eternity. But Jag had feared that tasting Karen's blood in order to mark her would drive him over the edge. Would push him to take more than the small taste of her life's blood needed to mate.

Jessica's hand went to his face. "Des," she whispered a second before her lips brushed his jaw. So tender, so sweet.

Des kissed her then, kissed her as he'd never kissed another. Kissed her as if she held his last breath within her. And perhaps she did. He understood none of this. He simply knew he had to have this woman, completely, entirely. Now.

Chapter 9

In the midst of that kiss, Des battled his primal side, working to smash it, to tame what he'd allowed to roam free. Sex as an outlet for the primal needs of his Beast. But not tonight. For the first time since he'd become a Knight of White, intimacy with a woman was not about sex. It was about *making love*. And the man in him demanded control. With a force born of all he was, all he would ever be, Des shoved aside his Beast.

Needing Jessica closer, to become a part of him, his hand slid up her skirt, beneath the sweet fullness of her ass, lifting her hips. She arched into him, moving against his hips, teasing him with how easy it would be to rip those panties away, to find his way inside her.

Had he ever wanted to be inside a woman the way he wanted to now? He felt a need to merge with her. A need to be one with Jessica.

He palmed her breast, remembering the way her nipples had hardened beneath his touch only hours before. She murmured his name, a sensual reward that played along his nerve endings, coaxing a rush of sensation to rip through his body.

A low growl escaped his throat. He nipped her lips. "Take off your clothes." It was an order he knew she'd obey, and he didn't wait for a response. He shoved off the bed and made fast work of ridding himself of his as well.

Naked, hard, raging with primal need, Des drew a breath, forcing himself to calm. To enjoy the glorious sight of Jessica naked. Her full breasts were high, her nipples pebbled, her creamy skin a drastic, sensual contrast to his darker coloring, a fact that aroused him beyond belief. His cock pulsed, throbbing.

"You're beautiful," he whispered, meaning his words. They weren't spoken for the seductive purposes he might say them to another female. Because whatever it was about Jessica that called to him, it did so completely. To him, she was the most beautiful woman he'd ever known. The most engaging, sensual beauty that existed.

Her gaze slid over his body, lingering on his erection, touching him with heat. Slowly, her eyes lifted. "So are you," she said, her teeth sliding seductively along her bottom lip, her voice husky with arousal.

She offered him her hand, inviting him to join her. The invitation felt bigger than the moment though, bigger than life. As if touching her now, taking her tonight, would somehow change his life, his world.

But he didn't stop to analyze those feeling, didn't need a second request. His knees hit the mattress and she met him halfway. Soon they were face-to-face, their eyes locked, the connection in that moment, soul deep, intense. Beyond words, even beyond touch.

Des drew a breath and settled his cock between her legs, easing her into his arms, air escaping his lungs, trickling past his lips. And then the oddest thing happened. He experienced the most intense sensation of calmness, of being complete. He could almost feel his Beast purring inside, as satisfied as the man.

He whispered her name a second before he kissed her. There was tenderness in the way their lips melted together, merged. The impact of that connection held no less potency than the devouring passion of their prior kisses.

Des was lost, hoping never to be found.

Somehow they ended up on their sides, lying on the mattress, legs entwined. He didn't remember how. Only that she fit his body perfectly, and he marveled at how sweet her flavor, how addictive.

Des had always taken pride in his ability to pleasure his partner, but it had been about his ego, not about his desire to give. And he so wanted to give to Jessica.

But Jessica had her own ideas, urging him to his back as she eased close to him, her breasts pressed to his side. One of her fingernails scraped his nipple. Her teeth scraped the other. Des sucked in a breath, molten heat firing his veins, threatening his willpower. It was all he could do to remain still, to allow her to work her magic.

Her hand slid down his stomach, her mouth finding his, teasing him with quick caresses of her lips. His heart kicked into overdrive as her fingers walked downward, and without warning, her palm wrapped around his shaft. Her touch sent a jolt of pleasure shooting through his groin and spiraling through his body. He let out a deep moan, his hips lifting.

Jessica smiled against his lips for a moment, clearly aware she was driving him insane.

"Witch," he accused.

"And you like it," she purred, sliding her palm up his length and then spreading the damp proof of his arousal at the head of his erection.

A second later, she released her hold, leaving him aching for the return of her hand. She moved between his legs, her mouth finding his stomach, tongue dipping into his navel, his cock pressed between those lush breasts.

He squeezed his eyes shut, fighting for restraint. Because as much as he wanted what he knew she intended, what he knew came next—the wet heat of her mouth around his shaft—he wanted inside her more.

Forcing himself to act before he lost the will, Des sat up. His fingers slid into the soft strands of Jessica's hair, guiding her lips to his, kissing her…taking her with his mouth, his tongue, his teeth. He pressed her for all she would give him, his demands fuelled by primal need—need that demanded he act, consume, claim.

Palming her breasts, he kneaded, and then plucked at the nipples. With satisfaction, he felt her shiver, her hand coming up to close over his, to urge him onward.

"I want inside you," he whispered against her mouth.

"Yes," she said and pushed on his shoulders, urging him onto the mattress.

He complied, easing down to rest on his elbows. Des

took in the vision she made, his stare hungry, devouring her beauty as she straddled him. She reached forward, closing her palm around his shaft. Des sucked in a breath as she guided him to her core. Slowly, she inched down his shaft, taking him inside her—wet warmth surrounding him.

For several seconds, they sat there, intimately joined, eyes locked. Something inside him moved with that look, with that shared moment. Emotion expanded in his chest, in his body, in his soul, a feeling of closeness, of belonging consuming him.

Suddenly, he ached to hold her. An ache that pressed, demanded. "Come here," he whispered hoarsely.

She eased forward, her gaze never leaving his, her fists finding the mattress beside his head. Her chest rose and fell, drawing his gaze.

"You drive me crazy," he told her.

Her response was to melt into his body, to kiss him with such passion, such utter desire, he could taste the urgency, the hunger on her lips. At the same moment, they began to move, in tune with each other's wants and needs. Her fingers rested on his jaw, as if she feared he would stop kissing her. Des took her in, his arms around her, melding her soft curves tighter against his body. He couldn't get enough of her.

The slow sensual dance grew frenzied. Faster. Harder. Almost desperate. He wanted deeper, wanted all of her. Wanted more. He couldn't get more. He needed more. They bucked together, even as their hands explored, guided, teased. Desperation began to build inside, clawing at Des, claiming him.

Abruptly, his primal side flared, roaring to life with

a fierce intensity. It was the kind of showing every Knight feared when off the battlefield. Because in battle the Beast demanded one thing… To devour.

Des struggled to smash his Beast back down. Struggled to claim the control he'd always reveled owning. He'd never before feared his darker side, but he did in that moment, feared it as he never had because the Beast cried out for Jessica, demanded she be claimed.

Des felt his teeth elongate. He pressed his face to Jessica's neck, hiding from her view, desperate. But the position put his mouth closer to her flesh, to temptation, and his internal war intensified.

What the hell was wrong with him?

"Des," Jessica murmured, her lips brushing his jaw. "Des, I…" Her body spasmed, clenching his cock with silky pleasure. Somehow, her satisfaction pulled him back into a place where only he and Jessica existed, where the Beast ceased to exist.

His arms tightened around her, his hips bucking into her, pumping into the tight recesses of her body. Sensations poured over him, into him, around him.

Jessica had somehow reclaimed both the man and his pleasure. Release came over him in an explosion of power, shaking him from head to toe, stealing his breath, his thoughts. Taking him to oblivion and back.

And when they finally stilled, their bodies melted together, Des didn't ever want to let her go. The problem was, neither did the Beast.

One of the many reasons, no matter how much he didn't want to, Des had to walk away from Jessica. He had to say goodbye.

She sighed as he pressed their bodies side by side so

that her back was to his chest. He pressed his legs to hers, enclosing her curves with his frame. And he wished things could be different, that this didn't have to be goodbye. But he didn't dare make love to her again. What if he couldn't control the Beast next time? Thinking about how close he'd come to biting her scared the hell out of him.

This couldn't be happening. Jessica couldn't be his mate. If she was, she would find out that he'd lied to her. Not a good way to start out forever. And she had a family, a life. The kind of security one didn't want to walk away from to fight demons, nor would he ask her to. The other option was no better. By trying to suppress his darker side, had he found out he didn't know how to anymore?

Either way, this was unfair to Jessica. He had to get through the tour the next day and then distance himself. No matter how painful that might be.

His gaze lowered to where his hand rested against the ivory perfection of her leg. Light where he was dark, in every way possible.

He had no choice but to walk away.

Excitement coursed through Greg's veins as he opened the lockbox, ready to retrieve the diaries. His hand even shook a bit as he shoved the key into the lock. The door opened and his eyes went wide.

Empty. The freaking locker was empty!

Greg's mind roared with rage. He'd paid, and paid well, for those diaries. Damn it! He should have just used his men. Fear about the Beasts had kept him from doing so. Fear about the unknown. If the Beasts took control of his men, they could take the diaries. But this plan hadn't gotten him anywhere.

He slammed the locker shut, not bothering to remove the key. His cell phone rang, and he checked caller ID. Unknown. He knew damn well who it was. Any fear he'd had of Black Dog disappeared. He was damn tired of being a whipping dog for the rest of the world. He'd been kicked one too many times.

Greg hit the answer button. "Where are my diaries?" he demanded.

He listened a moment, heard the bad news. It was all he could do to remain calm as he agreed to meet the Hell Hounds back at that bridge again. Oh, he'd meet them all right, but this time he wasn't going to let them cow him. This time he would get the results he'd paid for. One way or the other.

Greg punched the button on his phone. His fingers turned white where he still gripped the receiver. Without those diaries, he had no ammunition. He couldn't hand over that journal. Not without being killed. *Damn it!* He pounded the palm of his hand on his forehead. *Think!* He drew a breath. Thought a moment. Exhaled.

A plan began to take root. Segundo said he wanted the journal, but Greg knew better. It was what the journal would lead him to, what it held inside, that Segundo wanted. So Greg had to make sure he got to that list of bloodlines first. He laughed. Yes. He could still pull this off.

Considering his options, he decided he couldn't afford to trust the men working the catering event. They could already be influenced by Segundo. And he needed a team capable of chasing the trail that map would lead him on. He needed the Hell Hounds.

They owed him big for tonight, but despite that, he doubted they would feel inclined toward generosity. They'd want more money. Lots of it, too, he'd be willing to bet. Immediate cash was what he needed. And he was willing to take risks to get it. He had access to certain museum funds. By the time anyone missed them—well, he'd be long gone, and filthy rich with money and power.

When this was over, everyone who had ever doubted him, who had ever thought he wasn't good enough, would be begging forgiveness. He'd make sure of it.

An evil smile twisted on his lips and he started walking. Walking toward his new and improved future.

Chapter 10

Jessica woke to the sound of her alarm clock playing top-forty music, wishing it would go away, not sure she even remembered going to sleep. She rolled onto her back, blinking in the sunlight, her hand going to the empty space beside her. Disappointment shot through her at Des's absence, memories flooding her thoughts. Images of her and Des, intimately entwined, making love, replayed in her mind. She'd fallen asleep in his arms, feeling more at peace than she remembered ever feeling.

She sat up, searching the room for signs Des was still there, upset as she noted his clothes were missing. That he'd bolted surprised her. Their connection had felt so real, so alive, unlike anything she'd ever experienced. But then, she'd put the man through hell, and her father had been pretty damn rude.

Shoving away the covers, she walked to the bathroom and turned on the shower, thinking of how her father had talked to Des. Unlike most men she'd known, Des wasn't one to sing her father's praises. She stepped under the flow of the water and realized her father had been right on one account. Des had a lot of her mother in him. She sensed it. The wildness, the need to explore.

A lump formed in her throat as Jessica realized that for the first time in her life, a man had sparked the beginning of something special in her. A man she could feel something for, a man who would be gone in a few days, before they ever had time to get to know each other fully. This should be a fling, nothing more. How likely would a long-distance relationship be to succeed? So why did she feel forgetting him would be hard?

Part of her wished she'd never gone down this path because it was headed for heartache. Another part couldn't imagine missing having Des in her life, if only for the briefest of times.

Jessica dressed in a simple black suit-dress and heels, and spent a bit of extra time on her makeup to cover the dark circles under her eyes. Then she headed to the kitchen, assuming she needed to call a cab.

She entered the tiny dinette area just outside her kitchen to find Des sitting at the table, dipping graham crackers into a peanut-butter jar.

Her heart swelled with happiness beyond what his simple presence should offer. She knew that, but it didn't change anything.

The dark shadow of stubble on his jaw only served to enhance the rugged warrior image the night before had given him. Seeing the steely hardness with which he'd faced those criminals at her father's house, she'd known there was more to Des than met the eye.

He grabbed a spoon from the table and filled it with peanut butter. "Hope you don't mind. I was starving and I love this stuff."

She smiled and sat down across from him. "I do, too," she said. "I can't say I've tried it with graham crackers before, though."

He smeared peanut butter on a cracker and handed it to her. "It's damn near a delicacy. Try it."

Jessica bit into the cracker and approved, taking a moment to swallow. "Good stuff."

Des handed her his glass of milk and she accepted, thinking how intimate the act. "I thought you'd left." She set the glass down. "You were gone when I woke up."

He shoved the peanut butter aside and leaned forward, fingers laced on the table in front of him. Warmth radiated from his eyes and his voice lowered. "Only because I knew I wouldn't let you out of that bed if I stayed in it with you."

Jessica suddenly felt the warmth in his eyes spread through her body. The only thing that kept that warmth from turning to downright molten fire was the ringing of the phone.

With effort, she tore her gaze from his and went to grab the cordless phone off the wall. She returned to her seat and answered, to find her father on the other end of the line.

Five minutes later, she hung up the call. "My father," she announced.

"I gathered as much," Des commented, his attention

going to cleaning up the food, all the warmth from before gone. He glanced at her as he screwed the lid on the jar. "Any news?"

"Nothing." She hesitated. "I'm sorry for how he treated you last night."

His eyes glinted with a hint of steel. "He thinks you need a different kind of man. As much as I don't want to hear that, he's probably right." With his words, he pushed to his feet and she felt a door close, felt Des shut her out.

Her heart fell to her stomach. She knew Des wasn't here to stay, but she'd hoped to have more than one night. But that wasn't going to happen.

He'd made a decision just now. She'd felt it as if it were her own. Felt the finality.

Des had already said goodbye.

A few minutes after Des dropped Jessica off at work, he stood in the living room of the team's temporary headquarters—a rental house near the museum.

Des wasn't feeling his normal, smart-ass self. If anyone spoke of his night with Jessica, he might have to jack them up against the wall.

He found Max and Rinehart standing around a setup of folding tables arranged in a square, busy connecting wires to equipment. Judging from the cautious looks they cast his direction, neither planned to cross him today. No doubt he radiated abnormal edginess, because he damn sure felt it.

"Give us an hour and we'll be fully operational," Rinehart commented.

"And this won't be some back-of-a-van operation," Max commented, looking up from the red and blue wires he continued twisting together. "This is going to be a grade-A, techno sweet shop."

Rock stomped into the house and let the screen door slam behind him. "The seven trainees Jag sent are headed up the driveway. And holy hell, he sent Marco. That sorry bastard doesn't listen worth a crap."

Rinehart let out a bark of laughter. "Sounds familiar."

Any other day, Des would egg on the banter between Rock and Rinehart. He tended to keep the team light, even in the face of adversity. Not today. He wasn't feeling it.

Rock grimaced and opened his mouth to bite back at Rinehart. Des cut him off, fixing the young Knight in a direct stare.

"I want those Knights wired and in the field within an hour. I need Rinehart and Max free to prepare for the extraction of that journal."

Rock's frustration slid away, his focus on his job back in place. The Knight might be a bit of a livewire, but he knew when to toe the line with Des as well as the others did. "I'm on it," Rock said, turning to the door to detour his new team before they entered.

Rinehart stood behind a computer, looking up long enough to cast Des an amused look. "That assignment ought to bust Rock's ball back to size."

Des claimed a seat on a folding chair directly in front of a monitor now flashing through images of the museum. "That's the idea."

The computer screen showed Jessica walking down a hallway, and Des felt his heart triple beat. Greg came toward her, and she stopped to talk to him.

"Where's the volume?" Des asked, his gaze never leaving Jessica.

"Another ten minutes," Max said.

"Damn," Des murmured. He really wanted to hear what was going down, if anything.

Max walked around the table to eye the screen, but Des didn't pay him any attention. His muscles were taut, tense, his entire body filled with regret. He'd gone cold on Jessica, shut her down like a bad dream, when she was more fantasy than nightmare.

He watched as she swiped hair behind her ear, her movement jerky. Her lips were thin and she crossed her arms protectively in front of herself.

"Look at her," Max commented. "She's on edge. She knows what a bastard Greg is."

Greg and Jessica parted ways, and Des exhaled a breath he hadn't realized he'd been holding. He eyed his team. "We're sure Greg was behind last night?"

"Oh yeah," Max said.

"And the men who attacked the mansion? Who were they?"

Rinehart answered, "Hired guns."

"By Greg," Max added. "I have a taped conversation that's as damning as it gets."

Rinehart shoved his hat back on his head, then put his hands on his hips, one leg forward. "We nabbed one of the men and convinced him to talk, but he didn't know much." He snorted. "And believe me. We scared the man shitless. He would have talked if he had anything to say."

Rinehart knew a little too much about making people talk. Des knew he'd spent his human life in the military. Sometimes, he wondered what exactly Rinehart had done for the good ole U.S. of A. But then, they didn't talk about their own pasts, let alone ask about each other's.

"The diaries are in a safe in the back room," Max offered. Des didn't bother asking where they'd gotten a safe. His men were resourceful. Max continued, "Sonsabitches wanted those books in a bad way."

Rinehart pulled a short-bladed, six-inch saber from his belt, handling it with the ease most would handle a pocketknife, and used it to cut some wires. "Kind of seems like they know something we don't."

Des grimaced. "Information related to that list of bloodlines, no doubt. Jessica's mother had studied Solomon all her life. It makes sense her personal notes might be of value, maybe a guide to understanding the journal."

"Whatever might be in the diaries, it's only specula-tion," Max pointed out. "The journal is the true score."

"Right," Des agreed, "and we can't be behind the eight ball this time. We might not be so lucky as to recover the journal. We need to be there before the Beasts."

Rinehart added, "Greg's the key to when and how the Beasts plan to get that journal."

Des thought a moment. "I need to get closer to Greg." He had an idea. "Max." He waited until he had the Knight's attention. "Get in contact with that board member you played footsies with. Tell him his executive director can't seem to find time for me and it's causing concern. I'm scheduled to be at the museum for a tour at one o'clock. Tell your contact that if Greg can't make time for me, maybe our collection isn't important to the museum."

Max reached for the cell phone attached to his belt, but not before Des saw a hint of respect in the Knight's eyes. "Consider it done," Max said.

Des pushed to his feet, wishing like hell he had time

to give those diaries a glance. But he needed to shower and pull himself into some semblance of order.

He'd given up his last excuse to see Jessica before the party. And that night would be the one for goodbye. Because before that charity event was over, he would crush her by claiming her mother's life's work. Because he and his team couldn't leave without that journal.

Avoiding Jessica was for the best. So why did everything inside him scream with regret?

Jessica stepped out of her office and headed toward the elevator, planning to meet Des in the lobby. It was almost one o'clock, and he would be taking the museum tour. Anticipation charged her body. She wanted to see him again; hoped he would be different than he'd been on the ride to work earlier that morning. He'd barely spoken to her after that call from her father. No matter how she tried, Jessica couldn't shake how unsettled she felt about the way things seemed to be ending between them.

The elevator opened. Michael stood inside, a bag in his hand from the restaurant Des had gone to the night before. The minute Michael saw her, his eyes lit up. "Just the person I wanted to see."

"Not now," she said, stepping inside the elevator. "I have to give a tour."

"I'll ride with you," he said, feet planted. "Something is weird about your fiasco last night."

Sarcasm laced her voice. "Other than me being held at gunpoint, I'm not sure what you mean."

He waved off her smart mouth. "Besides what we've already discussed. I'm talking about Des Smith. I was just at the restaurant, and no one there remembers him."

He made a face. "And that isn't a man who's easily forgotten. Not to mention he was bleeding."

She frowned. "I don't have a clue where you are going with this. Des brought food back to us. He was at that restaurant."

They arrived on the ground floor, and the door opened. Michael followed Jessica into the hall, clearly determined to finish the conversation. "I know, but something is off. The way you described him handling those men at your father's house. It doesn't add up. *He* doesn't add up."

She stopped walking a few inches shy of the lobby. "What insanity are you talking, Michael?"

"Like I said. It doesn't add up, Jessica. I'm thinking he's with the insurance company. Some kind of security specialist maybe."

Her eyes went wide. "The insurance company!" She quickly lowered her voice. "What in the world would they gain by sending someone in as a donor?"

"There's been a theft attempt on the journal. It's not crazy to think they might be cautious." He shrugged. "You know, to check out the staff."

"Des's attention has been on me. I'm the last person they'd need to worry about since I am the reason the donation even made it to this museum."

"But he was originally set up to meet with Greg, right?"

Her brows dipped, the suggestion rolling around in her head. "You think he's here to check out Greg?"

"What about Greg?"

Jessica turned to see the man in question, Greg himself, behind her. She quickly feigned innocence. "I was just looking for you."

The glint in his eyes said he didn't believe her. "Well,

it just so happens, I was looking for you, too. I'm taking your appointment with Mr. Smith."

"What? Why?"

"The board said so, that's why. They want this donation, and after last night, they're afraid you're not up to bagging it."

Jessica didn't believe that for a minute. The board knew she could handle herself. Greg simply wanted to reel in the fish she'd caught and take credit with the board. "I'd rather finish what I started."

"I said I'd handle it. Besides, you need to prepare for that party. Scratch Mr. Smith off the long list of things I need you to handle today." He didn't give her time to respond, turning on his heels and sauntering away with a cocky air about him.

Damn it! Disappointment washed over her. She really wanted to see Des. All she could do was hope he'd ask to see her. He was taking care of her flat tire, so surely he would.

"I told you," Michael said. "He's checking out Greg."

Jessica rolled her eyes. "Greg is trying to steal the credit for my work." She started toward the elevator. "And I don't know why I let him get to me. I do this because I love history, not for pats on the back."

Michael fell into step with her. "I don't think so." He hesitated. "Of course, that's normal for Greg. I'm not denying that. But you heard him. The board wants him involved. This isn't Greg's doing. It's someone else's."

"Right. Like the board really talked to him." She waved off that idea. "You can't believe a word Greg says."

"Fine, then. Don't say I didn't try to warn you." He raised the bag. "Ham on rye. Want half?"

"Only if you promise to let me eat in peace. No talk of undercover secret plots."

"I said fine, then, already." He lifted his head with a prim air. "But just because you don't talk about it, doesn't make it untrue. Pretending it isn't so simply doesn't work."

She started to reprimand him, but his words hit home in too many ways to completely discount them. He was right. Pretending didn't work. She couldn't pretend her mother was away on a trip and make it so. Nor could she pretend those diaries would be returned. No matter how much she tried to block out the hard facts of recent events, they were there, a part of her life that wouldn't go away.

Nor could she block out the feeling that the whirlwind of the past year was about to end. Destiny had something more in store for her. Calling to her. The question was—why did Des, a man she barely knew, feel a part of that destiny?

Saturday night, Greg stood under the shower, warm water pouring over him, adrenaline pouring through him. Finally, the night of the charity event, the night when he would gain his rightful place in this life, had arrived. With Black Dog and his men covertly working for him, the journal would be in his possession, and he'd find the treasure the map inside led to. Then, he'd hold the treasure captive until Segundo turned him into a powerful demon, an immortal without human limitations. Tonight would be the beginning of a new and better future.

Abruptly, the curtain flew back, revealing Segundo.

All of the bravado from moments before washed down the drain beneath his feet, leaving him naked, exposed.

"What the hell are you doing?" he shouted, the words gone from his mouth before he could call them back.

Segundo's eyes flared red, his human mask distorting into that horrid half Beast, a snarl sliding from his lips. A second later, Greg found himself pressed against the tile wall, feet dangling above the tub's surface.

"Do not press your luck with me, human. I can cause you so much pain, you will beg for mercy."

Greg's hands went to his throat, to the beastly fingers cutting off his windpipe, clawing for mercy. And then, as suddenly as the Beast had picked him up, Greg was dropped.

His feet hit the wet floor of the tub and he slipped, reaching for support but to no avail. He fell hard, his shoulder taking the brunt of the hit, his head knocking against the porcelain side.

Segundo towered over the tub. "I've been patient, human, but no more. Bring me my journal before this night is over. If you don't, I'll tear you apart limb by limb and then find someone who will." He turned and walked away.

For several seconds, Greg didn't dare breathe for fear Segundo would return. When he did not, the tension in Greg's body slowly eased, but the humiliation did not. It was a familiar part of his life he'd long ago vowed to put behind him. Resolve formed as he pressed himself upward, fighting against the dizziness the head injury caused.

He would be humiliated no more. No more!

Chapter 11

Des straightened his silver Armani tie and then inspected himself in the mirror. His hair slicked back, his white shirt starched, his suit expensive: his appearance appropriate to mingle with the rich bastards he'd be around at the charity event.

Turning away from the mirror, he found the hallway and started walking, feeling on edge, ready to chew nails. He'd be seeing Jessica tonight for the first time in days. Seeing her long enough to watch her crushed by the events that were about to unfold, by the loss of that journal.

Jessica's feelings were only one of the many reasons uneasiness played in his mind, in the taut lines of his body. Their extraction plan had holes. Big holes. Based on limited surveillance feed from various locations, including the catering company's office, they knew an attempt on the journal would be made at the party. That meant the Knights' best strategy was to intercept the thieves as they tried to exit the building with the journal in their possession. Letting them get past the exits would be too risky. Des still planned to attend the party, which put him inside the museum, ready to respond where needed as the plan went into motion.

It had all sounded good as they'd rolled it out several days before. Right now his gut said differently, and if he could postpone their actions he would. But they were throwing down tonight no matter how much he thought they needed more time. Because one way or the other, someone was taking that journal home before the party ended, and it wasn't going to be the Beasts. And though they had found no direct proof Greg was working for the Beasts, it didn't really matter. Even if he wasn't, once he had the journal, the Beasts were near, and they'd take it from him.

Hoping for some sort of positive news from Max, Des completed the path down the hall and entered the surveillance area. Max sat in front of a computer. Which, now that Des thought of it, was where he always was. Des had yet to see the Knight sleep. Reluctantly, he admitted to himself that Max had earned his respect, if not his trust. The trust part of the equation just wouldn't come. He remembered that flash of red in Max's eyes and it gave Des pause. Was the red in his eyes as well? Could he and Max be alike? Had the Beast consumed Max as it had Des, and he simply didn't recognize it in himself?

Des shook off the thought and focused on the matters at hand. "Where do we stand?" he asked Max, hoping for something new, something extra to go on. Even with the bugs he'd planted in Greg's office the day of the tour, they'd gotten limited feed.

"No better than thirty minutes ago when you asked me last time," Max spat back, glancing over his shoulder. He was the only one left at the house. Rock and Rinehart were in position, their team with them.

"Chingado," he cursed in Spanish. "That's not good enough. We need more information." They knew the catering company, Greg and this man called Black Dog were in bed together and intended to switch the journal out with a fake at the party. One or all of them were likely being controlled by the Beasts. But that was the extent of their knowledge. Not enough as far as Des was concerned, considering the public forum this was all going down in.

Max scrubbed his face, a heavy stubble darkening his jaw. "I know. Believe me, I know. I've hunted for info on Black Dog but came up empty. These guys are good, some sort of special-ops team who really know the meaning of *covert.*"

Des grimaced and eyed his watch. "I have to go. This is going down wrong. I feel it. We can't draw swords on humans, and why do I think they know that?"

Max swiveled around to face him, his eyes hard. "Pain can be worse than dying. If anyone knows this, you should. No one says you can't cause one hell of a lot of pain."

The words, spoken with a sharp intensity, swept Des with the force of truth. Words that went beyond the surface meaning, deep into the recesses of Max's soul. Des saw it in the other Knight's eyes, and decided in that moment, he and Max had at least two things in common. They both had a past that refused to let them see into the future. And they both agreed on what had to happen tonight. If Greg or his men got in the way of saving that journal, they were going to have a hurting put on them.

Jessica stood in the main hall of the museum, the charity event in full swing, her nerves in a jumbled mess. The journal would be publicly unveiled for the first time in a mere hour. For some reason, she couldn't shake the sizzle of fear deep in her gut. If anything happened to that journal, she'd be crushed. Worse, her father would be crushed.

The insurance people had been thorough, she reminded herself. Borderline paranoid even. They'd checked out every detail of the party, even the new catering staff. She knew because they'd kept her beyond busy for days now, jumping through hoops that helped keep her mind off the fact that Des had disappeared from her life as suddenly as he'd arrived. Even her car keys had been left at the reception desk after his tour. Yet, he would be here tonight. Or so Greg told her. He'd be going to review the Smith collection the next week. Greg, not her. Des had shut her out completely.

Des. His name ran through her mind as it had a million times. Despite all that had happened, he simply refused to be expelled from her thoughts. Dating and the entire male-female relationship quandary occupied a tiny piece of her life, but even in his absence, Des consumed a big portion. Maybe it was the age-old temptation of wanting what you couldn't have, though that had never appealed to her in the past.

Michael approached, looking handsome in a black three-piece suit, tailored to perfection. The man had been her rock the past few days, juggling last-minute details that to some would be a crisis. To him, they'd been nothing but wrinkles that needed touch-ups.

He gave Jessica's dress—a pink knee-length chiffon—a once-over and let out a low whistle. "You've got style and class, sweetheart."

Her lips lifted in an attempted smile. "Thanks."

"I'm not feeling that smile and I'm wondering why?" His hand elegantly swept the decor of silver and pink. "The party is absolutely spectacular. You did your mother proud tonight."

She avoided his question. "*We* did her proud," Jessica corrected, loosening up a bit thanks to the familiar banter she often shared with Michael. "This would never have happened without you. Oh, and I *love* the pink ribbon cake. The catering company turned out to be excellent."

"Amazing, isn't it? I wouldn't have thought it was possible." He gave her a keen look and then glanced around the room. "Any sign of your father yet?"

"Not yet, but that doesn't surprise me. This entire night is emotional for him."

"And for you, I suspect," he commented. "Is that why I'm getting that tentative vibe off you?"

"You're right about this night being emotional," Jessica admitted, not at all surprised he pressed for answers about her mood. "But honestly, that's not what's bothering me." She flattened her palm on her stomach. "I have this funny feeling something is going to go wrong."

"Meaning what?"

"I'm worried about the journal."

He waved off her words. "Honey, the way the insurance people flocked around us this week, you have nothing to worry about." His attention went to the door. "Speaking of insurance people. Look who's here."

Jessica's gaze went to the door, where Des entered. Her heart fluttered wildly, the impact of seeing him again washing over her with far more intensity than she'd expected. Heads turned as he walked in, female heads. Unbidden, a tingle of jealousy played on her nerve endings.

"Des is not with the insurance company," she said sharply.

"Whatever you say," Michael said, rolling his eyes. "Insurance company or not, he's an attention grabber." His voice perked up with interest. "What's up with the two of you, anyway?"

Her gaze went back to Des's profile, noting the bosomy brunette who was trying to claim his attention. Her lips pursed and she cast Michael a nonchalant look. "Nothing. Nothing at all."

"Shouldn't you greet him?" Michael pressed.

"He looks well taken care of," Jessica commented before she could stop herself.

No doubt Michael would pick up on the bitterness in her tone. From the look in his eyes, she was about to get another round of questions, but a sudden rush of activity arose at the front door. Jessica and Michael, and a hundred or so other guests, turned toward the commotion.

Jessica spotted her father standing near the front door. Her lips lifted as she watched him work the crowd as an accomplished politician, shaking hands, smiling.

Though she was too far away to see his eyes, she suspected that smile didn't touch them. This night came with the pain of loss over his wife, over her mother.

She glanced at Michael. "Now, *there's* a man who needs to be greeted. I'll catch up with you in a bit."

She waved to Michael before working her way through the crowd, heading in her father's direction. But only a few feet away, she stopped dead in her tracks when she found him talking with Des. These were the last two people she'd expected to see in what appeared to be a pleasant conversation. She wasn't one to tuck tail and run, but she preferred to deal with her awkward reunion with Des alone. Not in front of her father.

She contemplated her options. She considered retreating, if only momentarily. But there was no escape as both men seemed to sense her presence, overwhelming her with their attentive stares.

Her father motioned her forward, and Jessica caved to expectations. She drew a deep, calming breath and started walking, refusing to meet Des's stare, but no less unnerved by his attention.

She hugged her father and kissed his cheek before inclining her head toward Des. "Glad you could make it."

His eyes narrowed ever so slightly, his expression guarded. "I wouldn't have missed it for the world."

"I was just thanking Des for his help the other night," her father commented. "I didn't exactly show my gracious side that evening."

"As I said, Senator," Des offered in a mild voice, "the night was full of emotional upheaval. We were all on edge."

Jessica cast Des a pensive look, her instincts telling her he wasn't overly receptive to her father's apology, despite the respect in his manner.

"May I have your attention?" Michael stood on a stage where a small orchestra had taken seats. "With us this evening is Senator Montgomery." The crowd clapped, heads turning to him. "The Senator will unveil an amazing piece of history. But not yet." Michael smiled and the crowd made sounds of teasing displeasure. "We don't want anyone to miss this, so we'll give people time to arrive. In the meantime, I'd like to introduce our entertainment." He went on to list the band's credits, then added, "Let the dancing begin!"

The crowd calmed and couples began to ease onto the dance floor directly in front of the stage. "Would you like to dance, Jessica?" Des asked softly, drawing her gaze.

His invitation surprised her. She wanted to dance with him, but then, she didn't. Des confused her. Des enticed her. He had also hurt her. And he would be gone tomorrow. She looked into his eyes, finding them warm and telling of the connection they still shared.

Business, and his donation, seemed a good excuse for rushing into the fire again, into his arms. Before she could speak, before she could accept the dance, her father interjected. "Actually, I'd love to have my daughter be my first dance of the night." He held an arm out to Jessica, as if staking a claim. His gaze went to Des, the kindness of a few moments before tinted with a hint of steel. "I'm sure you understand?"

A dark look flashed across Des's features, and for a moment, Jessica thought he was going to say no, he did *not* understand. Because, frankly, she didn't understand, herself.

After a long pause, Des inclined his head. "Maybe later then," he murmured, his eyes meeting hers for a fleeting second, ice where there had been heat.

Jessica tried to will him to look at her again, but he wouldn't. Whatever haunted Des, whatever made him respond to her father as he did, obviously had a deep hold on him. And she could do nothing about it in their limited acquaintance.

Jessica linked her arm through her father's and let him guide her to the dance floor, knowing she couldn't reprimand him. Not on a night like this one. There were more important things to focus on.

She refused to allow anything, or anyone, to get in the way of honoring her mother's life, her work. And that included Des, no matter how sexy and mysterious the man might be.

Des walked to the bar and dropped cash on the counter, barely glancing at the bartender as he covertly scouted for Greg. "Tequila, straight up." A shot glass appeared, filled with his drink of choice. Des downed the contents. "Oh yeah," he said when the bite slid down his throat. "Hit me again." He wouldn't get drunk, but he damn sure needed that kick.

He finished off his second shot and leaned on the bar, his eyes catching on his target. Greg stood in a far corner talking with an elderly man whom Des recognized as one of the museum board members. He couldn't wait to take that bastard, Greg, down. Eyeing his watch, Des checked his time lines.

According to the intel they'd managed to secure, Greg would be taking drugged refreshments to the two guards in direct contact with the journal. When they passed out, the catering staff would replace the guards and the journal, all before the unveiling ceremony started. Max had tapped into the museum cameras and would watch for Greg to launch into action, alerting the entire team.

Des's gaze landed on Jessica as her father twirled her around the dance floor, a vision of beauty in pink. Something inside him moved when he looked at her, and it wasn't simply about fire and attraction. It was deeper, more intimate, impossible to ignore.

Pushing off the bar, Des didn't give himself time to think. In a few minutes, all hell would break loose. He wanted his dance, their first and only dance, damn it. And he didn't care if the senator approved. Not this time.

In a few long strides, Des closed the distance between himself and Jessica, sidestepping several other dancers and stopping by her side. Jessica stopped dancing, her light blue gaze registering surprise.

"Can I cut in?" Des asked, focused on her, not the senator.

The soft piano music echoed in his ears as he waited for her response. She stared at him. One second. Two. She turned to her father, pushed to her toes. She whispered in his ear before stepping out of his arms.

Des reached for her, taking her hand in his, electricity shooting up his arm. Images of their naked bodies, entwined intimately, flashed in his mind. Urging her forward, he eased her closer, posturing them for a dance, his hand on her waist. It would be so easy to meld her tight against his body, to feel her soft curves pressed to his. It would also be inappropriate for their circumstances.

"You look beautiful," he said, his voice husky even to his own ears.

"Thank you," she said, her voice a bit tentative. "I'm surprised you broke in on a dance with my father."

"Why is that?" he asked.

Her eyes narrowed, her expression saying she didn't believe he'd even asked that question. "You seem uncomfortable with him. He's very opinionated about my life. I thought perhaps you preferred to avoid him."

"I never avoided him or his opinions," he said. "Just the opposite. I did what he wanted."

"Meaning what?" she asked cautiously.

The song changed, turned slower, softer. Des used the opportunity to close the distance between them, taking a step forward, their legs touching.

His gaze touched her lips, full and sweet, perfect. Lips he knew tasted of temptation. He fixed her in a sizzling stare, finding her look guarded. But he could smell her arousal, feel her heat.

He answered her question. "Meaning I stayed away when I didn't want to."

She pulled back then, staring up at him. "That sounds remarkably like an excuse." Her gaze delved, probed. "Somehow I don't take you for an excuse maker."

"I wanted to see you, Jessica." He spoke the words low, with conviction.

She studied him a moment longer. "Why are we dancing, Des? If you avoided me because of my father, why are we here now?"

Her father was just one reason to distance himself and he knew it. Perhaps Senator Montgomery was simply an excuse to avoid facing the truth. The primal side of him stirred to life around Jessica in a way he feared he couldn't contain. Even now, it clawed at him, rejecting the idea of just walking away, demanding he drag her off somewhere and claim her. It wanted her this moment; his assignment, this crowd be damned. He steeled himself inside, fighting the power of that demand. The Beast usually never rose unless he called to it. He gave it control during battles and sex, and it behaved the rest of the time. It was a deal between man and Beast, a pact of sorts.

"Des?" Jessica pressed. "Why?"

He stared at her, fearing the control he'd thought he owned over the Beast had become a facade. He had to distance himself from Jessica before he did something crazy. This feeling, this primal urge felt beyond mating. He was afraid he'd hurt her.

He drew a breath and began to formulate a method of distancing himself from her. "I'll be leaving soon."

Her expression didn't change, her face still registering cool composure. But Des felt her mood shift, darken. She stopped dancing. "Well, it's been nice meeting you. I hope I'll see your donation here in the museum. Enjoy the rest of the party."

She tried to step away but Des tightened his hold. "Don't do this, Jessica," he said, stopping her departure when he should have let her go.

"Do what?" she asked stiffly.

Turn to ice instead of fire. But he didn't say the words. Who was he to ask such a thing after the way he'd treated her? Besides, he was dangerous. He was on edge, out of control.

"Nothing," he said, forcing himself to let her go, regret rocking him inside and out. Des offered her a tiny bow. "Thank you for the dance."

He straightened, their eyes locking, and for a second he almost grabbed her again, almost pulled her close. His fingers balled into fists and then released, tension, desire, demand chasing his willpower, fighting for control.

Finally, he managed to incline his head and walk away. Not a moment too soon, either. Max sounded in his earpiece. "Greg's on the move. The game is in play. I repeat, we're in play, Knights."

Des returned the smile offered by an elderly woman as he paced the room in a nonchalant pattern, prepared to take action. All the while, he knew Jessica's exact position, determined to watch out for her safety and praying everything went down without a hitch.

Suddenly, the hair on the back of his neck stood up, a trickle of warning tightening his chest. His gaze rocketed to where Jessica stood next to the punch bowl. She was swiping at her dress with her napkin, a large wet stain on the front of it, a man obviously apologizing profusely. And then she started walking toward the elevator. Des started walking, too. Fast.

"Son of a bitch!" The words were spoken in his ear by Max. "I'm sure I don't need to tell you that if Jessica goes upstairs, she could walk right into trouble."

No, he did not have to be told. Des sidestepped several people and made fast tracks toward the stairwell. The brunette from earlier that evening stepped in front of him, stumbling. Des reached out and caught her, irritated. Trying to be nonchalant when his heart pounded so hard he thought his chest might explode.

He gently set the woman away from him, the scent of alcohol flaring in his nostrils. He murmured an apology about an urgent phone call, promising a dance on his return. Finally free, he took long strides toward his destination.

Desperate to find Jessica before that trouble found her first.

Chapter 12

Jessica stood behind her desk, the stain stick she kept in her drawer at hand, but there was no hope. Her dress looked as bad as she felt. She'd already been upset over Des's aloof treatment, but now she was downright near tears. Tears, good grief. That would make twice in a week. She tossed the stick back in her drawer and headed back to the hallway, disgusted with herself for falling apart.

Who knew if she would have reacted so intensely to Des, or any of this, if her mother's absence weren't such a predominant theme to the evening. Yes, they were honoring her mother, but in death rather than in life.

She eyed the end of the hallway, the double doors leading to the secure area where the journal was being guarded. Despite her grief, pride welled inside her.

Soon, it would be on the main floor, a vision for all to see.

Halfway to the elevator, she passed an office and heard a noise—whispering, she thought. A shiver raced down her spine, a premonition of trouble.

"Where is your other shoe?"

Fear slid away, anger in its place. So much for Greg's great catering company. A sexcapade during a high-security event was outrageously inappropriate. She shoved open the door, intending to blast the couple inside, finding herself a bit shell-shocked at what she saw.

Greg was in the room with another man who had discarded his pants but still wore the caterer's white-shirt-and-tie ensemble. "What's going on here?" she demanded, not sure what she had walked into, but quite certain it was far more than she'd expected.

"How about some privacy?" Greg demanded, moving in front of the other man as if protecting his lover.

Jessica eyed the clothes on the floor again, her heart pounding in her ears. Something was so not right here. "Sorry," she said, easing backward, trying to act embarrassed when she was freaking-out scared.

The stairwell doors burst open and Des appeared. "Jessica."

One look at his face and she could see the edginess, the tension. "Des?"

He started walking, long strides closing the distance between them quickly. The urgency she felt in him further ignited her own. She yanked the door shut on Greg and the other man, and rushed to meet Des halfway, a feeling of being chased pressing her onward.

"Hold it right there."

Greg's voice alone wouldn't have stopped her from her destination, but the sound of a gun being cocked brought Jessica to a dead halt.

"Turn around, Jessica," Greg said. "Nice and slow, and don't even think about making a sound. Right now, even as we speak, a sniper is in the crowd, ready to target your father. One word from me, and the trigger goes off."

Jessica's eyes locked with Des's and somehow his presence offered a sense of security, despite the gun at her back. "Do as he says," Des whispered.

Drawing a deep breath, she desperately tried to quell the rage racing through her. Slowly she rotated, staring down the barrel of a gun. This couldn't be happening.

"What is this about, Greg?" she hissed, but she knew the truth and it sickened her—he wanted the journal.

"Shut up, Jessica," he ground out between his teeth. "I am so sick of hearing you talk, always Ms. High and Mighty." He called over his shoulder to the man who had been with him in the office. "Secure the journal."

Suddenly, Des was by her side and Greg jerked the gun in his direction. "Stop right there," he said. "Don't think I won't use this."

"You won't risk the noise," Des said. "Not before you have the journal out of here."

Greg glared at Des. "You underestimate me. The gun has a silencer. I can put a bullet in your head—" the weapon pointed at Jessica "—or hers, without anyone knowing."

Des laughed. "There is no silencer on that gun. Do you even know how to fire it?"

Blood rushed to Greg's face. "There is a silencer and

I damn sure know how to shoot the damn thing. Want to find out firsthand?" He aimed at Des's knee. "How about I start at your legs and work my way to your arms?"

Jessica made a plea. "If this is about money, Greg, my father has lots of it. He'll pay you."

"He wants more than money," Des commented. "Don't you, Greg?"

He narrowed his gaze on Des. "You have no idea what I want."

Des ignored his statement and continued, "Any promises they made you," Des replied, "they won't keep."

"The journal is secure," came a voice from behind Greg.

Jessica's attention riveted to the man who appeared beside him, and she recognized him instantly. He wore all black as he had the night he'd raided her father's house. Her attention shifted to Greg. "You took the diaries, too, you bastard."

Abruptly, the doors behind them burst open. Jessica found herself thrust behind Des as two men moved to either side of him, both pointing guns at Greg and the man in black. Somehow, Des managed to arm himself as well, a gun now held in each of his hands.

Her stomach lurched, fear dancing along her nerve endings. Who were these men and how did Des know them? Had Michael been right? Was Des some sort of security specialist? With the insurance company? Or was he more—something dangerous? She started to take off for the stairwell when she remembered the threat against her father.

She couldn't leave without knowing her father was

safe. Jessica pressed herself tight into the corner and squatted down, managing to get a good view of what was going on. Hopefully, positioned as she was, any bullets would fly over her head.

Des fixed his weapon on Greg. "All right, Greg," he said. "Let me tell you how this is going to play out. You're going to bring me that journal. If I don't have it in sixty seconds flat, I'm going to let my partner here—" he motioned to the man on his left with a slight incline of his head "—shoot out one of your knees. See, he loves torturing people."

Three more men in black charged the room. Jessica recognized them as well from the attack at her father's house, including the one called Black Dog.

"Well, well," Black Dog said. "Look who we have here." His forehead crinkled. "Someone is playing both sides of the field now, aren't they?" He narrowed his gaze on Des. "You pretend to save the senator and his daughter, but your men stole the diaries from us." Black Dog eyed Jessica where she cringed in the corner. "You didn't know your boyfriend here stole from you, did you?"

"Wait," Greg said, his voice fired with anger. "Are you telling me he took my diaries?"

"Oh yeah," Black Dog said. "He took them."

Jessica could barely believe what she was hearing. She surged to her feet, knots twisting in her gut. "Des?" Everything inside her said she could trust Des, but there were things that didn't add up, things Michael had picked up on. "Tell me that's not the truth. Tell me."

"Don't listen to him, Jessica," Des said. "He's trying to upset you." The men beside Des moved in a flash of inhuman speed, knives flying across the room and into the thighs of the two men flanking Black Dog. They gasped, moaned, legs buckling even as they reached for the blades.

"Give us the journal," Des said, his voice low, deadly. "Now."

"The only thing we're doing is walking away," Greg said. "And if you so much as blink, the senator and every guest around him will get a bullet in their heads."

As Greg and the men in black started to back away, Jessica sucked in a breath, fearful that bullets were about to fly, worried for her father, for the guests. She'd never felt so helpless in her life. So completely without resources. So completely out of control.

She didn't know if she could trust any of these men, not even Des. Didn't even know which of them would shoot at her, which would protect her, if any of them.

A night meant to celebrate her mother's life might well be stained in blood. And at this moment, she wasn't so sure it wasn't going to be her own.

Fury ate away at Des in the few seconds he had to think through his actions. In those seconds, the enemies backed off, preparing to slip away, and conflicting agendas pounded on Des's mind. He wanted to end this—no, needed to end this. Right here and now, he and his team could take down these men and secure the journal.

But at what price? What if there really was a sniper in the midst of the guests? Sacrificing innocent human life wasn't an option. It would violate every responsibility he possessed as a Knight of White.

He watched as the men turned a corner and then disappeared out of sight. "Damn it!" he cursed, shoving his weapons in his waistband. "Son of a bitch. I can't believe I had to let them go."

"It was the right choice," Rinehart said in the earpiece. "The *only* choice."

Jessica spoke then, drawing his attention, her anger more than evident in her hissed words. "Tell me you didn't take those diaries."

Des turned to her, forcing himself to look into her eyes, knowing what she would see in his. That she would know he'd lied.

He took a step toward her. "Jessica—"

She backed away, hit the wall. "Don't come near me. Answer the question. Did you take those diaries?"

"There are things—"

Her voice lifted. "Did you take them?"

What could he say? "They're safe."

She shook her head. "You bastard. You lied to me. You…used me."

Des barely contained his flinch. He'd been called a bastard plenty of times in his life, and learned to let it roll off his shoulders. This time it stung. He remembered her calling Black Dog a bastard back at her father's house. Now he himself was no better than a criminal to her. But then, that didn't surprise him. "Call me what you must, but I was protecting the journal."

"Trying to steal it is more like it."

Des kept his focus on Jessica. "There are things going on here you don't understand, and I don't have time to explain them now."

He thought of the diaries, of Jessica's study of her mother's work. If there was any hope of finding that list of bloodlines without the journal, the diaries were the answer. And Jessica would understand her mother's notes. She had to come with them.

The elevator dinged. Someone was coming. Des cursed and grabbed her, covering her mouth with his hand. In a stealthy maneuver, he pushed her into the stairwell, his team following.

Outside the door, Michael's voice sounded. "Jessica?"

She fought against Des, landing a solid blow to his groin that had him barely containing a grunt. Frustrated, he shackled her legs with his and pushed her against the wall.

His mouth went to her ear, his voice a hissed whisper. "I know deep down inside you trust me, but I don't have time to make *you* see that. People will die if the contents of that journal get into the wrong hands."

He reached for his tie with his free hand, the other one still covering her mouth. They needed her help and it was clear she wasn't giving it willingly. He had no choice but to take her by force.

Muffled sounds came from her, attempts to shout, her body stilled by his stronger one. All the while, Max was yelling through his ear mic, warning him to hurry up. He had Michael on camera, and he'd spotted the pile of clothes the fake catering person had left behind.

Des managed to yank his tie free. "Sorry, sweetheart," he said a second before he wrapped the tie around her head and gagged her mouth. Fear radiated off her, and he drank it in, hating it, but having no option but this one. They had limited time to recover that journal and find that hidden list before the Beasts. Without that journal, those diaries were their only hope.

If anyone could find an answer in them, it was the daughter who knew her mother well; it was Jessica.

Des bent over and lifted her over his shoulder, eyed Rinehart and motioned them onward. Part of him screamed with the rightness of carrying her away, of taking her with him. Another part of him thought goodbye would be easier to swallow than the contempt he'd seen in her eyes a few moments before.

At least that contempt would keep him—and his Beast—at a distance. Jessica wasn't likely to let him anywhere near again. Not tonight. Not ever.

Jessica found herself sitting in the back of a van full of computer and tech equipment. A rugged-looking cowboy she recognized from the museum confrontation sat directly across from her.

The cowboy tipped his hat. "Name's Rinehart, ma'am." He spoke as if this were a casual meeting and she hadn't been forced inside the vehicle. "You can take that gag off now." He grinned. "And feel free to work those vocals and call Des as many names as you see fit. I imagine he pretty much deserves them all."

A mixture of fear and confusion took hold as a sense of actually liking this man came over her. He was obviously trying to ease her apprehension. Despite that fact, this man should scare the hell out of her, as should all of her captors. So why did she feel her situation, simply her lack of control, scared her far more than this man or any of her captors for that matter?

She reached up and yanked away the tie. "Where's Des?"

"He thought you might prefer he keep his distance."

His eyes narrowed on her face. "Personally, I thought you'd want answers from him, not me."

He was right, but she said, "I want answers, period."

"And you'll get them."

"Just like that?" she asked. "I find that hard to believe, considering I was just gagged and thrown in the back of a van." A choked laugh escaped her lips. "This is insane. It's a bad dream. Any minute, I'm going to wake up and promise never to drink caffeine before bed."

"I said that myself for damn near a hundred years." He shrugged. "I keep waking up and nothing has changed, so I figure I'm needed in this particular nightmare." He gave her a meaningful look. "I think maybe you are, too."

Her brows dipped. What a bizarre thing to say. "I don't understand any of this."

His lips twitched. "I suspect you will soon." He leaned forward, elbows resting on his knees. "Here's the thing. We need your help. See, that journal is supposed to have a map to the—"

"The box holding the list of bloodlines," she said flatly, anger starting to form. Now she understood. "You're treasure hunters. I'm sure the box alone is worth a pretty penny to the right people."

He jerked back as if slapped. "Don't go jumping to conclusions and working yourself into a huff. This *is* about that list of bloodlines, but not for the reasons you're thinking. If you believe in the legend of the journal, surely you believe in angels and demons. Because ultimately that is what that list of bloodlines is all about. Think about how dangerous that list would be in the wrong hands."

Wait. Surely, he wasn't saying what she thought he was saying. "You're saying demons are after the box." It wasn't a question because she was certain she misunderstood.

"You've entered into a battle as old as time. A battle of good versus evil."

The craziness of this night grew with each passing second. "And I suppose you expect me to believe you're the good guys."

"That's right."

She shook her head and this time she laughed for real. "And those men who stole the journal are what? Demons?"

He didn't look amused. "Not even close. They're pawns in a demon's game. I don't doubt they think they're acting on their own accord, but I promise you they aren't."

"So I'm supposed to believe a demon is controlling my boss, Greg, and that's why he's behaving so irrationally?"

"Greg is who Greg is. The demons simply took advantage of the evil that is already a part of their character. But the reason for Greg's involvement comes down to necessity. A demon can't touch that box without it self-destructing."

"If you go by what my mother believed, human evil will be an issue, too." She swallowed at the sudden dryness in her throat, frightened by how easily she'd shared that information, about how much she wanted to believe this man. "And what will you do with that list if you find it?"

"Protect it. Protect the family names it will identify." The van came to a stop and Jessica stiffened. "We're here," he said.

"Where is here?" she asked, fingers curling around the bottom of the bench.

He slid off the seat, squatting, obviously preparing to open the back door. "Our temporary headquarters. We have your mom's diaries locked up inside. Which, by the way, we weren't trying to steal. We simply intercepted them before they were stolen." He climbed out of the van and then offered her his hand. "Will you help us?"

She stared at his hand, not sure what to make of any of this. "How?"

"Help us find that box and the list," he said. "The only map that existed was said to be inside the journal. No one knows your mother's work as you do. The diaries could hold clues to the location of the box."

Des appeared behind the cowboy named Rinehart, his dark eyes capturing hers. A sudden rush of adrenaline shot through her body. Jessica drew a deep breath, trying to calm down.

And when she spoke, despite looking at Rinehart, her words were meant for Des. "I make no promises to help, but I'll read the diaries." Her attention returned to Des. "But I won't help unless I have reason to believe I should. Right now, I have no reason to trust you and every reason not to."

She stared at Des, holding her breath, willing him to speak, to give her some sign, something that gave her hope. She didn't even know what it would be, just that she needed it more than the breath she held. But he said nothing, gave her nothing. His dark eyes probed, lingered, seemed to see through to her soul.

His gaze lifted to Rinehart's. "Take her to the back bedroom and give her the diaries."

Jessica watched him turn away without another look in her direction, feeling as if she had been punched in the gut.

She'd been so sure what she'd felt with him had been special, and as real as anything in her life. It appeared she had no idea how to tell what was real and what was pretend. How was she supposed to trust her judgment from this point onward?

An auburn-haired beauty with full breasts and lush curves pressed tight against Segundo's body, her soul lingering between worlds, feeding his hunger. Her will was no longer her own, but his. Soon the human male, Greg, would deliver the journal, and she would help him celebrate his prize.

Segundo stood on the balcony of his luxury hotel suite, damn near salivating at the thought of wielding the same power Adrian possessed. Soon, Cain would know who his true leader of the Beasts should be. Segundo would prove that he alone, not Adrian, had claimed the journal. And rightfully, he alone would hunt those bloodlines to honor Cain.

The sudden sound of a snarling Hell Hound, Black Dog in his beastly form, had Segundo pushing aside the female. The Hound eased from the darkness, white fangs dripping, red eyes fixed on Segundo.

He reached for his sword, ready to slit its throat if it attacked. Adrian's new pets were a gift from Cain. Where there was a Hound, there was a master.

As if on cue, fire flashed in the air before Adrian appeared. His gaze went to Segundo's hand where it rested on his weapon. "You would kill my pet?" he challenged. "The pet who saved your incompetent ass tonight?"

Segundo quickly retreated, taking a step backward. His hand left his weapon, a chill rushing over him. But he didn't dare speak. Adrian might well cut out his tongue if he did so. Whatever trouble was about to blindside him, he had to take it in silence.

"Your human museum worker double-crossed you, Segundo. He has left with the journal, intent on finding that box himself."

Segundo ground his teeth at this news. He'd kill Greg when he got his hands on that piece of shit. "I expected nothing less of him," Segundo commented. "My unit will have the journal in an hour and the human will be disposed of."

"My Hounds can smell betrayal in my enemies. What do you think Black Dog smells on you, Segundo?"

With a quick snap of his fingers, Adrian sent the Hound forward, charging at Segundo. His eyes went wide, his body tensing as he prepared for the impact, not daring to challenge his master's pet.

The Hound slammed into him and he flew backward, landing with a hard thud. Huge clawed paws pressed into his chest. Slimy jaws settled inches from his face, rank breath biting at his nostrils. It took every ounce of control he owned not to reach for his blade and slice the creature's neck.

Appearing in Segundo's sight, Adrian glared down. "At a minimum, he smells your stupidity. No Beast can touch the box holding that list, you fool. We need this human."

He waved his hand and the hound became a man, one booted foot on Segundo's chest. "Black Dog watched Greg and waited for an opportunity," Adrian stated. "He manipulated Greg with ease, tricking him into thinking he was a human who could serve Greg's needs, when Greg is the one serving our needs. Even the Knights cannot sense Black Dog is not human. In you, they smell the stench I do—the stench of failure."

The Knights couldn't sense the Hounds because in human form, they were useless and possessed no magic. But Segundo didn't vocalize his thought. The Knights would spay those Hounds without blinking, and then Adrian would see who had failed, and it would not be him.

Adrian glared at Segundo, his words spoken like a slap. "You and your unit will be the Hell Hounds' backup."

Segundo wanted to scream with fury. He would not back up a bunch of worthless Hounds! He'd kill every last one of those damn canines before this was over, starting with Black Dog.

"Your partnership with Black Dog can start tonight," Adrian said. "His Hounds have tracked the Knights. I want them taken out so we can get on with business."

Segundo yearned to tell him to go back to hell, to do his own dirty work. The truth of the matter was Adrian was forbidden from taking part in the actual foot-soldier wars. Just as his counterpart, Salvador, was forbidden from aiding the Knights in battle. But if he pointed that out, Segundo knew he wouldn't live to see tomorrow.

Adrian motioned to the auburn-haired beauty who stood in the shadows, waiting to be called to duty. His gaze swept her body with primal heat before his attention shifted to his second-in-charge. "Excellent taste, Segundo." His gaze returned to Black Dog. "She is your reward, my pet. For good service. Take her."

An evil smile touched Black Dog's lips, his eyes flashing red. A second later, he had the woman inside the hotel room, primal noises filtering into the air.

Segundo didn't get up from where he lay, knowing Adrian wasn't done with him. He couldn't move until he was told to move. Tonight would be filled with pain. Pain he vowed to endure as he always had before. But when it was over, he would find a way to turn this around. To convince Cain this was part of his plan. And one day, he would return all the pain Adrian had caused him tenfold.

One day soon.

Chapter 13

An hour after leaving the museum, the screen door behind Des opened and shut. He turned to find Rinehart approaching. "Rock and his team just got back from the museum."

Des had left Rock behind hoping for a lead on Greg's location. Every wire they'd had on Greg was inactive. It was as if the man had fallen off the face of the earth. "Any luck?"

Rinehart held up a dagger. "They found this." He handed it to Des. "Note the initials on the handle."

Des frowned. "H.H." He eyed Rock. "Any clue what it means?"

His lips settled into a grim line. "None. I'm going to do some research on it myself. Max is busy trying to track Greg and this Black Dog. He's even checked credit-card activity and the OnStar computer linked to Greg's car, and come up empty."

Des had spent the last hour beating his head against an imaginary wall, trying to figure out answers to several serious dilemmas. One of which was how Black Dog, and now Greg, had evaded their resources. The other, a multitude of complex issues involving Jessica.

"Huh," Des said, uncomfortable with the unknowns involving Max. He'd started to trust him but now he wasn't sure. If Max was so good with technology, why couldn't he nail this surveillance.

"What does 'huh' mean?" Rinehart asked, obviously encouraging Des to speak his thoughts out loud.

"It means I want you side by side with Max, making sure our bases are covered. I want you to be his shadow."

Rinehart looked as if he wanted to argue, but he didn't. He retreated toward the door, pausing to look over his shoulder.

"There might be something in the diaries," he said.

Which were with Jessica, and Rinehart knew as much. He also knew Des was avoiding her. Des drew in a long, calming breath. "I'll handle it."

Rinehart stared at him a moment and then gave a nod before disappearing into the house. Des watched his departure, forcing Jessica from his mind. Reporting their failed mission to Jag had to come first.

Des flipped open his phone and dialed, receiving voice mail on the other end. He left a message and waited, dreading the moment of truth.

The night had been filled with insanity. No, she was filled with insanity because Jessica really wanted to believe Des and his men were the good guys fighting evil.

She sat on the twin-size bed in the tiny bedroom she'd been in for the past hour, her mother's diaries stacked around her. Though she'd barely skimmed the surface of the thousands of passages each book held, Jessica had confirmed what her father claimed. Her mother had believed that demons would come after the journal.

What Jessica didn't understand was why her mother had been so secretive about her work. The thoughts her mother had merely hinted at in conversation ran much deeper in the diaries. It was clear she had been passionate about her beliefs—the words jumped off the page, full of conviction. Yet, she'd been quite selective about the bits she'd shared with Jessica.

Any other time, Jessica would have been absorbed by the task of scouring the diaries, to relive her mother's work. But her thoughts were a jumbled mess that persisted in waylaying Jessica's focus on her reading. Thoughts of Des and of her father—she wanted answers from Des and she needed to call her father. Her poor dad. He must be going insane with worry.

Setting the diary she held in her lap to the side, she shimmied off the bed and found her shoes. It was time to find out how much of a prisoner she really was here. Could she walk through that door without being stopped?

Sure enough, she turned the knob and found herself in the hallway. The sound of male voices drew her attention and she followed them. She'd seen the house upon entering and knew the men were likely gathered around the computers and televisions set up in the living-room area.

She glimpsed Rinehart and the man she'd met upon

arriving called Max. Both oozed warrior-like power
and dark danger. It was almost enough to make her turn
and head back to the other room. Almost.

She straightened beneath their cutting gazes and delivered her words with a confidence she didn't quite feel.
"I need to let my father know I'm safe." They simply
stared at her. She frowned, irritated at the lack of response
and feeling a bit urgent to have them understand her circumstances. "If you really meant what you said and want
my help, then I don't see why this should be a problem."

Rinehart finally spoke. "I'll see what I can arrange."

Now she was upset. "Arrange?" she challenged.
"What is there to arrange? You hand me a phone and I put
my father out of the misery of worrying that I am dead."

"It's not that simple," Rinehart countered.

"I see all this equipment you have," Jessica said. "I
know you can get me through without being traced. If
you want to."

Rinehart started to speak. "Ma'am—"

Suddenly, her hellish night slammed into her emotions. She deserved answers and by God, she would
have them. "Am I a prisoner?"

"You will return home safely," Rinehart said. "You
have my word."

She stared into his hard eyes and found nothing but
blankness, but she desperately wanted to believe him.
Maybe because it was easier than accepting she might
not ever go home again, that her life as she knew it was
over. Because deep inside, she felt that to be the case,
just as she had felt Des was a part of her destiny. None
of this made sense. The urgency to understand built
inside her.

"You didn't answer my question," she countered. "Right now, at this moment, am I a prisoner?"

Jag orbed onto the porch only seconds after Des had left a message on his voice mail. Des felt the shame of letting his friend and leader down, wishing he could crawl under a rock and hide. Instead, he met Jag's gaze head-on. "I have failed you."

"You have not nor will you ever fail me."

Jag spoke the words with so much confidence that Des vowed to make them true. No one had ever believed in him as Jag did.

Long minutes later, he finished telling Jag of the past few days' events, about the knife with the initials H.H. and about his plan to overcome the loss of the journal. "I brought Jessica here."

"If anyone can find a path to that list of bloodlines, she would be the one," Jag concluded, giving his approval of the decision. "Is she willing to help?"

"I believe she will. If I can earn her trust. She's been through a lot and—" he hesitated, turning away, resting his arms on the wooden railing "—things between her and me got a little out of control."

Jag was silent several seconds and then took up a position next to Des, his arms on the railing as well. "Are you telling me you got personally involved with a female?"

Des stared up at the moon, the stars glistening almost as if they laughed at him. "I don't know what I did. I…yeah." He glanced at Jag. "It just happened."

"You've lived in this world of ours long enough to know nothing *just happens*."

Mate. The word played in his mind, and he wondered if Jag knew the truth about Jessica. If his leader, his friend, knew that Jessica drew him beyond what another female could.

"I don't understand any of this," Des said. "Jessica and I don't make sense. We're from different worlds."

"It seems to me your worlds are intertwined. That journal has touched both of your lives. Perhaps that is the tie that binds you."

Des pushed off the railing, facing Jag, seeking confirmation that Jessica was his mate, and if so, what it all meant. So many questions flew through his mind, he didn't know what to ask first. What did their bond really mean? If he walked away would she forget him? Would she go on and be happy?

"Are you saying—"

A female voice filled the air, demanding, upset. "Jessica," Des explained, his gaze locking with Jag's.

Her voice sounded again. "I want to talk to Des."

"Demanding. Fearless. Ready to kick your White Knight ass." Jag smiled. "I like her already."

Jessica glared at Rinehart and Max, waiting for her answer. Her fear had taken flight, replaced by an urgent need to get a grasp on her situation. She felt no physical threat from these men, but she felt a sense of unease inside that set her teeth on edge. She didn't deal well with the unknown. It made her feel the floor might fall out from beneath her at any moment.

She repeated her question and would do so as many times as it took to get a direct answer. "Am. I. A. Prisoner?"

"Jessica."

The deep voice from behind her resonated along her nerve endings with potent impact. She turned to find Des standing at a patio door.

Des. Everything inside her wanted to believe he was a good guy. But she wasn't raised a fool, either. She deserved answers and she deserved them from him.

"We need to talk," she said and cast him a look meant to say that she wasn't taking no for an answer.

"Agreed," he said. "But first, there's someone who'd like to meet you."

Her chest tightened. Why did this moment feel profound in some unexplainable way? "Who?"

"Our leader. The one who would defend the list in place of Solomon."

"And why would he be the choice to take Solomon's place as protector?"

"Why don't you ask him that question yourself?" Des suggested.

"Where is he?" she asked.

Des lifted a curtain to expose the patio door. "Outside."

She wanted answers, whatever it took to get them. Tentatively, Jessica stepped forward, aware of Des's heavy stare, his absorbed attention. She didn't look at him until they were shoulder to shoulder. Their gazes locked. Torment and regret flashed in his eyes. She saw it. Felt it. Felt him. Damn it, she wanted to hate him for how he'd used her. But Lord help her, she didn't. She didn't hate him at all. Her reactions to this man were without reason.

"I need to call my father," she said softly.

He inclined his head. "Of course, but we need to discuss what to tell him first."

"Hello, Jessica," a man's voice said. He spoke with a hint of Spanish accent. "I'm Jag."

Jessica stepped onto the porch to find herself face to face with a ruggedly handsome man. A goatee and dark hair that touched his shoulders framed a strong face and square jaw.

"You are the leader of these men?"

"'These men' as you call them are the Knights of White, an elite group of warriors. And yes, I am their leader."

"The Knights of White." She repeated the name flatly, a bit numb at this point, not sure what to expect. This night got more and more bizarre at every turn.

Jag smiled. "You don't like our name?"

"The name is fine." She hesitated. "Different. Unique. But fine." Her hand motioned to his ring and she frowned. "Your ring. It's...interesting."

He held out his hand, welcoming her to view the object of her interest. She bit her bottom lip and peered at the ring. He motioned her forward. "Come closer," he said. "I don't bite."

Stepping forward, she eased the distance between her and the ring, noting it was shaped as a five-pointed star. "It's Solomon's seal."

"It is. Solomon was a protector of humanity, just as I am. It was a gift from my mentor when I took on the leadership role of the Knights. My mate wears the same marking on her shoulder as well."

Jessica frowned. "Your mate? You mean wife?"

"We are not like you, Jessica. On some level, I think you know this already. There is a ritual for our kind, which bonds us together, linking our souls. We live and die together. We are one. The star appears when that ritual is completed." He smiled, his handsome face taking on a tender quality that softened the harsh lines of his features. "Her name is Karen. I think you'd like her."

Her knees trembled as she asked her next question, somehow feeling it would have a profound impact on her future. "Why are you telling me this?"

"Because what is different is often frightening. I need you to see us as who we are. It is our duty to find that list and protect those bloodlines, and we need your help to do that. Your mother was a great warrior in her own way. She knew that list had to be protected. She sensed evil hunted it. And she was right."

She shook her head. Her mother had believed all of this. Deep down, Jessica did, too. But still. The strangeness kept growing, getting bigger, far beyond what she had accepted as reality in her day-to-day world. "I keep thinking I'm dreaming. Studying something you think is a myth and deciding it's all real are two very different things."

Jag reached out and touched her hand, and Jessica gasped at the impact. Suddenly, images flashed in her mind. Des fighting some horrid creatures—oh God, demons! She sucked in a breath, experiencing the same pain Des felt as a knife sliced his hand, feeling his will as he'd pushed past it. The night he'd come to the museum, she realized. That was how he had been injured.

Battle after battle played in her mind in fast forward. Des fighting demons. She saw all the men she had met, swords as their weapons, demons as their enemies. These were the Knights of White. They were demon hunters.

Abruptly, the images changed, replaced by visions of her and Des in her apartment, and again emotions wrapped around Jessica. She knew the torment Des had felt over lying to her. Then the picture in her mind shifted and she saw Des running up the stairs earlier that night, trying to get to her before Greg did. And she knew the fear he'd felt for her safety.

And then her mother was there, her mother writing in her diaries, fretting over a secret she had to hide, a secret that affected her family. Jessica's chest tightened at the vivid image. *Mom. Mom!* But the picture faded and she couldn't get it back. Everything went black.

Jessica blinked against the dampness in her eyes, realizing she was crying. Her gaze latched on to Jag's. "Now you know why we need your help," he said. "Will you help us, Jessica?"

"Yes," she whispered. "I'll help." Through those visions she knew this was her calling, her destiny.

"Thank you." He smiled, a smile that touched his eyes with sincerity. "You'll have to meet my mate, Karen, someday soon. I think the two of you would find you have a lot in common."

He inclined his head slightly. "Until we meet again." Jag didn't say more, nor did he give her a chance to ask anything else. He eyed Des over her shoulder. "I'll see what I can find out about those initials you mentioned."

Jessica wished Jag farewell and then turned to face Des, noting the questions in his eyes. She knew he had no idea what Jag had shown her. She hadn't thanked Jag for the insight, she realized, and turned back to him only to find he was gone. She drew a breath, head spinning with the bizarreness of this world she had entered, with the magnitude of the information Jag had shared in such a short time.

She turned back to Des, her gaze resting on his handsome, rugged face. She wondered how the scar above his lip had happened. Wondered why she hadn't noticed more scars on his body when they'd made love. She'd seen the countless battles he'd fought. She'd felt his loneliness both in those visions and in this moment. She found she wanted to be the one to erase that feeling from Des, to heal him.

"What just happened with you and Jag?" he asked.

"He showed me the truth."

His eyes darkened, grew more alert. "Meaning what?"

Jessica walked toward him, stopping when they were toe-to-toe. "Enough to more than earn that commitment I gave to help you," she said, and quickly amended her statement. "I *want* to help."

Several seconds passed before he answered. "I hated lying to you," he said, his voice a bit husky. "If I'd told you the truth and you'd called the police—"

She cut him off. "You couldn't risk losing the journal. I get that after Jag showed me those things."

"Which was what?" he prodded again.

Enough to know Des hadn't used her, that he cared about her. That there was something profound about their meeting and she was no fool. Jag had told her of his mate for a reason. But she didn't say that. Didn't question Des about their bond. The time wasn't right.

She ignored his question. "You had to pretend to be a donor, Des. I get that." Still, one thing bothered her and she couldn't simply put it aside. A part of her was hurt and angry. "But you didn't have to sleep with me in the process."

"I know," he said. "Believe me, I know. And I don't blame you if you hate me for it. But right now, looking at you, feeling what I do, I don't know if I could have changed that night no matter how hard I tried. I wanted you."

The rough way he spoke the words, full of conviction, washed over her, igniting a mixture of passion and anger. "You think wanting me makes what happened okay?"

"No, but it doesn't change the truth." His voice was low, a primal quality lacing the tone. "I wanted you too much to walk away."

He pulled her close then, mouth slanting over hers, tongue darting past her lips, hungry, sliding against hers, drinking her in. She melted into the kiss, wanting it, wanting him. God, how she wanted this man. Her hands slid around his waist, her chest pressed to his. She couldn't get enough of him. His smell, his taste.

The sound of a throat being cleared barely broke into Jessica's lust-filled haze. Then she heard, "Sorry to interrupt."

Des tore his mouth from Jessica's, and they both looked toward the door to find Max standing there. "I've got something to show you."

"Now?" Des snapped.

"Uh, yeah. You're both gonna want to see this."

Chapter 14

Jessica followed Des into the living room to find Max and Rinehart staring at a television screen, and Jessica's eyes went wide as she realized her father was the main attraction.

"Oh good Lord," Jessica said. "I *have* to call him before he has the damn National Guard looking for me."

Max eyed Des for approval and then handed her a cell phone. "It's untraceable."

"You can't tell him the truth," Des warned.

"I can handle my father," Jessica assured him, dialing the phone.

A few minutes later, she hung up, her father dealt with. Jessica had given him enough detail to assure him she was safe, while convincing him that Des's private security people had saved her from her attackers and were helping her hunt down the journal. Apparently, Michael was worried sick and her father promised to update him. Her father's relief over Jessica's safety had him promising to help her deal with the police for her. Eventually, she'd have to explain everything to them, but for now, he'd arrange a temporary reprieve.

Des motioned her to the kitchen. "I set the table up as a work area."

"Great," she said, casting him an appreciative look, thankful to be treated as part of the team, not a prisoner. "I do have a suggestion, since time is obviously of the essence." Only Max and Des remained in the room. She had no idea where all the other men had gone. "If my mother had any theories about the location of the box and the list, she would have planned expeditions through her research teams."

"I assume her team was part of a company?" Max asked.

Jessica nodded. "Yes. My father set up a privately held corporation that he funded for my mother's work— Montgomery Enterprises. My mother's last wish was to find that journal, so he kept the operation alive, even though nothing was going forward. We should be able to get a list of expedition locations through the company. Anything of importance found in the diaries can be cross-referenced to her planned dig sites."

"Excellent," Max said. "If I get that information, I can work up a series of data queries that will tell us which is our best bet based on numerical probability."

Des looked at Max as if the man was insane. "Numerical probability."

Jessica couldn't help but smile. Des and Max had a bit of an oil-and-water vibe flowing from them. Absently, she wondered a bit about Max herself. He'd mastered the rough-and-tough renegade look, but spit out information as if he should be wearing glasses and a suit.

"Numerical probability is all we have right now," Max snapped back at Des.

"I can say with ninety-nine percent certainty we're looking at a Mexican location," Jessica commented, but hesitated as she considered the best approach. "I'll need to talk to my father in person. He's already pretty on edge, but I know I can get the information out of him once he sees me."

Max perked up at that. "There's a chance I can pull what we need remotely if I have the right data. Key employees of Montgomery Enterprises, addresses and phone numbers to start." He grabbed a pad and pen. "Give me anything you can."

Jessica wrote down what she knew, which took some thinking. Task completed, she followed Des into the kitchen and sat down at the sturdy wooden table.

Side by side, they began to read. The silence that fell between them was remarkably comfortable, and Jessica couldn't help but sneak an occasional peak at his handsome features. Every once in a while, their gazes would lift and connect, her stomach fluttering with the contact.

Needing distraction, she looked around the tiny kitchen, which had no decor aside from the fast-food bags the men had left on the counters. And suddenly Jessica had the most amazing feeling of belonging. A feeling her mother had described experiencing when she was at certain dig sites.

Jessica's gaze slid back to Des, and a sense of being needed overcame her. Des needed her. Funny thing was—she thought she might just need him too.

Hours passed as Des and Jessica pored over pages and pages of writing, until Des felt he had finally found something worth seeing. He'd stumbled onto a few passages noting potential dig locations. The ones that were circled and highlighted had several smudged notations he couldn't quite decipher. Rock picked that moment to return from his run to the corner store. Des cast him a sideways look and noted the tray of foam coffee cups. Rock stopped at Des's side and tossed him a peanut-butter cup.

Jessica accepted coffee, though Des waved off the offer, trying to focus. That didn't stop him from ripping open the candy, though.

"You love that peanut butter," she said.

He glanced up and smiled. "It's addictive," he said, *but not as much as you,* he added silently.

Des held out the package and offered Jessica one of the two candies in it; she accepted. He stilled a moment as he watched her take a bite. It had been so long since he'd shared more than sex with a woman. Such a small act was amazingly intimate and warm.

She swallowed a bite. "I forgot how good these things are," she said. "Or maybe I'm just that hungry." She glanced down at her diary and refocused on Des. "I've been through everything I have here. Please tell me you found something."

He finished off the last of his snack. "Actually, I think we finally have a destination. Based on what I'm reading, I'd say we've got a long drive ahead of us. We're headed to Guerrero, Mexico." He handed her the diary and pointed out the illegible text. "Can you make out any of that?"

Jessica studied the diary Des had been reviewing for several seconds, a grim expression on her face. "No." She gave him a look filled with concern. "And not only is Guerrero a long drive, it's a big state." She thought a moment. "My mother often kept maps with handwritten notes. I can try to get my hands on those. My father would know where they are." She reached for the phone that was still sitting on the table from her earlier call with him.

Des covered her hand with his, stopping her action. "It's four in the morning. Why don't you get some sleep and call him in a couple of hours?"

"Shouldn't we leave now?" she asked.

"Sunrise is soon enough," he said. "We'll need to pack up and make some arrangements anyway." He called out across the room. "Max!"

"I'm already here," Max spoke behind him, "and yes, I got into the company database Jessica mentioned and there is a reference to two cities in Guerrero. Tepecoacuilco and Ixcateopan. They were on a list of planned digs that never saw funding."

"I remember her talking about Tepecoacuilco," Jessica commented, before glancing back down at the page and starting to read, her finger following text as if she feared she'd miss something.

Scrubbing his jaw, Des didn't see there were many travel options. "Greg's a wanted man. He won't risk the airport. It's a two-day drive. We could make up time by flying."

"We need our equipment and weapons," Max argued.

"True," Des said, his gaze catching on Jessica as he noted she had gone pale, her attention on the text inside the diary. "Jessica?"

She flipped the page and read for several more seconds before her lashes lifted. "Now I know why my mother was so obsessed with the journal that final year before her death." She swallowed, as if she might be fighting emotion. "Finding the journal had become personal."

"Go on," Des prodded, not sure what to expect, though his instincts had gone on alert.

"I have notes here regarding the reason the box is so important. My mother references finding writings she believed to be Solomon's and some perhaps that were written by another person close to him. She was quite certain the list will be encoded to protect the innocent. That it will take months, if not years, to figure it all out."

"What do you mean by encoded?" Des inquired.

"She gave several examples of the type of text used, and none of it is easy to understand." Jessica found a passage and read, "The fifth family born unto the Temple of Solomon." Her gaze lifted from the book. "In other words, anyone who found the journal would have to do some serious research to figure out what they were reading. They wouldn't just read a list of names and be able to hunt down the descendants of these bloodlines."

Rock chimed in then from where he stood at the kitchen counter making a sandwich. "So that's good, right? That means if we get the journal back before it can be fully translated and researched, we at least have a chance to track those families and offer them protection."

"I would say, yes," Jessica agreed. "Even great scholars would need time—as my mother said—maybe even years, to decode the list." She bit her bottom lip. "A demon though. I don't know. Maybe they would understand the information?"

"Let's hope Solomon came up with something they don't understand," Des commented. "But none of this explains why you think this had gotten personal for your mother."

Jessica hesitated. "My mother believed her family name to be on that list of bloodlines."

Des felt as if he had been punched in the gut, the implication of her words washing over him. Thank God they'd retrieved the diaries. If the Beasts found out about the suspicions that Jessica's family was on that list, they would kill her.

"Why did she think that?" he asked cautiously.

"She'd pieced together the writings I mentioned she'd found and seems to have gathered certain family names who hold high positions on the list for some reason. She didn't know for sure if her name was on the list, but she was strongly inclined to believe that it was. She also felt anyone on that list would be—"

"Hunted," Des said softly, trying not to scare her.

"Yes," she said. "She references demons in a few excerpts. She was tormented by that prospect, afraid to leave the journal buried and afraid not to. Afraid it would fall into the wrong hands." Jessica swallowed against the sudden dryness in her throat. "She didn't voice a lot of this to those around her, worried she'd sound insane. But she felt driven to follow up on this."

"Rock," Des said, his tone low and calm, though he felt anything but. "Call Jag." He refocused on Jessica. "You'll be safe at our training facility."

Her rejection was instant. "I'm not going anywhere but after that journal."

Oh, she was going. She might not think she was going, but she was going. He wasn't letting her step in harm's way. "It's the only place you'll be completely safe."

Rock's voice could be heard, talking on the phone. An instant later, Jag orbed into the room and the other men slowly eased out of sight. "Rock says Jessica faces imminent danger," Jag stated, his gaze shifting between Des and Jessica.

Des watched Jessica eye his leader, her expression indicating no surprise at his dramatic entrance. At this point, Des doubted much would shock her. "I'm fine," Jessica informed Jag. "Des is overreacting."

Des leaned on the table, his hands flattening on the wooden surface. "I'm not overreacting." He cut Jag a sideways look. "Her mother believed their family to be descendants of angels."

"If this is true," Jag said cautiously, "Des is right. You're in danger, Jessica. Your mother's bloodline will be a target."

She inhaled a heavy breath and let it out. "If I'm in danger so is everyone else on that list."

"Risking your own life will not save theirs," Des countered, ready to tie her up and hand her over to Jag. He was not letting her get hurt.

Jessica's eyes flashed with anger. "You only have two options." She glanced between Jag and Des. "One being to find the journal before Greg hands it over to the Beasts."

"He probably already has," Des argued.

She gave him a challenging look and countered his remark. "Then you need to find another way to the treasure box holding that list. And it is a treasure to the Beasts. We all know that. If my mother's work is the key to this search, I am too. I can stumble my way around this Hebrew text better than any of you."

Des ground his teeth. "This isn't a discussion, Jessica. You are going with Jag and that's final."

"Who are you to tell me what to do?" she challenged, her finger pointed at her chest. "I decide what I do." She grabbed the diaries. "I'm going to that bedroom you shoved me into when I first got here. And I'm going to read my mother's diaries and find a way to get to that treasure before the Beasts."

Des watched her depart, fighting an urge to go after her. Who was he to tell her what to do? *I'm your mate, damn it!* Unbidden, the words screamed in his head, barely contained as he watched her leave.

Jag leaned against the wall and crossed his arms in front of his chest. "She's right, you know. She can help."

"She has no idea what she is getting into."

"She knows." Jag spoke with confidence. "I showed her the battles. I showed her the Beasts."

"I won't let her risk her safety."

"Her choices are her own."

Before he could stop himself, Des threw out a challenge. "If this were Karen, would you say the same?"

Jag's response wasn't instant; his eyes narrowed on Des's features. "Are you claiming Jessica as your mate?"

Des let his head fall forward a moment. "Yes. No." He lifted his gaze to Jag's again and studied his friend. "How can she be? I thought you and Karen were a one-time deal. You're our leader. She's your wife from a past life. There has never been any mention of mates for the rest of us, no matter what we might dream of."

"Time will give you the answers you seek," Jag assured. "If Jessica is your mate, you will know. Your Beast will hunger for her pure nature as much as the man does. The urge to claim Karen was almost impossible for me to fight."

It was more than an urge. More like a command. But Des didn't say that. "If I claim her—what then?"

"She has your protection. Your immortality."

"My life," Des said flatly, reality playing hard in his mind. "She could never deal with what I am. She shouldn't have to."

"Perhaps she can deal with it better than you do."

Des's lips thinned, his defenses going on alert. Everyone knew Des embraced his Beast while the other Knights suppressed theirs. "I deal with it fine."

"By pushing the man out of the way," Jag said. "But when will the man be lost?"

"Hiding from that part of myself won't make it go away," Des proclaimed. The truth was, he'd been a slave in his mortal life, but had often felt more like an animal. He understood the Beast and, until Jessica's arrival in his life, had managed its presence with ease.

"Claiming the Beast so readily is dangerous, Des. Let Jessica help you find the man again."

"What if she finds the Beast instead?"

"Perhaps you're more afraid she'll find the man than the Beast. It's the man you don't want to face. The man—and his past. You have to let go of what was and find what is."

Jag pushed off the wall. "You know how to reach me if you need me." He disappeared.

Des stared at the empty space Jag had stood in a few moments before, unsure where to go from there. Part of him wanted to storm down the hall and demand Jessica go to the ranch, to safety. The other part wanted to pull her close and never let her go. Wanted to tell her who and what he really was—-to explain both man and Beast—and believe she could accept him, even embrace their bond.

But Des had long ago embraced hard-core reality and that allowed him to cope and thrive, to survive the eternal battle of good over evil. If he let Jessica in, if he let down his guard and she turned away from him, would he find his way back to sanity, to control of his Beast?

He'd found a way to push the darkness aside without Jessica's help for this long, he could continue. He couldn't risk losing complete control. He would fight evil and win, both on the battlefield and within himself.

No other option existed.

Chapter 15

Jessica stayed in the bedroom long enough to become paranoid, which amounted to barely an hour after her confrontation with Des and Jag, fearful she might get left behind. Which was nuts, of course. Des wanted to ship her off to some ranch, not leave her behind.

The minute she entered the living room, her worries kicked into overdrive. Almost all the equipment was packed away, and there wasn't a man in sight.

She stormed toward the patio where the door stood open, intent on finding Des and confronting him. The revelations made while reading her mother's diaries had only served to solidify what she knew deep in her gut anyway. The events of the past week were part of her destiny. A destiny that had started long before her mother's involvement, and continued onward. A destiny she had to serve, and that meant going after the journal and that list.

Light rain pelted down on the ground as Jessica stepped outside and made her way to Rinehart's side, as he loaded equipment into a van. "Where's Des?"

Rain began to fall harder, and Jessica's hair was plastered to her face, but she didn't care. She wasn't seeking shelter until she found Des.

Rinehart motioned to a metal shed, two vans sitting near it, which Jessica hadn't noticed before. "I wouldn't bother him now," Rinehart suggested, straightening as he nudged his cowboy hat out of his eyes. "He's going over field plans with some of the Knights."

"What plan?" she asked. "When are we leaving?"

"I'm not sure when you and Des are leaving. The rest of us leave in thirty minutes."

"What does that mean?" she asked. "Why would Des and I leave separately?"

The rain turned to a downpour and Rinehart made a frustrated sound as he looked skyward. His gaze lowered and he quickly surveyed Jessica's clothing. "You better go inside. Your, ah, dress is going to get a lot of attention."

She looked down, appalled to realize the pink material had become translucent. Embarrassed, she rotated toward the door, her gaze landing on Des as he approached from her left.

He covered the distance between them with stealth speed, his hand closing around hers as he tugged her inside the house.

"You might as well be naked," he said, eyes sweeping her body, lingering on her chest, where her nipples peaked against the sheer material. "There are ten men running around here."

She shoved a clump of wet hair off her forehead. "It wasn't raining this hard when I went outside."

"Why were you even out there?"

"Why wouldn't I be?" she demanded. "Am I a prisoner, Des? Is that it? We're back to that?"

He ignored her question, his hands sliding around her waist, pulling her tight against his body. "If that's what I have to do to keep you from running around half-naked in front of my men, then yes." Possessiveness laced the words, and damn the man, it made her hot. She didn't want to be. Didn't want to respond to such caveman-type behavior, but there was no mistaking the distinct ache forming between her thighs. And when his hand slid down her backside, molding her tight against his hips, against the proof of his arousal, she moaned before she could stop herself.

A wicked smile played on his mouth as his lips drew closer, teasing her with the kiss to come. Her lashes fluttered, her nipples peaking beneath the cold, wet fabric. "Des," she whispered. "I—"

Suddenly, his hand went over her mouth. Jessica's eyes flew open. He cast her a warning stare, his body stiff as he walked her to a corner to retrieve a stash of weapons that had yet to be loaded in the vans.

She felt his arms release her, and she wanted to pull him back, a bad feeling twisting her in knots. A sinister charge suddenly laced the air. The sound of the rain seemed to magnify, louder, louder. No other sound existed. Even from Des, who lifted the lid of a box to display five guns. Thanks to her father's military background, and insistence she learn to defend herself, Jessica knew they were all Glock handguns. And she knew how to use them.

Suddenly she heard a shout. Des cursed, clearly getting more out of that shout than she had because he grabbed two guns and pointed them. At that same moment, the ceiling crashed in, two beastly looking creatures hitting the ground as if the fall had been nothing. They wore shiny suits she remembered from the vision Jag had given her, half their faces distorted, grotesque.

Des fired both guns, one round after the other, unloading the weapons in their snarling faces, between their eyes. The creatures stumbled, fell.

Turning to Jessica, he offered her the guns. "You know how to use them, right?"

She nodded, accepting the Glocks, kneeling down to reload. Des followed her to a squatting position, his face intense, the look in his eyes primal and hard. His movements seemed effortless as he flipped open another case and removed a magnificent sword with detailed engraving on the handle.

Impossibly, the creatures Des had shot in the head stirred, one already on his feet, a sword drawn. "Oh my God," Jessica said, barely finding her voice. She raised one of the guns, unable to handle both at once, ready to fire.

But before she could act, another Beast crashed through the sliding glass door, shattering it. She ducked, her hands covering her face as glass pinched at her skin. She peered between her fingers, afraid to be blind to what might come next. Des was in control, his moves swift and certain as he sliced the Beast's head off with the weapon.

Jessica jerked her attention away before the head hit the ground, unable to bear that sight. She aimed at the other two Beasts and fired, missing on her first attempt.

Before she could make another shot, Des was in the middle of the room, matching blades with the two Beasts.

She fired at yet another creature as it entered the broken sliding glass door, and this time she hit her target but the Beast didn't slow. A second later, she was being dragged through the door, her gun crashing to the ground outside.

"Des!" She screamed his name over and over, kicking as hard as she could and landing her heels on the Beast's knees several times with apparently no damage.

Suddenly, Rinehart and Rock were in front of the animal, swords in hand. The Beast laughed, low and deep. Evil. "You'll have to go through her to get to me."

A gunshot rang in the air, once, twice, three times. The Beast stumbled and let go of Jessica. She fell down and scrambled around to face the thing. Its head hit the ground, followed by its body, Des's sword swiping through the air. Her eyes locked with his, as the rain began again, pelting at their skin.

The relief Des felt over Jessica's safety was short-lived. Low growls filled the air, and big black dogs charged at them. Only they weren't dogs. They were huge monster-like animals; fangs protruded from distorted faces, their eyes glowing red.

A scream ripped from Jessica's throat and Des raced forward, then grabbed her and shoved her behind his back. Rinehart, Rock, Max and Des formed a circle around her.

"You have got to be kidding me," Rock said.

"What the hell are these ugly bastards?" Des asked.

"You don't know?" Jessica shouted only to be ignored.

"Best guess?" Max asked, his tone dry, unaffected. "Greg thought he hired men. He hired Hounds. We know what those double H's stood for. Try Hell Hounds."

"Great," Des said. "This party gets richer every day. I'm betting they die about like the Beasts. Anyone got any other suggestions, speak up now!"

One of the dogs charged at Rock, and he sliced his blade through the air and took the animal's head. It disappeared as if it burst into flames. Des and the other men prepared to charge at the dogs only to find the Hounds retreating.

"Let them go," Des said, eyeing the group. "I want everyone out of here in ten minutes." He tossed his weapon to the ground and reached for Jessica at the same moment she pushed to her feet. She rushed into his arms.

He held her for several seconds, held her so tightly he knew she could barely breathe, but he couldn't seem to help himself. He had come so close to losing her, and it was the first time he'd felt this type of fear, this utter terror, since the day he'd watched Arabella die at the hands of the Beasts.

When he loosened his hold, he couldn't quite talk himself into letting go of her completely. His hands slid down her hair, framing her face. "Are you okay?"

She swallowed and nodded, watching the flaming Hound body. "How does it burn in the rain?"

"It's fire straight from hell."

"Were they after me?"

"Using humans as a shield is their way," he said. "I don't think they came for you."

Her eyes went wide. "They came for the diaries!" She started running for the house, but Des grabbed her hand. She turned to him, rain running down her face. "The diaries!"

"Don't leave my side," Des said, yanking her close. The woman was trying to get herself killed. "Do you understand?" But he didn't give her time to answer. He started walking, her hand still tightly circled by his. She followed him inside the house, and thankfully they found the diaries untouched.

Jessica grabbed a plastic grocery bag from the kitchen and wrapped the notebooks in it to protect them.

Once they were safely inside the Porsche, ready to depart, fears began to form. "They weren't after the diaries, were they?"

He shook his head. "They were here to kill us. They don't want us anywhere near that box."

And Des didn't want the Darkland Beasts anywhere near Jessica. Nor could he stand the idea of her being away from him. Yet, his life was about the Beasts, his destiny fighting their evil. He couldn't keep Jessica close without exposing her to the Beasts, and he felt selfish for wanting to.

His gaze slid to the clock radio, then to the sky. It was pitch dark outside despite the 6:00 a.m. time. In the middle of all of this blackness, was she his light? But even if this was true, how could he ask her to live in a world with Beasts and creatures from hell?

Greg felt every nerve ending in his body like a live charge, every hair standing on end. He kept expecting Segundo to show up, to detour their progress. But hours had passed since they'd taken the journal and departed Dallas for Mexico, and Black Dog's covert skill had proven more than respectable, even with a group of four Jeeps carving a path as one.

The piece-of-shit Texas back road they traveled held more potholes than solid ground, but it also kept them off the radar. Away from the police and, it appeared, from demons as well.

He'd found the pertinent map inside the journal without challenge, and was pleased it was legible—for the most part anyway. He at least knew what city they sought, what general destination. There were Hebrew notes to be translated, which meant a detour through Mexico City. The rich history of the city drew enough exploration that he'd find someone to help, willingly or unwillingly. Either way, he'd find someone.

Because whatever else of value was inside that journal, he planned to unravel it before he handed it over to Segundo. One never had enough ammunition. The journal and the magical box should give him enough leverage to obtain the power he wanted, to ensure he would be turned into one of Segundo's kind, but he wasn't taking any chances.

Greg clutched the bag in his lap a bit tighter, the bag holding his prize. No one else had seen it, and they wouldn't be seeing it, either. The journal was his. And soon much more would be, too.

Chapter 16

Jessica ended a call with her father and dropped the cordless phone on her living-room couch. She and Des had stopped by her apartment to pack and clean up before a flight to Mexico later in the day. "He's meeting us at the airport. That gives us a few hours until we have to leave." An image of the evil red eyes she'd stared into less than an hour before flashed in her mind and she shivered.

Des ran his hands down her arms, his touch sending an electric charge through her body. "You should take a hot bath," he suggested. "Get rid of that chill."

As much as she found the suggestion appealing, she couldn't help but worry. "You're sure those 'things' won't show up here?"

"It's safe. I promise. The Beasts shy away from public places, and a busy apartment building during the morning rush hour qualifies."

"Check," Jessica said. "Stay in public places. Less chance of dying."

Her life would never be the same after all of this, she realized suddenly. From this point forward, she would wonder what lurked in the shadows. Wonder who might be hurt if she didn't warn them, if she didn't act.

She shoved aside the thought, deciding to deal with the present for the time being—a bath and dry clothes and sensible shoes being priorities. Des didn't have that luxury, though. He was covered in mud, his pants and shirt soaked, and had no change of clothes.

"I have a washer and dryer in my utility room," she said. "You could throw your clothes in to wash." Shyly, she added, "You could join me in that bath if you like."

Heat flared in his eyes, but as quickly as it appeared, he schooled his features with reserve. Abruptly, he dropped his hands to his sides and took a long step backward.

"There are things about me you don't know, Jessica."

"Then tell me," she urged.

"Jessica." He hesitated.

Obviously, he didn't think she could handle whatever he had to say to her. Sure, she was a little frightened of what he might reveal. The unknown had a way of unsettling her. She'd pretty much surmised Des couldn't be wholly human, but there was a sense of rightness to being with him that kept her grounded despite the uncertainties.

She fixed him in a level stare, urging him to see the truth in her eyes. "You can't tell me anything that will scare me away, Des."

His mouth set in a grim line. "Don't be so sure of that."

"But *I am* sure," she countered, without hesitation.

"Think about what you saw back at that house. I live in an eternal war. What do you think it takes to do what I do? To kill as a way of life?"

"To kill monsters? Bravery. Most of us would hide under the bed and pray it was a bad dream. You're a hero, Des."

His eyes flashed with disbelief. "You have no idea who and *what* I am. When I raise my sword in battle I become one of those Beasts."

Instantly, she rejected that statement. "You are not one of them."

He sat down on a footstool; the action was laced with exhaustion and defeat. "You don't understand, Jessica." His head dipped between his shoulders.

She squatted down before him, her backside resting on her heels. Her hands settled on his knees, the dampness of his jeans pressing against her palms. "Make me understand."

When he looked up at her, his eyes were stormy. "You should go take that bath before you run out of time," he told her.

Frustration took hold. After all she'd been through, the fact that Des was shutting her out hit a bad note. There wasn't time to plead for answers. They were in the midst of intense circumstances. She didn't want to be in the dark. Didn't operate well that way, in fact. Jessica could deal with a lot of turmoil but not without some semblance of control. And knowledge was control.

Her voice was low and tight as she resisted the urge to yell. "I deserve answers, Des. You say I don't know what you are, then tell me. You fight those Beasts." She decided to be direct. "Those Beasts aren't human. Are you?"

"The less you know, the better off you are. The easier it will be to go back to your life when this is over."

Her eyes widened in disbelief. "Surely, you don't think I can ever go back to the way things were before this? I am a part of this war now, whether you choose to acknowledge it or not. And if what my mother believed to be true is true, that we are descendants of angels, then we were born into this battle."

"There are others chosen for battle, Jessica."

"Like you."

He drew a breath. "As I said, the less you know, the easier—"

She cut him off. "I'm not buying that. Not after everything I've seen already. I have a right to know." She didn't give him time to argue, charging forward with her question. "You are one of those chosen for battle, right?"

Though his reluctance was evident in his features, he responded. "The Beasts have a mission. To grow their army by stealing souls and converting men into Beasts."

Jessica blinked. "I don't understand. What do you mean by *convert?* How?"

"They drain the victims of their blood, stealing their souls in the process. All that is left is pure evil."

Realization came over her with grim reality. "So those Beasts you were fighting were once men?" He nodded. "Evil men who were targets for that reason?"

"No." His lips thinned. "The Beasts thrill at claiming what isn't theirs. They often target happy families, forcing the man to watch as they use his woman, tormenting him before they convert him. After he's converted, he doesn't know love. He knows nothing but evil. He feels none of the loss. Just a desire to create it for others."

Her stomach turned. "They kill the woman when it's over."

"Yes," he said softly.

Thinking these Beasts were simply demons from hell was one thing. Finding out they were once men, turned into monsters who preyed on innocent people was another. It scared her, but it also created resolve.

"I don't want to run away, Des. I want to fight. I can't go back to where I was before, pretending none of this exists. I won't."

His hands circled her wrists and he leaned close, fixing her in a hot stare. "Look into my eyes, Jessica. Look into the depths of my soul. Because I think if you try hard enough, you'll find a reason to run. Because my soul is stained, and I am no longer human. A Beast stole that part of my life and still lingers inside me. I was one of those they converted, saved by a higher power to serve humanity. But the Beast remains, a part of me that allows me to face my enemies on a level playing ground. But it does more than help me fight. It battles the good in me and it makes demands." A second passed, his eyes darkening further. "And that Beast demands you, Jessica. It wants you just as much as the man."

His words washed over her and logic said she should be afraid, but her heart and her soul told her differently. Over the years, she'd touched pieces of history and felt a rush of evil that had sickened her. Her mother had spoken of such a reaction as well. She felt the evil in the Beasts. But not Des. Des made her warm with emotion and hot with desire.

"Then let the Beast have me," she whispered.

Sexy, wild hair framed her face, accenting the dark passion in her light blue eyes. She was beautiful and everything inside him screamed that she was *his*.

Des barely contained the roar of primal desire burning a path through his body. "You have no idea what you are saying." The words came out a hoarse whisper.

He straightened at the waist, trying to put distance between them before he lost control, before he did something they might both regret later.

Countering his action, she lifted off her heels, to her knees, closer again. Too close. Not close enough.

"I'm not afraid of you, Des," she declared.

The soft words playing on his emotions, seducing him, taking him, demanding he act. He moved without conscious thought, pulling her into his arms and claiming her mouth as he wanted to claim her body. He'd contained the Beast the last time they'd been together, but as his tongue swept past her teeth, man and Beast were united in demand.

The sweetness of her taste did nothing to sate his hunger. A hunger that reached deep into his core, an emptiness only she could fulfill. Hunger to claim the other half of his soul coming to life in physical need. His body pulsed with adrenaline, with molten fire.

Des slanted his mouth to deepen the kiss, pulling her closer. Her soft moan almost did him in. He was hard, ready to find his way inside her, his zipper stretching to the limit, just as his resistance had before this kiss.

She tugged at his shirt, and somehow the action jerked a tiny part of Des's mind back to reality. He tore his mouth from hers, his hands framing her face. Their eyes locked, their breathing heavy and oddly in unison.

"We have to stop, Jessica. I can't promise to control myself."

"I don't remember asking you to," she said instantly.

"You don't understand."

"Explain later. After you make love to me." She pressed her lips to his and then slid off his lap. Before he knew her intentions, her dress fell to the floor, shoes kicked off and discarded. Next her bra and underwear.

She stood there, a goddess with pale skin, a vision too lush, too tempting for any man or Beast to ignore. He reached deep, fighting his urges, trying to regain control. He knew how to control his Beast, he reminded himself. Perhaps it was this, the unnatural way he suppressed it with Jessica, that was wreaking havoc on him. Perhaps the Beast had flared out of control because he hadn't allowed his primal side freedom to explore her.

Before he could reconsider, he pulled his shirt over his head and then pushed to his feet, completing the process of undressing. Jessica stepped forward the instant he'd completed his task. Des sat down on the stool, reaching for her, temptation delivered to his hands. He pulled her between his legs, the Beast in him wild, ravenous and free.

He covered one of her breasts with his hand, the hard peak teasing his palm. His mouth worked the other nipple, sucking and licking. Jessica arched into his touch, her soft sounds of pleasure licking a sizzling path along his body and settling in his groin. Her fingers slid into his hair, her touch soft and seductive.

She tilted his head up, her eyes locking with his, passion overflowing in the look she cast him. "Des," she whispered, and he swallowed the word with a kiss.

Somehow, she had made it to his lap, her legs straddling his hips, his cock pressed to her core. Their tongues tangled, their kiss passionate. Their upper bodies melted together, her breasts pressed against his chest, her hands traveling, exploring. She offered herself freely, no fear of the wildness his body, his kiss, expressed. And the more he took, the more she gave, the more he wanted.

Forcing his lips from hers, Des murmured, "This isn't enough," and reached between them to encircle his erection.

Jessica's hands went to his shoulders, her gaze to where he intimately slid his cock along her core. She gasped as he stroked her clit and he glanced up at her, taking in the beauty of her passion-filled expression— the impact like the striking of a match.

Des had to have her now. In one fast move, Des slid the head of his erection along the wet core of her body and entered her. The minute he felt her warm, wetness, her tight confines squeezing him, his hands went to her hips. He thrust upward as he pressed her downward, forcing her to take all of him, not willing to wait. Not willing to go slowly. Not this time. This time was for the Beast. And the Beast wanted more.

A thick feeling of lust and desire surrounded them,

a haze that fed the pumping of his hips, the sway of hers. His fingers slid around her ass, caressing her cheeks, urging her to move with him. Harder. Deeper. But…it wasn't enough.

He pushed to his feet—the footstool restrictive—intending to go to the couch. Her legs wrapped around his waist; her arms around his neck. Des thrust several times, unable to wait, unable to find the couch. She arched backward, her nipples peaked in the air, his hands tightly wrapped around her waist, protecting her from falling.

Suddenly, he realized the trust that she had put in him. The confidence she had that he would hold on and not let go, that he was strong enough to be the force that held them both. The impact of that thought sent him to the couch, the man beginning to surface where he'd let the Beast take control. And that was where his battle began. The battle of man and Beast.

Jessica rocked on top of him, her curves, her soft moans surrounding him, pulling him into the passion. She was close to orgasm, he could feel it in the tiny spasms tightening around his cock, feel it in the desperation of her movements. And with each pump, each thrust he, too, felt desperation. Because he felt the rise of the mating call, felt the desire to claim what was his.

He pulled her close as he'd done before, burying his face in her neck, his hands on her back, holding her next to him. Hiding from her vision, afraid she would see how his teeth were elongating, afraid she would see the Beast burning in his gaze.

Drawing a calming breath, he tried to get lost in their movements, in the sexy sway of body melting into body.

She felt like heaven. She felt like home. Like a place of belonging he'd never experienced. His chest tightened as her body milked him, her orgasm coming hard and fast, and he knew from their last encounter this would be the moment of ultimate temptation. Knew her pleasure somehow called to the mating urge. He'd been crazy to think letting the Beast free would save him from this. Because the truth was, when it came to Jessica, there was no separation of man and Beast.

His breath lodged in his throat as he fought the urge to sink his teeth into her shoulder and mark her as his mate. But once he did that, there would be no turning back. Her lips brushed his ear, her breath whispering against him. He pumped his hips, again, again, one last time, forcing the desire to claim her into a sexual burn. And then he exploded, shaking with the intensity of release.

Seconds passed, their foreheads pressed together, her fingers gently caressing his jaw. She leaned back a bit and stared down at him, emotion in her eyes, tenderness.

"You can't scare me away," she whispered.

His heart squeezed with her words and he pushed to his feet, blocking his expression from her view as he carried her toward the bedroom so she could shower and dress.

In his mind, he responded to her words: *I wish that were true.*

Jag's words came back to him then. *Perhaps you're more afraid she'll find the man.* Tonight, he'd shown her his Beast. She had yet to see all of him. The man, the slave boy, still hid. Jag had been right. The present was about the past. It created a separation between him and Jessica. And Des wasn't sure he could change that.

Chapter 17

Dressed in black jeans, a pink T-shirt and her favorite leather sneakers, Jessica sat on a love seat in the airport Wi-Fi lounge waiting on her father.

She eyed Des, who sat next to her as she took a sip of her triple-venti white mocha. "Lack of sleep has officially taken hold. Every inch of my body hurts."

"You can sleep on the plane," he said, no mention of being tired himself.

It turned out Des had had clothes in the trunk of his car, so he'd been able to change. In faded jeans, a black T-shirt, and worn black boots, he looked wholly male and quite delicious. The three Quarter Pounders she'd watched him down before they'd gotten their coffee had been another story. Lack of sleep had her stomach feeling downright queasy.

She studied him a moment, amazed at how simply

looking at him warmed her inside out. His sexy, dark looks were the kind that turned heads, and plenty of them. But Jessica, like most women, had seen her share of hot men. Des thrilled her in a way beyond what another man could. She'd had relationships in her life, but none that had felt instantly comfortable. Instantly right.

The events of the past week were frightening, and out of control in a way that would normally make her uneasy. But that sense of destiny and rightness filled her more with each passing minute, a sense of these events being what her entire life had been about.

A crazy urge overtook her and Jessica didn't fight it. She reached out and ran her hand over Des's freshly trimmed goatee. There was a hint of auburn mixed in the darker beard that matched his hair. Her eyes lifted to his, and she felt the connection clear to her toes. Felt him all over. Wanted to know everything about him.

Jessica ran her finger over the scar above his lip. "How did you get this?"

His throat bobbed. "You wouldn't believe me if I told you."

"Try me," she urged.

A flash of darkness crossed his face, quickly hidden behind a mask of indifference on the subject. He took her hand and kissed her fingers. "Ask me another day." He cut his gaze away. "Not now, when your father is about to be here."

Obviously, that scar held a bad memory, and she wanted to know what it was. But she didn't press. Not now. She sipped her coffee. "You don't seem tired at all." She hesitated. "Do you, uh, well, you know, people like you—" she lowered her voice despite the secluded corner location they held "—immortal and all—do you get tired?"

He laughed. "Of course I get tired."

"So you sleep?" she asked, her voice back to her normal tone.

"Yes." Now he was smiling, his dark mood gone and she was glad. "I eat. I breathe. I sleep. So do the other Knights. In fact, I plan to sleep on the flight as well."

She bit her bottom lip. "You don't get all Beast-like do you? You know. Big red eyes and all that." Quickly she added, "Not that it matters! I just want to know."

His expression darkened again. "No, Jessica. I don't look like a Beast. I just feel like one."

Well, that had not gone well. But she had him talking and she still had questions. "Do you age?"

He cast her a sideways look. "No."

She swallowed. "And you're how old now?"

After a moment of hesitation, he looked at her. "Ninety-nine."

Her jaw dropped open. "Ninety-nine," she repeated flatly, hoping she'd misunderstood. Des gave her a nod of agreement, confirming his age. She thought of Rinehart's words in the van. Something about being nearly a hundred years old. She'd thought he was joking. Apparently not.

Okay, this could be a real problem. "In other words, when I'm old and gray you will look like you do now?"

"Jessica—"

Before he finished his sentence, her father walked through the doorway. Jessica waved him forward. He gave her a nod of acknowledgment but no smile. As he approached, she frowned, noting the way his khaki pants and polo shirt were a bit rumpled. Her father was always well pressed and pulled together.

His strides were long, rushed. Not at all the gentle pace he'd always favored. Jessica pushed to her feet and greeted him with a hug. He held her long and hard, as he had when he'd called her to his house that evening not so long ago.

"Hey," she said, inspecting his features. His eyes were tired. No doubt he'd worried all night, fretting over her safety. "You okay, Dad?"

"It's been a long night, but I'm fine." Claiming the leather box-shaped chair directly beside their love seat, he offered Des a nod as he laid a long envelope on the rectangular cube-style table sitting between them.

"You found the maps?" Jessica asked.

"The map," he said. "The only map you need."

"What?" she asked, confused. "But I didn't give you a specific location."

"You don't have to. Your mother did."

"But I read her diaries. She had several possible cities listed."

Her father laughed then. The kind of laugh someone uses when they think they are going crazy. "Trust me. This is the only map you need. It won't give you the specifics that the journal would, but it's the map that holds the answers you need." He glanced at Jessica. "Your mother said to tell you she wrote all over the map and hopes you won't have trouble deciphering her notes."

Jessica blinked. "What? She told you to tell me when?"

He hesitated. "After you called this morning, I took

a short nap. I…had a dream and…" He pressed his fingers to his temple, "I know this sounds insane, but your mother came to me in that dream."

Reeling from his words, Jessica frowned. She was about to ask him to repeat himself when he spoke to Des. "And she told me I was an ass to you and should apologize. She's right. I was, and I am, indeed, sorry."

Jessica didn't give Des time to respond. Her heart was about to explode in her chest. "Mom came to you in a dream?"

Her father reached out and took her hand. "It was as real as you are sitting here right now."

Her mind went back to the times she'd thought her mother was near, urging her onward. Like that first dinner with Des at the museum, when she'd felt as if her mother was urging her to share her work with Des. Jessica turned to Des. "Is this possible?"

"I believe it is," he said. "I've learned to keep an open mind."

Her father spoke, pulling her attention back to him. "I still don't want you to go chasing this journal, but your mother insists that you have to." He glanced at Des. "And that Des will keep you safe." He leveled a stare on Des. "You're no anthropologist, geologist or anything of the sort, are you, son?"

"No, sir," Des said. "But I do have a vested interest in protecting the journal." He paused. "And your daughter."

"So I hear," he replied. "And for that reason I am trusting you with my most precious gift." He raised Jessica's hand. "Don't make me sorry I did."

An announcement sounded for their boarding group. Jessica made a frustrated sound. "I have questions."

Des pushed to his feet. "I need to call our team with a specific destination." His brows dipped. "We're still going to Mexico, right?"

Jessica watched her father nod. "Tepecoacuilco." He followed Des to his feet and offered him his hand. "God's speed, son."

Des's expression didn't change, but Jessica felt something pass between him and her father, and noticed how they shook hands a little longer than she would have expected.

Whatever her mother had said to her father, it had affected him profoundly. And whatever had passed between Des and her father had impacted Des just as much.

She hugged her father and noted the calmness that seemed to come over him, as if delivering that map had somehow taken away the frazzled state he'd been in since his arrival. But there was still worry in his eyes, worry born of a father's love as he watched his daughter set off to conquer the unknown.

Jessica left him with a promise to call home soon, a promise to be safe. And as she walked toward the airline gate, Des by her side, she had a sense of everything falling into place. But she also felt a need for expedient action.

Her mother had spoken from the grave, and for that to happen, Jessica had to believe the stakes were high, the clock ticking.

They'd been on the runway for thirty minutes, another rash of thunderstorms passing through with fierce results. Des sat on the plane, edgy and ready to rip away the restraint of the seat belt as he waited for takeoff. The cabin was stuffy, the air stale, the stench of hot bodies wrenching his gut.

Des hated small spaces, and he most especially hated any form of confinement. It brought the demons of his past to life. Memories of being tied up and tortured. No matter how he tried to destroy those parts of his past, they haunted him.

Beside him, Jessica tried to study the oversize map by folding it in pieces. With a frustrated sound, she stuffed it back in the envelope. "This is useless. I can't make out anything." She sat next to the window, peering outside at the clouds above. "God. At this rate we are going to be sitting here for hours."

Des hoped like hell she was wrong. "Try and rest," he suggested, though he knew he wouldn't. It was bad enough his past was pounding on him, but the present wasn't being so gentle, either.

She gave him a scrutinizing look and her hand went to his. "Are you okay?"

Her touch rushed over him with warmth, and a sense of calm overcame him. The feeling was so distinct, so total, he could do nothing but stare at her. The rage of pain and emotion inside somehow lessened with a mere touch from Jessica.

He reached forward and brushed a strand of her raven hair from her eyes. She was lovely, pure. So unlike him. Could she ever love him? Could she deal with his world? Did she even have a choice?

"Des?"

"I'm not a fan of flying," he said, refocusing on the moment. "I guess I prefer being in the driver's seat."

"It's safe," she said quite seriously and then whispered, "even for us mere mortals."

God, how this immortal wanted her to join him for eternity. She calmed him in ways he didn't think possible. Before she'd touched him, he'd been ready to climb out of his skin.

He laced her fingers with his. "I think I'll hold onto your hand anyway. If that's okay with you?"

"I have a better idea," she said, leaning forward to slide the envelope with the map into the seat's back pocket. She raised the armrest separating their chairs. Then she lifted his arm, snuggled beneath it and settled her head and hand on his chest.

She sighed, the sound full of satisfaction. A strand of her hair tickled his nose, and he rested his cheek on her head. If he had any chance of happiness in this world, Jessica was his slice of heaven. But what if he was her slice of hell?

His eyes slid shut, and he let himself imagine, if only for those few moments, that there was a way to merge their worlds. That the past and the present could come together—and so could he and Jessica.

With that peaceful thought, with his mate in his arms, Des allowed himself to fall asleep.

Des lingered at the edge of the woods, just beyond sight, taking in the beauty of Arabella's profile as she waited on him. He was back in his human life, the day he'd been bitten by a Beast, the day that had changed him forever. She stood beneath an oak tree overlooking a pond. It was their tree, their pond, their place to escape. Here he wasn't a slave to her rich father. For over a year now, this had been the solitude where they'd found each other, where they'd escaped the rest of the world.

A light breeze lifted her skirts slightly, her dark hair blowing with the wind. He inhaled, almost certain his nostrils caught the sweet scent of her.

Des stepped forward, eager to see the light in her eyes that she saved for him. But as he neared, she kept her face hidden, cast downward, and he knew something was wrong. His stride quickened, a sudden feeling of dread in his stomach.

"Arabella," he called out, but still she did not look up.

Des stepped into the clearing beneath the tree, and out of nowhere it seemed, Spanish soldiers, her father's men, circled Des, rifles pointed at his body.

Arabella turned to look at him then, and for an instant he saw guilt and pain, apology. But then her father's voice blasted through the air, and with it, she stiffened, her expression going cold.

"Stay the hell away from my daughter."

Des stiffened his spine as General Martinez, Arabella's father, parted the circle of men and showed himself. A short, stocky man, he used brutality and money to intimidate and strike fear in those around him. Des fixed the general in a hard stare, refusing, as he always did, to show fear. He knew how much it infuriated the general but he didn't care.

The general stopped directly in front of Des. "I should have you shot right here and now. What have you done to my daughter?"

Des had to look down on the general, who was a

good five inches shorter than him. He'd often thought that bothered the man. Right now, he hoped it did. "Done?" Des asked, his gaze going to Arabella, who refused to look at him. "I've done nothing to her."

The general punched Des in the gut. "Don't dare even look at her. What threats did you make to force her to give herself to you? Tell me now or I might cut your tongue out, so you can never tell anyone else!"

Des straightened again. "I threatened nothing. I love her." He looked at Arabella who stared at the ground. "She loves me."

The general turned to his daughter. "What trash is this sorry slave talking?"

Arabella hesitated, hugging herself. "Father—"

He cut her off and grabbed her by the hair. Des fought to contain himself. The brutal bastard treated everyone like nothing more than his trash.

"You want him?" her father demanded.

She whimpered, crying. "I—"

He glared at her, the air crackling with his anger. "Do. You. Want. Him?" A shaky, heavy breath blew from his lips. "Think hard about your answer, daughter, because if you disgrace me, you may well die by this slave's side."

A sob filled the air and then silence, father and daughter staring at each other. Abruptly, Arabella shook her head, her voice firming. "I don't know what he's talking about, Father. I was afraid. I was…" She bowed her head. "I didn't want anyone to get hurt."

Des felt the blow of her words before he felt the general's fist pound into his gut, over and over. Des doubled at the waist as he heard the general order, "Tie him up."

Des didn't fight the soldiers who dragged him toward the tree. He never fought his beatings. Never feared the pain. Before finding love with Arabella, he'd often wished they'd hurt him enough to kill him.

Moments later, he found himself tied to the tree he'd considered special. Tied to that same tree, about to be beaten. The general held a knife in his hand as he approached Des. He shoved the knife to Des's cheek. "Admit that you threatened her. I will not have my daughter disgraced by the likes of you." The knife pinched into Des's cheek and slid downward, biting into his upper lip. "You sorry Mexican bastard."

Des ground his teeth against the pain, blood dripping down his face now. It had been years since he'd seen his Native American mother. Des had been sold to the general as a way to punish her for Des's actions. Because Des had dared to defend her. To try to stop her beatings. And he had failed her; he'd been sent away where he could do nothing to protect her. Des didn't even know if she was alive or dead.

"I'm no bastard. I not only knew my piece of shit *Spaniard* father, I knew him well. And like you, he cared for no one but himself." He was angry now. Angry that Arabella had turned away from him. Angry at being called a bastard. Angry at being sent away from his mother. "You might as well face it. I might be Mexican, I might be a slave, but I am the man your daughter loves."

"He didn't threaten me, Father." The general turned to Arabella. Her tears were gone. "It started as a game. I was just having fun with him. Teasing him a little. It was nothing more than that."

Des's heart kicked into double time. The way she

said the words, her face devoid of sorrow, a smile hinting on her lush lips, Des almost believed her. Which had been real? The whimpering claims of love or this? Was she trying to save him or save herself?

The general let out a fierce noise and motioned to Des with the knife. "This is not a game." He said *this* as if Des were a thing, not a person. He eyed a guard and shoved her at the man. "Lock her in the house and I will deal with her later."

Returning to Des, the general stood in front of him, shoving the knife to his throat. "I'd kill you right now but that would be too good for you." His chest rose and fell several times before he spit in Des's face. "My daughter could never love an animal like you."

He stepped backward and eyed one of his men. "Hurt him and then get rid of him."

Des felt the butt of a rifle hit him in the gut, the first of many blows. But those blows didn't cause him the pain Arabella had. Was it true? Had she been using him? Playing with him? Had she laughed behind his back at his foolishness? He imagined that laughter with each slap, each cut, each fist. And when the beating ended, his battered body standing only because ropes attached it to that tree, their tree—Des knew the truth. Arabella did not love him or she wouldn't have allowed this to happen.

His head hung between his shoulders. He'd been a fool to believe their worlds could come together. His eyes drifted shut and he prayed they wouldn't open again. He was…done.

Des's lashes snapped open. Disoriented, he stayed completely still, reaching for his location. He inhaled.

Honeysuckle. He smelled honeysuckle, felt warmth, not pain. His gaze drifted downward, to the dark head resting against his chest. *Jessica.*

Glancing to the right, he noted the plane window, the clouds beyond. They were in the air and he'd had a nightmare. It had been years since he'd last dreamed of Arabella's betrayal. Years of blocking out what he didn't want to remember.

It had been later that day that the Beasts had come. Des had managed to free himself as the hell broke loose around him. Men and women running, screaming, fighting. He grabbed a gun from a soldier, running with all his might, desperate to get to her, to save her. But when he got to the house, to her room, the general was already in battle with a Beast. Des hesitated, part of him wanting the general to die. It was only an instant, one flash of thought, and then he acted. He battled the Beast to save the general, only to see another Beast burst through the doors and kill Arabella.

Her death devastated him and he stumbled in battle. A Beast grabbed him, biting his shoulder, sucking his soul out. He rose a Beast, hungry for one thing…. The general's blood.

Salvador appeared then in a flash of glorious light, his hand going to Des's chest, returning his soul. Des fell to his knees, devastated by the poison he'd felt in those beastly moments.

And he'd never forgotten that need for blood and vengeance. That feeling, he realized suddenly, had come closer and closer to the surface lately. What he saw as controlling his Beast was really the Beast controlling him. He lusted for battle in an impure way. It was the biggest fear of all the Knights that the Beast would somehow claim them again. It was the reason most of them suppressed their Beast as much as possible.

Yes, he feared Jessica's rejection. Yes, he feared that she could not accept his life. But if she could, if they had found something special, a gift to be claimed, then there was far more to worry about.

Because more than anything, Des feared the Beast had already claimed too much of him. What if he tried to reclaim control, to bring the man in him forward, and he found out there wasn't enough of him left? That he would bite Jessica to claim her as his mate, and take too much. Together they would become victims of the Beast. He let Arabella die at the hands of the Beast. He'd lost his mother, never able to find her again— Lord only knew what had happened to her. Des was afraid of failing Jessica. Afraid of realizing his worst fear…loving someone else, and losing them.

Deep in the Mexico Mountains, only a day after stealing the journal, Greg clutched the bag in his hands as the Jeep pulled to a stop, the Mexican sun blasting down on their heads, sweat beading on his upper lip. "Here," he said as the caravan of vehicles pulled up behind them. "This is it."

To be certain, Greg retrieved a piece of paper from his pocket, a copy of certain sections of the map from one of many copies he'd made of the journal when he couldn't find a translator. He wasn't about to pull the journal out and risk Black Dog's grubby hands touching it.

After a few seconds of scrutinizing the paper, Greg nodded. "Yes. This is the first location."

Irritation flared in Black Dog's face, his words as sharp as a knife. "*First* location. What the hell does that mean?"

"There are several stars on the map and they are numbered." Fortunately, he had a book to reference the denominations. "I assume one map leads to another map or some sort of clue."

Black Dog pounded the steering column. "You didn't tell me we were freaking going on a scavenger hunt. This treasure box better be worth all you say it is."

Greg cringed at the volatile response, forcing himself to straighten, to try and come off strong. "You'll get what you've got coming to you," Greg snapped back, aiming for an unaffected air. The man had a dark side that set Greg on edge. He didn't want to be killed before he claimed his immortality. That would seriously mess with his plans. "Besides. It's not like I haven't paid you well."

He shoved open the door with those words, irritated, and afraid he might say more than he should to Black Dog and get hurt. Greg had cleaned out the discretionary fund at the museum for this. If anyone had thought he was an innocent victim, that discovery would prove he was not. There was no turning back. He was going to find that list, and he needed Black Dog to do it. When Segundo gave him his power, he'd dish out what Black Dog deserved and then some. He'd put him in a nice big mansion in the graveyard.

Greg stared at the landscape before him. Hills and trees lined Mexico's Cocula River, and lots of them. He glanced at the drawing in his hand, reading the text next to the *X* again. He couldn't be sure what it said. Maybe "two that are alike." Glancing around, he noticed two huge rocks that appeared the same.

Black Dog stopped next to him as the rest of their group began to impatiently gather. "Well?"

Greg pointed at the rocks. "Dig there."

"You're sure?"

"I'm sure," Greg said.

"You don't seem sure."

Greg hesitated. "I'm sure about the rocks." There was another problem that had begun to weigh on his mind. "We might have another issue. The legend says that the box holding the list protects itself from evil. It self-destructs. Or that's what the legend says."

Black Dog laughed. "And you're no choirboy, now, are you? But don't worry. You hardly qualify as evil."

"We can't take a chance," Greg said, feeling insulted for some unfathomable reason.

"What do you want me to do?" he asked. "Go snag a nun?"

"I'd settle for the choirboy."

Hours later, Segundo stood in the trees beyond the dig site, tired of following Greg and the damn Hell Hounds as if he were the dog. Darkness surrounded him, not a star in the sky, the light obscured by the storm clouds overhead.

Abruptly, out of nowhere Black Dog charged through the trees at him, in his animal form. Segundo refused to move, to show any response. The Hound snarled at him, that disgusting breath engulfing Segundo. His hand itched to slice the damn thing's throat. "Afraid to face me like a man?" he challenged.

Black Dog flashed into human form. "It's you who are afraid," he said. "I can smell it all over you. The fear that I will replace you by Adrian's side."

"You mean at his feet where a good dog belongs?"

A primal growl slid from Black Dog's lips.

Segundo crossed his arms in front of his body and stepped to the side, displaying a human female tied to a tree. "She should do nicely as the pure one to open the box holding the list. She's a schoolteacher, father's a preacher. You should like her. She bites."

Black Dog sniffed. "Damn, I hate the scent of 'nice.'"

"I guess your delicate nostrils will just have to deal."

In the distance, Greg called out for Black Dog. "We found something!"

Segundo eyed Black Dog. "He's not needed anymore."

He copied Segundo's stance, arms in front of his chest. "Adrian says he is."

Tension raced up his spine. The Hound was just trying to bite at his nerves and he knew it. Too bad it was working. "Adrian?"

"That's right. Greg understands the map."

"At least stop playing house with him. Take control."

"Adrian doesn't want him spooked. He's afraid he'll hold back information then."

Greg yelled again and Black Dog eyed the woman. "I'll be back for her."

Segundo watched Black Dog depart, his teeth grinding together. Greg wasn't needed. Adrian was punishing him. Forcing him to endure this charade with Greg and Black Dog, powerless to do anything but play along. And he knew how Adrian worked. He'd dangle Segundo along, and then kill him.

Which meant he had to possess that list and take it to Cain so that he could overtake Adrian's position. If Greg and Black Dog died in the process, it might just make his day.

Chapter 18

Jessica sat on the Mexico City hotel bed, shoes off, legs crossed, listening as Des talked on the phone to Max as his team traveled to the dig destination her mother's map indicated. She waited until he hit the end button. "Well? Any sign of Greg?"

"They're still about an hour out from the location you gave them."

A knock sounded on the door. Des went to answer it as Jessica started to open up the map again, afraid she'd missed something. Des rolled a room-service cart forward. "Eat, woman. You've eaten hardly anything. Some food and some rest might help your mind work better."

The sweet scent drew a rumble from her stomach, and she pressed her hand to the offending part of her body. Des's brow inched upward. "See. You need food."

She ignored the comment. "Shouldn't we be meeting the guys down at the river?"

Des sat next to her and lifted the steel cover off the Reuben sandwich she'd ordered. "Looks good." He sniffed. "Smells better. And we'll meet up with the rest of our team soon after you eat and get some rest. Thanks to our flight, we aren't that far behind them."

She grabbed a fry and dipped it in the little ketchup container provided. "I admit I need food." She bit into the fry. "Hmmm. Yeah. I need food." She eyed the hamburger he'd ordered. "I gather burgers and peanut butter are major staples of your diet?"

"I never get tired of a good burger," he commented, checking the bun to ensure he liked what the hotel had put on it. "I could eat them every day and be happy."

"I like a good burger, but I don't think I'd go that far. Though when I was nine, I went on a French fry binge. I refused to eat anything but French fries from my favorite restaurant. My parents were not pleased, let me tell you."

He laughed. "What'd they do?"

"They bought me French fries." She laughed. "I was spoiled." She finished off a big bite of her sandwich and held it out to Des. "Want to try it?"

Surprise flashed in his eyes before they filled with warmth. She held the sandwich to his mouth and he took a bite. She waited for his appraisal. "Well?"

"I like it," he said.

They talked about favorite foods and favorite movies. When she'd finished off her meal, she scooted up onto the bed and found a pillow, tiredness creeping over her.

"We have to find that list before the demons."

"We will," Des said, pushing the tray away from the bed.

"What if we don't?" she worried. "Maybe I'll take a fifteen-minute nap, but no longer. We should go."

He climbed onto the bed and settled beside her, pulling her close, her back to his front, his body curving around hers. One leg trapped hers as if he was afraid she would try to leave. Possessive. Protective. She loved it.

"We'll find the list," he said. "I set the alarm so we won't oversleep. Now rest."

She smiled to herself, peaceful in a way she couldn't describe.

The world was going crazy around her, a race against demons underway, and she didn't care. Not in that moment of time.

She snuggled closer to Des and fell asleep.

Des was having the best dream. Jessica was beneath him, naked and perfect, soft curves melting into him. Soft lips pressed to his. His tongue slid over hers, sweet like honey. He couldn't get enough of her.

Deepening the kiss, the hunger turned to fire. Her fingers were in his hair, and for some reason, it aroused him beyond belief. Everything about Jessica aroused him. He palmed one of her breasts, pinching the nipple. She moaned and he rewarded her for the sweet sound by lapping at the tip with his tongue. Her back arched as he nipped, kissed, licked.

He continued to pleasure her, but felt the growing fire of need and slid his palm under her backside, lifting her hips tight against his erection. The wet proof of her arousal surrounded him, begged for penetration. A deep groan escaped his lips as she rubbed up and down his length. This was his version of heaven.

"Des," Jessica whispered, her body arching upward, pressing closer. "Des." She tugged his mouth to hers, aggressively claiming a kiss.

He let her pull him into the kiss, wanting inside her any way he could get there. For now, he'd settle for his tongue. For now, but not for long.

But when he thought he was lost, sucked into a dream too good to be true, the alarm clock started to beep. The sound penetrated the lust-filled fog and Des's chest tightened. He raised up on his elbows, pulling away from her. She stared up at him, a question in her eyes. He answered with his own question. "This isn't a dream, is it?" he asked.

Jessica laughed. "I guess that depends on how you look at it."

"Holy shit," Des murmured under his breath, quickly scrambling off her, finding his way to the edge of the bed, his hand running through his hair. What if he had lost control? What if he'd hurt her? Why hadn't he?

Her hand stroked his back. His cock hardened with the touch, his body burning for more of her. "No," he said. "Don't touch me, Jessica." His gaze swept her naked body and he groaned. "And put some damn clothes on." She yanked her hand back as if smacked. "Don't you see?" he asked her. "I'm dangerous, Jessica. I'm dangerous to you."

He shoved off the bed and took long strides to the bathroom, then slammed the door and turned on the water icy cold. Stepping under the spray, he swallowed hard, emotion in his chest, in his throat. God. What if he had hurt her? He'd been asleep, unable to control what he was doing. It was a damn miracle things hadn't gotten out of control.

Jessica sat on the bed for a minute, staring at the closed bathroom door, stunned by what had just happened. What was that? She didn't know. But she did know she was tired of being left in the dark.

She stood up, marched toward the door and turned the knob. The door opened and she didn't give herself time to reconsider. She stormed to the shower curtain and flung it open. "We have to talk."

Shock rushed over Des's features. "Damn it, woman, I told you to put some clothes on."

"You're not wearing any."

"I'm in the shower."

"Now I am, too," she said as she stepped into the tub. Frigid water touched her skin and she hugged herself, shivering. "Good grief, it's freezing."

He leveled a stare at her. "Get out of the shower, Jessica."

"I'm in here now. I'm not getting out until you tell me what is going on. What is all of this about?"

"Jessica—"

"I deserve answers. I've said that too many times and this time I am not leaving until I get them."

He hesitated, clearly waging some internal battle.

"Fine. I think we might be mates."

There it was. That thing in the air between them she'd wondered about but felt odd asking. "Think or we are?" she demanded.

"Yes. Okay. I know we are."

She absorbed that a minute. "What does that mean?"

He shoved the wet hair back over his head, out of his dark eyes. "It means I freaking love you and can't stand the idea of hurting you. So please. I'm begging you. Get out of the shower and get dressed. Because I have to tell you, the cold water isn't working anymore."

Jessica didn't know what shocked her more, his words or the fact that he, indeed, was getting erect again. She swallowed hard. "And when we make love. That's when you think you're dangerous to me?"

His hand went to the wall, as if he was keeping himself in place, holding himself back. "Exactly."

She had to understand, had to have answers. "Will you talk to me about this when we're dressed?"

"Yes! Just get out." He stared at her. *"Now, Jessica."*

Something about the way he said the words put her in action. She stepped out of the tub, grabbed a towel and headed for the door, where she paused. She looked over her shoulder. "And I freaking love you, too."

She left then, not giving him time to respond, but she was quite certain she heard laughter as she pulled the door shut. A miracle, considering how on edge he'd been.

Warmth filled her. She'd never said those words to anyone before, never felt them until now. But though she'd known Des only a short while, she had no doubt they were a match—mates, as he said. She felt their bond in every part of her being, inside and out.

She pulled a pair of shorts out of her bag and then grabbed a T-shirt, nervous about what came next. About what all this meant. Sitting on the edge of the bed, she waited for the bathroom door to open.

A moment later, Des appeared in jeans and nothing

else. His towel-dried hair hung around his face. He was a gorgeous man. Broad shoulders, nice pecs sprinkled with dark hair, rock-hard abs that she'd like to press her lips to right about now.

He leaned against the wall, space a barrier between them, but he didn't speak, didn't seem to know how to start.

"You would never hurt me," Jessica told him, and she believed that.

"You don't understand," he said.

"You always say that," she countered. "Stop telling me what I don't understand and tell me what I need to know."

He made a sound and looked at the ceiling. "You are so stubborn."

"Apparently, you are, too."

He laughed at that, but it held a bit of sadness. "I guess I am. In fact, that's probably part of how I got where I am today. Jag has told me for years I walk too close to my dark side. That I'm pushing my luck, and that one day I might not find my way back to the man. And he was right. I can't control the Beast inside me anymore. When I'm with you, the part of me that is more Beast than man starts clawing at me, trying to get me to take you."

She wanted to go to him so badly, but she forced herself to stay sitting on that bed. "What does 'take me' mean?"

"To mate, the male bites the female on the shoulder. The bite heals in the star formation Jag spoke of."

"Oh. Well. Hmm. That sounds a little painful."

"I think it's more…erotic."

A distinct ache began to build between her thighs. "That sounds interesting."

Silence. One second. Two.

"You want to be linked to me, Jessica?"

"I already am, Des. We both know it." She tilted her head and studied the frown between his eyes, realizing he needed more than that. "And yes. I want that."

"You have no idea who I am. No idea of my past. And I'm walking on the edge of darkness, Jessica. I don't know if I can even come back."

"The past makes us who we are today."

Torment laced his words, filled his eyes. "Exactly my point. I am not in a good place."

"Maybe it's my bloodline, I don't know, but I was serious when I told you I feel evil when it's around me. Perhaps that's why I never liked Greg. And Des, you are not as close to the edge as you think you are."

He dismissed her words. "I am. Believe me, I am. I'm not sure how much of the man is left. If I bite you—" he looked away and hesitated "—I'm not sure the blood won't push me over the edge. I might kill you."

She pushed to her feet then, crossed the distance and hugged him, her head pressed to his chest. He held himself stiff at first, but slowly his hands settled around her. Beneath her ear, his heart beat a steady rhythm. She could almost feel hers falling into the same pattern, finding synchronization. He was part of her and she hurt for him. God, how she wanted to take away this pain eating away at him.

After a good minute of standing there in silence, holding him, she tilted her chin upward. "You won't kill me, Des. You see, I've felt both Beast and man, and I love them both."

"I won't risk hurting you. I won't."

"Then tell me how we solve this. Because I'm not going anywhere. You can't get rid of me. I belong here. I know that with every fiber of my being."

"Your life—"

"Led me here, to you. So let's find a way to solve this."

"It's not that easy."

"It never is." She touched his jaw. "Have faith, Des."

"Faith," he said softly. "I think I left that on the battlefield about fifty years ago."

"Then we'll find it," she whispered. "We'll find it together."

Two days after joining the Knights on the dig site, Des woke with a startled gasp. The days had been long, hot, without answers. The nights, for him, restless. He sat straight up, sucking in air, his hand going to his chest. His pulse was in overdrive, his body hot. Sweat gathered on his forehead.

"Des?"

Jessica's soft voice raced over his frazzled nerves and started to calm him. She slept with him, a soft presence that both taunted him with what he could not have, while also offering comfort and hope. His chest expanded, and he let the air blow through his lips. He quickly took in his surroundings. Tent. Dig site. Jessica's hand around his arm.

"What is it? Are you okay?"

He looked at her, touched her hand. "Fine. I… A nightmare." That same damn dream about the day he'd become a Knight. About Arabella and the Beasts. About wanting to kill her father. God. He'd been vicious. Ready to murder another man. Why had Salvador saved him?

Jessica tugged lightly on his arm, and he let her ease him onto the air mattress beneath them. They slept together fully clothed, and Des had managed to keep his hands to himself.

She rested on one elbow, staring down at him. "Do you want to talk about it?"

And say what? That in his human life, he'd considered killing another man? That he'd been a slave who couldn't take care of the woman he loved? "I can't," he said. "I just can't, Jessica."

Disappointment flared in her eyes. "All right, then." Slowly, she lowered her body, her head resting on his shoulder.

Her touch, her presence calmed him. Her voice was like soothing salve on a wound. Dimly, he recognized that as hope. She got to the man on some level, or that wouldn't be possible.

Jessica touched the arrowhead necklace around his neck. "You wear this all the time. Does this mean something special to you?"

Chingado. So much for calm. His heart crashed against his chest in heavy thuds. He swallowed. "It reminds me of my mother."

She lifted back up on her elbow to look at him, her eyes lighting with interest. "Will you tell me about her?"

No. Yes. Damn it! Jag's words rang in his ears. *Let Jessica help you find the man again.* He didn't want to relive the past, yet somehow he knew it was part of finding his way to Jessica. But that didn't mean he had to like it. So he blurted out the truth, told her of a time when he was human, before he'd become immortal. "My mother was a Native American slave. I was the bastard son of her master."

Des sat up, grabbed his shirt and pulled it over his head, giving her his back. He couldn't look at her. He just couldn't. "I need to check on the team." He still wore his jeans and boots in case a quick departure was needed. It was.

Three days into the dig, Jessica stomped up a hill to the shaded area where tables, equipment and supplies were kept under a tent. She grabbed a bottle of water from the cooler and then stuck a second one in her cargo pants for later. In various pockets, she kept digging instruments, a trick she'd learned from her mother.

Max joined her, climbing the hill and taking a bottle of water for himself, having returned only a few minutes earlier from a scouting mission with Rock and his men. He'd ditched the leather coat he favored for a white T-shirt and jeans. He had a rough, hard edge to him, the kind that made a woman want to tame him. Not this woman, but others. But there was something else there, too. Something that made her a bit uneasy and she didn't know why.

"You love this, don't you?" Max asked.

She smiled. "Yeah. I forgot how much. Still, nowhere near as much as my mother did though. What's the latest on Greg?"

He finished off half the bottle before responding. "Still nothing and we've covered ten miles in all directions."

Jessica sat down on the ice chest, frowning. "Something is off. If I'm right about our location, and he has the real map, why isn't he here?"

"You did say Solomon would likely code the map and the list. Maybe Greg can't read it, and he's chasing his tail."

"Yeah, well," she said, apprehension forming, "I'm starting to doubt myself. Maybe I'd better hit the books again." She took another long swig of her water.

"You do that. We'll keep diggin'. Besides, seems wrong to have an angel digging in dirt."

Jessica just about choked on her drink. "I'm no angel. Besides, we don't know for sure my ancestors are on that list. And even if I am, it's just a name on paper." She gave him a probing look, hoping to open up a little conversation about Des. "You Knights are the ones who face off with demons, Beasts, dogs, whatever they all are."

He looked toward the horizon, acting as if he was inspecting the sky, but she could tell he was avoiding eye contact. "Sometimes, it takes a demon to kill a demon."

"So it's like that, is it?"

His gaze drifted her way. "What are you talking about?"

"Des thinks he's all dark and demon-like too. Sounds like you feel the same way."

He looked at her. Just looked. No blinking. No change of expression. Then, out of the blue, he asked, "Do you love him?"

The question took her off guard, and not because he asked it. The intensity of his words rattled her a bit. "Yes," she said softly. "I love him."

"Then believe him when he tells you there is something dark inside him. Because there is. Love him enough to believe in it but not fear it, and you might have a chance to save him."

"Save him from what?"

Des stomped up the hill before Jessica could ask Max for more details, and she wanted to scream at him to go away for another minute or two. She wanted to save Des, but she didn't know how or even what she was fighting against. Some abstract beast-inside thing was hard to battle.

"What's cooking besides me?" Des asked, grabbing the bottle of water in Jessica's pants rather than making her get up. His gaze narrowed as he eyed the two of them.

"Jessica was just telling me how we're two of a kind," Max said. "You know." He pretzeled his fingers. "One with our Beast and all. I was telling her that's not true. We're not alike." He dropped the empty bottle of water in the trash bag. "There's still hope for you. I never had any." Without another word, he turned and walked down the hill.

"Holy shit," Des said. "What was that all about?"

Jessica watched Max depart, and for just a moment, she felt a flutter of unease in her stomach. A hint of evil coming off Max. A shiver washed over her despite the hundred-and-ten temperature.

Des kneeled down in front of her, one palm pressed to her forehead. "Are you sick?"

She shook her head but didn't explain. For some reason she didn't want to tell Des about Max. "The cold water mixed with the heat. It's nothing."

His palm moved to her cheek. "You're sure?"

She grabbed his hand and kissed it, thinking how tender his actions. Des was not evil. If only he knew that. "I'm sure." Jessica settled his hand in her lap. "Un-

fortunately, I'm not so sure we are at the right dig site."
She went on to explain her concerns.

When she'd finished, Des asked, "Where does that leave us?"

"I need to study the map and the diaries again."

"Ah, *mi amor,* you've been over them so many times."

A secret smile played in her mind. She loved when he forgot his fears enough to call her that. "I'm missing something," she insisted. "I have to try and find out what." She pushed to her feet and he followed. "I'm going to get started now. I hate for us to waste any more time here than necessary."

Jessica stood on her toes and kissed his cheek, pleased when he looked at her with surprise followed by warmth. She started toward the tent to do her research, satisfied she was getting through to Des on some level. That was something.

"Jessica, stop!" It was Des, and instinctively she did as he said. "Stay completely still."

And then she heard it. The telltale rattle of a rattle-snake. Her heart sank to her stomach so fast she could have been at the top of a roller coaster going down. The snake was nowhere in sight, and though it defied every-thing she'd been taught, the intense desire to start running overtook her. The idea of being a sitting duck damn near unglued her.

She might well have broken into that run if Des hadn't appeared in her peripheral vision and grabbed the snake, which was apparently right by her leg. Jessica screamed as the snake bit him once, then again on the hand, before he used a knife to slice it in half.

"Oh God, oh God, oh, God!" She rushed at Des. "You're hurt! You need a doctor."

"That snake can't kill me but it could have you." He grabbed her and pulled her into his arms, his face in her hair as he drew in a deep breath. "Damn it, woman, you scared the hell out of me."

"I'm fine, but—" Des swayed a bit, cutting off her words.

"You're not fine!" She looked over her shoulder and screamed, "Help! I need help!"

Des sat down on the ground. "I'm fine. It'll wear off." He steadied a look filled with apprehension on her. "Do you have any idea the kind of fear I feel at the thought of you being hurt?" His lips thinned. "Especially by me."

Jessica knelt beside him, noting the white coloring around his lips. "Help!"

Rinehart showed up, shoving his hat back on his head. "What the hell happened?"

"Snake," she said, starting to panic. Des was getting paler by the minute. "He needs a doctor. Can we take him to the city?"

Des lay back, arm over his face. "Shit. Yeah. See if you can get Marisol. Damn snake is kicking my ass." Rinehart flipped open his cell phone and dialed. Des peeked beneath his arm at Jessica. "*Mi amor.* I won't die, woman. Immortal, remember?"

She tried to swallow that concept. "But it's making you sick."

A shimmering light, almost like glitter, filled the air and then a beautiful Hispanic woman appeared, dressed in a summer dress of white with a knee-length skirt.

Beast of Desire

She knelt next to Des and glanced at his injury. "You're always finding trouble."

Des lifted his arm off his face and his lashes fluttered, his voice weak now. "It finds me."

"Hmmm. Don't think I buy into that." She glanced at Jessica. "I'm Marisol, the Knights' Healer. You must be Jessica."

"Yes," she confirmed, a bit spellbound by the woman. She had this warmth radiating off her, almost like, well, goodness.

"He'll be fine in a minute. Promise. Can you hold his arm up across your lap since he seems a bit out of it?" Marisol asked.

Jessica nodded and moved to lift Des's arm. "I am going to hold my hand over his injury, and you'll see a little light. Then presto—" she snapped her fingers "—he'll be fine."

When Jessica nodded her understanding, Marisol did as she described. Jessica marveled at the amazing sight of the light spilling into Des. She could see it climbing under his skin, neutralizing the snake's venom.

When Marisol completed her task, she smiled. "All done."

Des shook his head, as if he were trying to get rid of cobwebs, and then sat up. "Don't know what we'd do without that beam of light of yours."

"You know just the right thing to say to steal a girl's heart, Des," Marisol said, getting to her feet. "I'm going to say hello to everyone and then get out of here."

Des winked. "You mean Rock."

She gave him a warning look. "I mean *everyone.*"

Jessica read between the lines. Marisol and Rock had

something going on. She also saw Marisol as a female who would be easy to talk to and maybe offer some answers. "Can I talk to you a minute?"

Marisol didn't look surprised. "Of course."

Jessica eyed Des, and then glanced at Marisol. "Give me a minute and I'll catch up with you."

With a nod, Marisol turned away and Jessica refocused on Des. He spoke before she could. "What's that all about?"

"Sometimes a girl needs a girl to talk to." She ran her hand over the place that had sported the bite marks, amazed that they had disappeared. "You're okay now?"

"Yes," he said. "I'm fine."

A thought had occurred to her in the midst of all of this that she really wanted Des to consider. "Can I ask you something?"

"Of course." But his expression said he was tense, nervous about what secret she might want revealed. His walls remained up, and formed of steel.

"When you saw that snake about to bite me, what did you feel?"

"What?"

"Were you afraid for me?" she asked.

"Freaking terrified."

"Relieved when I was okay?"

"Beyond belief," he confirmed. "Why are you asking these things?"

"Just answer," she insisted. "Did you want to kill that snake?"

"Of course."

"And you were happy when it was dead?"

His jaw tensed. "Yes."

She leaned forward, pressed her palms to his cheeks and looked into his eyes. "How very human of you." And then she kissed him and rose to her feet, not giving him time to respond.

After leaving Des, Jessica immediately searched for Marisol. She found her talking with Rock, and as she expected, the sparks between the two were obvious. Marisol was quick to break away, however, and give Jessica some private time.

They found a pair of folding chairs by some metal tables and sat down. "What troubles you, Jessica?"

"Several things, actually," she said, rubbing her palms over her pants. "One is, well, Max. I think something is wrong with him. I thought maybe you could check him out before you leave."

"I can't heal what ails Max."

"Which is what?"

"Give me your hand," Marisol said.

Jessica did as she said. Marisol held her hand a moment, her lashes falling to her cheeks. When she opened her eyes again, she released Jessica's hand, clearly having made some decision.

"You love him very much. You see this as your destiny."

"Yes."

"No hesitations? No regrets?"

"None. I can't explain it, but I know I am where I am meant to be."

Marisol smiled. "Because you are." Those words hung in the air for a moment. "What I am about to tell you must be kept between us. You cannot tell Des or anyone else. Not yet."

Jessica felt nervous about it, but agreed. "Of course."

"Are you aware that Max is new to the Knights?"

"Yes," she said. "Des has voiced a few concerns about not knowing his history."

"That's because Des doesn't need to know his history. Not yet. Because you see, what ails Max is no different from what ails Des. They are both close to the darkness."

"I keep hearing this talk of darkness. What exactly is this darkness, this Beast inside?"

"Their souls were touched by evil, toxic in all ways possible. The man must be pure enough to dilute that or he will not survive."

This made no sense. "Why leave that Beast inside them at all? If the soul can be returned, can't the Beast be extracted?"

"They would never have the ability to fight those demons if they were in human form. Besides, certain physical conversions took place when each was bitten by the Beast."

Max's words came back to her. *Sometimes it takes a demon to kill a demon.* "Are you telling me Des and Max are not strong enough to fight that darkness inside?"

"Make no mistake," Marisol said. "Each of these men were picked because they are special. Each has more good in them than most will ever know. They are brave, courageous, full of willingness to fight for those they love."

"But the darkness could take them over?"

"Yes. They could fall to the dark side. Once the soul is consumed, they return to beastly form and answer to the underworld." She hesitated. "Max knows this well.

Des does not. He feels it but he does not know it. We chose not to tell him for a reason."

He deserved to know. "Why? Why would you not tell him?"

"Max comes from a group of fallen Knights. All succumbed, all but a select few, to the darkness. If Des knew this, then he might well decide his fall is inevitable and then he'd be lost."

Nausea overtook her. "Is his fall inevitable?"

Marisol squeezed her hand. "He has you now, my dear. There were no mates to the Knights before. No hope. You are the pure-blooded mate who will defeat his darkness. But he must claim you. Once that happens, all Knights will have hope. They will see they can hang on until their mates are ready for them. I only wish those before them could have been saved."

"Why not tell them when Jag found Karen?"

"So it felt real to them, not merely a mate given to their leader. Now, there will be two females, two Knights mated."

"Des thinks he will feel some sort of bloodlust if he mates with me. That he might kill me."

"It is true that the taste of human blood could destroy his soul, but you are his mate. To drink of you is the ultimate bonding of heart, body and soul. But man, *not Beast,* must control during the mating."

"How do I make sure that's the case?"

"I see love in his eyes when he looks at you," Marisol said. "As long as that love guides the mating, you will both be fine." Her expression turned serious. "But Des must face his past and forgive himself. He thinks he knows his purpose but he does not. He fights for vengeance, and because he thinks he is some sort of killing machine. He's lost the reason that defines his existence, which is to protect humanity and defeat evil. He must stop seeing himself as a Beast."

Jessica swallowed, nervously thinking of him biting her shoulder. "Or he might become one," she whispered.

They talked a few more minutes and Jessica hugged Marisol. About to depart, she had a final thought. "What of Max? I can feel how close he is to the edge."

Marisol's expression filled with sadness. "He is four hundred years old, Jessica. He's very strong and has fought hard to save himself. But he's been alone a long time. Max, I'm afraid, is a walking time bomb."

Chapter 19

Hours after Marisol had left the dig site, Des stood by the river, lost in his thoughts. A light breeze offered relief from the burning temperatures, his skin welcoming the cool touch. But nothing offered him relief from the torment he felt.

He'd tried to work out his frustrations by helping the team dig, and for a while, it had worked. Jessica had been studying the map and diaries for hours and he'd wanted to help. But he knew in his heart of hearts that he had some soul-searching to do. That knowledge had driven him to seek a bit of solitude. Jessica shouldn't have to go to Marisol for answers, and the fact that she had proved he had to deal with what was between them, one way or another. He wasn't being fair to Jessica.

Over and over, he replayed her words. Replayed her saying "how very human of you," trying to convince himself that was true. He loved Jessica and had no doubt she was his mate. But wasn't love about protecting that person? And how would he ever live with himself if he hurt her?

The sound of gravel behind him put him on alert. But he didn't reach for the blades sheathed at his hips. He knew instinctively who was there. Knew Jessica had sought him out.

He turned as she stepped into the clearing. In her hands she held one of the diaries. "Hi," she said softly. "I was hoping you might look at something for me. Since you seem to know this territory so well. I swear you guide us better than the map."

She'd given him an opening, and Des didn't let himself back out of what he knew had to be done. "It was near here that I lost my human life."

A stunned expression took over her features. "Will you tell me about it?" she asked tentatively.

A sudden dryness destroyed his voice, so he nodded and swallowed. "I will."

He motioned to a shade tree, and they sat down beneath it. She placed the diary on the ground beside her and hugged her knees to her body. Des leaned against the huge oak tree, needing support in an out-of-character way. And then he started talking and talking. He didn't stop until he'd told her about his mother, about being sent away from her, about Arabella and the day he'd lost her and then his life. When he was done, his chest expanded with emotion.

"Do you know what I think?" Jessica asked. No, and Lord help him, he wasn't sure if he wanted to know. He shook his head slowly. She continued, "I think a lot of feelings you attribute to the Beast are really quite human. I think over the years you dealt with the pain of that day by deciding it was all about the Beast. And I think you have to deal with the guilt you feel and face it like the man you are. When you do, Des, I believe you will be free of the darkness."

"I wanted to *kill* him," Des said, speaking of Arabella's father.

"I know," she said and reached for his hand, releasing her legs and tucking them beneath her as she sat on her heels. "I do. We all have those types of feelings. The difference between good men and bad ones is that the good ones deal with those emotions and don't act on them. And I might remind you that you had those feelings as a man. Not as a Beast. But I don't think you want to remember that part, do you?"

His gut twisted. God, how right she was. "I wanted him dead. I don't even know why Salvador saved me."

"Because you tried to save his life despite all that anger and hurt. Forgive yourself, Des, but in the process realize you are forgiving the man. No Beast is a part of this equation."

He squeezed his eyes shut. This was the thing he'd tried not to remember. The part of his life he'd buried beneath the Beast. Suddenly, he felt the soft touch of Jessica's lips on his eyelids. When she pulled away, he gently eased her to her back, settled beside her, legs aligned. He kissed her then, long, hot and passionate. "I want you so much," he murmured between kisses.

Her lips parted, the charge of arousal thick between them, wrapping them in a blanket of warmth. "Enough to keep me around for eternity?"

God, yes. "I'd die if I hurt you," he said, his voice hoarse with emotion.

"You won't," she promised, her lips brushing his. "You won't."

"I so want to believe that," he said, their breath mingled together, "to make love to you the way you deserve to be made love to." He pressed his forehead to hers. "I just have to be sure I won't hurt you."

Her fingers slid into his hair, stroking his scalp, soothing his nerves. The sound of rocks falling and the men yelling drew their attention. "So much for convincing you now," she said, in the midst of a sigh.

Reluctantly, Des agreed. "I would have enjoyed letting you try a little longer." He sat up and helped her to do the same.

"You say that now because you have your escape."

Des funneled his fingers through her hair, framing her face. "I don't want to escape. Okay?"

She nodded, her eyes filling with emotion. "Good. Because I don't plan on letting you."

Jessica walked with Des to the dig site, her hand in his. She smiled to herself, having the distinct impression he didn't want to let her go, amazed and thankful for all that had transpired.

They found Rock and Rinehart arguing. Why, Jessica didn't know, but no one seemed hurt so that was enough for her. Apparently, not for Des. He stepped forward and got in the middle of it, quickly drawing the harsh words to an end. "Knock it off before I knock your heads together."

Jessica shook her head. Diplomacy evidently wasn't his high point. Good thing it was hers. She glanced at the sky, noting the sun quickly disappearing into the horizon, not surprised when Des called an end to work for the night.

Claiming a seat under a canopy covering folding tables and coolers, Jessica was pleased when Des joined her only a few minutes later. "Frustrations are high and everyone is tired," he commented.

"I feel to blame," she said. "I found this location in her work on Solomon's son, Prince Menelik. She'd somehow come across many of his personal affairs. Anyway, the prince wrote that when his father gave him the box to hide, he took it to a far-off land, which somehow my mother surmised to be modern-day Mexico."

"I remember reading that," Des commented. "And the section about the river meeting two mountains fits this location perfectly. And she even had this spot marked on the map."

"Yes, but look at this," Jessica scooted the diary toward him. "Several pages back she had a note with a question mark. River, mountain, pond. There are some coordinates as well but they're smudged. Maybe Max could run some searches and see if there is a place like that nearby, still within the radius my father marked?"

Des stared down at the page for several silent moments before looking at Jessica. "He doesn't have to." His voice was scratchy, hoarse. "I know that area well. It's still inside the mountains your father marked, still in Guerrero. This is the city of Ixcateopan." His lips thinned. "This is where the Beast stole my heart."

Time to hit the road and face the ghost of the past. "Load up, everyone," Des yelled. "We're leaving. Now!"

* * *

Greg paced back and forth in front of his tent, trying to figure out where he'd gone wrong. They'd finally gotten to the last spot on Solomon's map, finally unraveled all the clues, but no box, no list. He'd taken them so far, so fast. Decoded five clues and each led to another, the final, here. If he had the other clues right, why not this one?

He ran his hand over his face, his eyes tired. He couldn't look at the map or the text anymore. He was seeing double, and it was getting him nowhere fast.

When he thought it could get no worse, Segundo appeared in his Beast form. That oversize eye of his glared at Greg, his intention to cause pain gleaming in the red center.

Panic overtook Greg, his heart almost jumping out of his chest. "Black Dog!"

Segundo laughed, evil. "You're such a fool, Greg. You live only because I've let you live."

Black Dog appeared, a gun in his hand. The minute he saw Segundo, he shoved it into the holster at his shoulder and made a primal growling noise that had Greg backing away.

"What the hell are you doing here, Segundo?" Black Dog demanded.

"Game's up," Segundo said snidely. "Seems you were so busy chasing Greg's ass, you didn't cover your own. The Knights just arrived. They're only a few miles down the road setting up camp."

Greg had no idea who the Knights were, but he suspected they were those men from the museum. All he knew for certain was he'd been a fool. Black Dog obviously knew Segundo. To think he could hide from a demon. But then, what choice had he had? Segundo would have killed him if he'd handed over the journal. He was going to kill him now.

Black Dog cursed. "Do they know we're here?"

"You mean, has your stupidity caught up to you yet?" Segundo asked. "Not yet, but it will." He snapped his fingers and five additional Beasts charged forward, all wearing shiny suits and swords. "Adrian wouldn't want me to sit by and see you destroy this mission. I plan to take care of things." He smiled. Evil. "I plan to take care of you, Black Dog."

Without warning, Black Dog turned on Greg, grabbing his shirt and yanking him forward. Greg's teeth jammed together and he bit his tongue. Blood spilled into his mouth.

"I don't like being made a fool," Black Dog half spoke, half growled. "We've been here longer than any other location. You said this was the final spot. Where is that damn box?"

Greg could barely breathe, let alone speak. He was shivering from head to toe. He was going to die. He knew it. He didn't want to die. "I... It should be here."

"Wrong answer," Black Dog said and shoved Greg to the ground. He looked at Segundo. "He's worthless now. This is the end of the road on that map. We don't need him."

Out of nowhere, two snarling black Hounds charged at Greg, their faces horrid and distorted. He backed up on his hands, scrambling as best he could from his ground position, no time to stand.

"Wait!" he screamed, certain he was about to die, his survival instinct kicking in. "You need me!"

The Hounds stopped at his feet, their teeth bared. "For what?" Black Dog asked.

"Kill him or I will," Segundo challenged.

"No!" Greg screamed. "I've studied Solomon," he lied. "That's how I got here so fast. The list will be encoded like the map. You need me."

"The list we don't have," Segundo said dryly. He fixed Greg in a hard stare. Seconds passed. Seconds that felt like hours. Then, "Keep the human alive for now," Segundo said, shifting his gaze to Black Dog. "Send your Hounds to scout the Knights' camp. We need to know if they have the list." He glanced at Greg. "Get him digging with the rest of your men. If that box is here, we need to find it now."

"My Hounds are digging. Send your Unit."

In a flash of movement, Segundo was in front of Black Dog, his hand around his neck, lifting him in the air, feet dangling. "Do not test me, Hound. You've screwed with my plans all you are going to." He dropped Black Dog with a hard thud. Segundo turned then and walked away, his men following in his footsteps.

Greg watched the whole thing in awe, almost forgetting the Hounds perched at his feet, ready to attack. He wanted to be as strong as Segundo, to have that power.

He still had the journal, which he had to hide and do it fast. And he still had the leverage of decoding that list. One way or the other, he'd get his immortality.

And then no one would push him around again.

Chapter 20

Des started the hunt for the box as soon as they arrived at their destination in Ixcateopan. Based on the diary notation, Des had them begin searching on the side of the pond closest to the river. It seemed the most logical choice.

With nightfall fast approaching, they'd set up spotlights in order to keep going. Des knew deep in his soul, this was the location. The coincidence was too extreme for it not to be. What were the chances he knew this location would be significant to him and show up in those diaries if there wasn't a connection. Very little, in his opinion.

When they had found no signs of Greg upon arriving, Des had sent Rock and his team to scout. They didn't need any surprises and it made sense that Greg would be near if they had the right location this time. After all, Greg had the map. But Rock had been gone damn near two hours without communication. The deep canyon had cut radio connection and Des was starting to get worried.

His gaze settled on the oak tree on the other side of the water. His tree. The one symbolic of so much in his life. Around them, mountaintops sculpted the horizon. It was a beautiful location, a perfect location for love, if not for the taint of death. He could almost still smell the blood of that day. Almost hear the screams, as the Beasts attacked.

Jessica's hand touched his back. "Hey," she said. "You okay?"

"I'm fine," he said, taking her hand. He'd told her what the location meant to him, about the day he'd been turned to a Beast. That he'd been saved by Salvador. "Any word from Rock?"

"Nothing," she said. "Should we look for him?"

Des had been thinking the same thing, but he didn't want to leave their camp with limited security. "We'll give him a few more minutes."

"That's the tree?" Jessica asked softly, her attention on the big oak.

"Yes," he said. "That's it."

She slid her arms around him and joined him in his inspection of the tree. The gentle but unyielding strength she possessed calmed him beyond belief.

"I'm here if you need me," she whispered.

He was about to tell her just how much he did, indeed, need her, when Rock charged into the clearing. "We had Hounds snooping around the camp."

"Chingado," Des cursed under his breath, pulling Jessica close, his hand going to the saber sheathed at his hip. "How many?"

"They're gone," Rock said. "Took off the minute they caught our scent."

"They'll be back," Max said.

"And where there's a Hound, my guess is there's a Beast or two," Rinehart added.

"Or ten," Max said with a grimace. "You find their camp?"

"I found more than that," Rock offered, setting a bag on the ground. "The journal's inside. I saw Greg hide it." He snorted. "Not very well, either. In a rotted tree trunk."

Jessica dropped to her knees and unzipped the bag. "Oh God. It would have been destroyed by weather and animals." She pulled out the journal, running her hands over it. "The map is inside."

Rinehart smacked Rock in the head. "Good work, kid."

"I need light," Jessica said. "Quick. Before they come back."

Des waved one of the trainees forward, and he stood over her, holding a flashlight. She flipped through the pages with less care than Des expected she would have used under different circumstances.

When she found the map, she studied it in silence, the Knights surrounding her, the one female among them. And Des had the strangest feeling she held all their destinies in her hands, not just his. He wondered if the rest of them felt it as well.

When Jessica finally looked up, her eyes locked with Des's. "It's under your tree."

Des felt his breath lodge in his chest. He couldn't even find his voice. Had that box been beneath his feet the day of his beating, the day the Beasts had come? It had to have been. Destiny, this day, his life, had been set in motion long before now.

The last of his fears over mating with Jessica fled during that moment. He knew, like that box, that she was his destiny. Des helped her to her feet and kissed her before grabbing a shovel to dig. Twenty minutes later, despite many others working by his side, Des was the one who hit something solid in the ground. And Des was the one who uncovered the exterior of the box.

Jessica walked to the side of the hole and stared into it, tears coming to her eyes. "I don't believe it. We did it."

"Yes, *mi amor,*" he said softly, "we did."

Now they just had to get it to the ranch safely.

Black Dog lay on the ground, having returned from the Knights' camp to be beaten by Segundo. "Adrian will make you pay for this," he proclaimed vehemently.

"See. There's where you're out of luck," Segundo said, slicing a saber down Black Dog's stomach. "While you were scouting, Adrian departed for the Underworld. He's visiting Cain, promising him he will soon have that list of bloodlines I had intended to deliver." He cut Black Dog again, barely containing his desire to kill him. Black Dog grunted with pain. "If you want to live, tell me everything you know. If that list becomes mine, if I am the one to hand it to Adrian, then I'll consider letting you beg for mercy. But if you dare cross me, Hound, I will kill you."

Segundo started to slice Black Dog again. "Wait!" Black Dog held up his hands. "The woman from the museum, that Jessica lady. She was at the Knights' campsite, helping them. I saw her myself. She's using her mother's research on Solomon to find the box. I can bring you that research. I've seen it. I know what it looks like."

Segundo cut Black Dog again, deep this time. Black Dog cried out in misery. When Segundo was satisfied he'd caused great pain, he added, "You just don't get it, do you? I want it all. The journal. The research. The list. The woman. And while you're at it, I want Greg dead."

He sheathed his blade and kicked Black Dog. "Now get up. We have work to do."

Segundo grimaced as he walked away, beyond angry, beyond frustrated. He had no choice at this point but to earn Adrian's favor back. His chance to steal Cain's favor had been destroyed.

He'd use Black Dog and kill him. And he'd use this Jessica and kill her, too. As for the Knights, they were nothing but a pain in his ass. They would be the first to die. He might be beat, but he wasn't going down without punishing everyone who had taken his glory.

None of the Knights would touch the box. They were all afraid to find out what would happen: if they were dark enough to cause its destruction.

It took an hour for Des to clear enough dirt around the box so that Jessica could lift it out of the hole. Too long when they knew those Hounds had been a sign of more to come. But Jessica had the box now, and they were preparing for departure. With relief, Des watched her climb into the back of one of the vans, the box in her lap.

He stood outside the door, keeping an eye on how the

team's progress was coming. He was beyond edgy; he was ready to leave this place in the past. As tempting as it was to take Jessica and the box ahead of the group, he wanted every layer of protection in place and that meant traveling as a group rather than splitting up.

"Once we get the communications lines back up, can Marisol take the box back to the ranch?" Jessica asked. "It makes me nervous having it out in the open like this. Or…er…is Marisol all dark side and stuff, too?"

"I don't know Marisol's history, but it's a damn good idea. It makes me nervous, too. We'll have to drive it out of this canyon, though, to get phone reception."

A warning filled the air. "Incoming!"

Terror squeezed Des's heart. Fighting the Beasts was second nature. Fighting them with Jessica in the middle of the battle was not. The ironic nature of a battle at this location, with her present, didn't escape him, either. It struck fear in his heart. Fear for her.

"Do not leave this van," Des said, hands going to her waist, and he set her inside. "I mean it. Whatever happens. Stay here. I'll be close."

"Des—"

He didn't let her finish. He slammed the door shut, and she scrambled to the window. Des had drawn two swords just in time. A Hound charged at him. He side-stepped and took its head, relieved when it turned to ash.

His gaze swept the surrounding area, his men all in combat with the Hounds. But the yell had warned of Beasts. Where the hell were they? Another Hound came at him—no, two. Des rammed one in the heart and pivoted around to take the other's head. The one he'd stabbed was back already, lunging at Des. It managed to latch onto his arm. Pain splintered up to his shoulder as the Hound rolled and took Des with him.

Max came to the rescue, planting a blade deep between the animal's ribs. The jaws snapped open and Des was freed. Max finished it off. Des gave Max a quick nod of thanks about a second before a group of Beasts and Hounds charged through the bushes.

"Son of a bitch," Max said, and Des knew why he was cursing. He had damn good reason. There were at least fifteen Beasts and another five or more Hounds coming at them.

From inside the van, Jessica watched in horror as the Knights battled one Beast after another and not without injury. She'd never felt so helpless. She wanted to fight, to be of use, but she knew she couldn't. Knew she was no match for these creatures. But she also couldn't stop watching. The idea of Des being hurt, or worse, killed, struck terror in her. Not to mention her concern for the other Knights, all of whom had started to take on big-brother roles in her mind.

The sound of the front door opening had her pivoting to see who was present. Black Dog was in the van and he had started the engine. "Hello, Jessica."

Her heart kicked into double-time, and she lunged for the back door. The doors flew open before she could exit, one of Black Dog's men showing himself. He held a gun on Jessica, and with that weapon, he stole her opportunity for escape. The van was moving with Jessica and the box inside.

And there was nothing she could do about it.

* * *

Des saw the van take off, fear for Jessica turning to pure fury that he unleashed on the Beast he battled. He sliced through its neck and surveyed his travel options. Too many battles were going on around him to risk trying to get to a vehicle.

He sheathed his swords and started running, faster than he had ever run in his life. When that wasn't fast enough, he ran even harder. Faster. He felt the van pulling away from him, stealing Jessica beyond his reach. His heart pounded in his temples; his muscles strained. Still, he ran. Still, he hung on to the visual of that van.

The sound of a motorcycle didn't register at first. But as it grew louder, Des knew who it was. He turned to find Max approaching on the "rice burner" he kept in the back of one of the vans. Des had bitched about that bike taking up needed space. Now he was damn thankful for both it and Max. When the bike was level with Des's position, he hopped on the back. Max turned on the speed, pushing the bike to its limit. And Des prayed it was fast enough.

Chapter 21

Black Dog shoved Jessica to the ground in the center of their camp. She landed on the box, a jewel slicing through her side. Obviously they only cared about the list inside. Jessica hated the idea of damaging that box more than she did the pain from her injury. Beside her a woman cried, her knees pulled to her chest. Apparently, she, too, had been abducted.

To the girl's left was Greg. Since he was sitting with Jessica and this girl, he'd clearly become prisoner in his own camp. Served him right. Jessica could barely stand the sight of him. "What kind of person does what you've done?" she demanded of him. "And it got you nowhere but in trouble."

"Don't push me," Greg said snidely. "I've had enough of you to last a lifetime."

Jessica set the box between herself and the girl, as

her stomach rolled. The presence of evil, thick and pungent, was everywhere. It damn near consumed her. Evil that seemed to expand as a Beast approached and stopped directly in front of them.

"This must be Jessica," he said, smiling. He was in human form, but it did nothing to disguise his nastiness. "I'm Segundo. But you can call me *Master.*"

Black Dog approached again, her mother's diaries in his hand. He tossed them at Segundo's feet. "Just as I expected. That's the research. They were in the van with her."

Jessica would have objected, but she never had time.

"Excellent," Segundo said. Then, without warning, he pivoted and pulled a sword. With one sharp slice, Black Dog became ash. Two guards transformed into Hounds and Jessica, like the other girl, gasped as they hugged each other. The two Hounds charged at Segundo with vicious snarls. The fight lasted only seconds. Segundo killed the Hounds with ease, as if he were playing a game, not fighting ferocious animals.

He faced the three prisoners. "Who's next?"

Greg didn't wait to see if it was him. Suddenly, he was behind Jessica and the other girl, a knife in his hand. He held the blade between their faces, positioned to turn on either of them.

"We had a deal, Segundo," he said, his voice shaking despite his bravado. "I want my immortality. You want this box. So this is what is going to happen. I'm going to get into that van and drive away. Otherwise, I kill the women and your chance at getting inside that box. Push me and I'll touch the damn thing and destroy it. In three days, I'll leave a message for you at the Hotel

Mexicano. Then, and only then, will I tell you how to get the box back."

To Jessica's relief Des and Max chose that moment to charge the camp. They battled Beast and Hounds.

Greg intended to take advantage of the distraction. He motioned for them to move. "Pick up the box and go, now!"

Out of the corner of her eye, she sized up the situation. Des and Max had their hands full, and Segundo was Lord-only-knew where, waiting to challenge them. Jessica had to deal with Greg on her own. There was too much on the line to let him have the box. Too many lives that could be in danger.

"Leave it on the ground and he can't win," she told the girl. "He can't touch it himself." She glared at Greg. "He's evil. He'll destroy it if he touches it."

Greg's face turned sour. "Pick up the box before you get us all killed." He bent down and yelled in the girl's face. "Do you want to die?"

"No," she whimpered. "No."

"Then pick it up!" Greg blasted back.

The girl reached for the box, clearly too scared to say no. Jessica blocked out the fighting around her and focused on saving the box. At the same moment, Jessica and the other woman reached for it. Jessica managed to get a firm grip on the box, taking possession of it and pushing to her feet. Greg followed, to stand directly in front of her, a knife flashing in his hand a second before he thrust it at her. Jessica gasped as pain shot through the left side of her stomach—pain like nothing she had ever experienced in her life. Pain that consumed and suffocated her.

Remotely, she was aware of what had happened, of being stabbed.

Spots started to appear in front of her eyes, and she frantically searched for Des. She wanted to see him one more time before she died. Because she was dying. She knew she was.

She dropped to her knees as he appeared in front of her. She could hear him saying her name, hear the panic. Didn't want to leave him. "I'm sorry, Des," she whispered, but wasn't sure if she spoke the words in her head or out loud.

A roar from Max permeated the fog; the pain somehow gave her a moment of clarity. She saw Max grab Greg. Saw Greg's face distort with pain. But then the image was gone, replaced by the warmth of Des's touch. Replaced by darkness.

"Jessica!" Des screamed, agony lacing his voice.

He was dying inside as he held Jessica in his arms, shaking so badly he could barely dial Marisol. *Need* Marisol, he thought. Need help. He would never forgive himself for not getting to Jessica in time. No. No. No! He refused to believe he wasn't in time. She had to be okay.

He looked to Max for help but the Knight was on his knees next to Greg, rocking back and forth. He'd totally lost it. "I killed a human," he whispered over and over.

Des tried the cell again but it was worthless. No signal. He'd never felt so helpless in his life. Des stood up with Jessica in his arms, her limp body and pale skin downright terrifying him. Blood poured from her wound. If she died, he was going to die with her. He had to get out of this area, to a place he could call Marisol.

Max was the only hope Des had of assistance. "Max!"

he yelled. "Max." Nothing. The Knight just kept rocking, kept murmuring. Des yelled again. "Screw that evil bastard, man. He stabbed my woman. Look at her. *Look* at Jessica. Help me, man. Snap out of it and help me."

Max's gaze lifted but the expression in his eyes was absent, checked out. *Damn it!* Des started running toward the vehicle. How he would drive and tend her wound at the same time, he didn't know. Then out of nowhere, Max appeared by his side and Des said a silent thank-you.

By the time Des got Jessica into the back of the van, Max had jammed the engine into gear. Tugging his shirt over his head, Des used it to cover her gaping cut and attempted to stop the bleeding. Max dialed his phone over and over, driving like a bat out of hell, hitting the bumps with the force only speed could deliver.

But somehow it wasn't fast enough. He couldn't do anything fast enough.

Emotions raging wildly, Des pulled Jessica close and touched her face. *So cold.* He leaned down, ear to her mouth, checking her breathing. His chest damn near exploded as he waited for the barely perceptible trickle of breath. "God. She's barely breathing." He inhaled a breath and tried to calm himself, tried to think. He leaned over her, his body draping hers, and prayed. He prayed as he'd never done in his life. With all his heart and soul, the man, the human, begged for forgiveness for the past and asked for Jessica's life.

Suddenly, Max slammed the van into park, jerking the vehicle with an abrupt stop. A second later, he was in the back of the cab, jacking Des against the wall. "What the f—"

Max tightened his grip on Des's arms, his strength in some sort of superhero mode, because Des couldn't budge him. "Listen up, man, and listen good," Max said. "There were Knights before the ranch. Good men who lost themselves to the darkness. I know because I watched it happen. I know because I'm barely hanging on. Save Jessica and yourself. Claim her and *do it now*."

Max let go of Des with as little warning as he had grabbed him, and Des fell forward onto his knees. By the time he hit the floor, Max had already climbed back into the driver's seat and had them moving again.

Des didn't have time to question; he simply acted. He pulled Jessica into his arms and shoved her shirt off her shoulder. "Are you sure it'll work like this?" Des said, concerned for her safety. He'd assumed they needed to be making love.

"Just do it!" Max screamed.

Right. Just do it. Des inhaled and reached deep, calling for the Beast he'd spent days trying to suppress. His teeth had elongated only twice in his immortal life, both times in bed with Jessica. He prayed he could bring them forward. Inhaling again, he took in her scent, the soft womanly scent so familiar, so Jessica. And he imagined claiming her, making her his mate.

Amazingly, he felt the sensation of his teeth changing, and he wasted no time planting them into her shoulder. Her blood touched his tongue like sweet honey, and he drew it within him, cradling her like a baby, willing her to return to him. There was no Beast in his mind, only a man pleading for his woman's return.

How he knew when to withdraw, when to stop, he

didn't know. He simply did. The instant he pulled his teeth out of her shoulder, the wounds began to heal. As he watched, a star began to appear.

"Jessica," he whispered. "Talk to me, *mi amor.* Please."

"It's ringing!" Max yelled, holding up the phone. Then he said, "We need you now."

Marisol appeared in the van, her concerned gaze settling on Jessica. She quickly knelt down and touched Jessica's arm. Her hand extended to Des. "Come, Des. We will save her together."

They shimmered out of the van.

Segundo stood on the outside of the camp watching as a group of Knights charged the site. The one called "Rock" rescued the school teacher and used her to retrieve the box. Segundo didn't see a point in joining the battle. Not now. Not with his plans destroyed.

He didn't even turn around when Adrian materialized behind him. He knew what was next and he would depart this realm a soldier. Segundo dropped to his knees and waited for death, for the blade to slice his neck.

Behind him Adrian laughed. "You think I will make it that easy on you, do you?"

Segundo's worst fears became reality with those words. A second later, he found himself flashed into a pit of snakes. A pit he would be in until Adrian had mercy on him. A pit he would be in for all eternity.

Chapter 22

Jessica's lashes fluttered and lifted. She blinked into the sunlight, trying to find her bearings. Trying to remember anything through the heaviness of her limbs, the fog in her mind.

Slowly, she eased into a sitting position, noting she wore her favorite burgundy pajamas, their familiar touch offering a sense of being grounded and safe. The room was small, with rich blues and bright white decor. When her eyes settled to the left of her, to the chair in the corner, she knew her pajamas had nothing to do with her feeling of safety. Des rested there, his eyes shut, his long legs stretched in front of him. He looked uncomfortable, his face shadowed, unshaven. But he also looked good. So damn good. The sight of him filled her with warmth, and instantly she knew that something had changed. She felt him inside and out. Felt him as if he were a part of her.

"Des?"

His eyes shot open and he was on his feet in a flash, rushing to her side, settling on the bed beside her. A second later, he pulled her close and kissed her. "I thought I'd lost you."

She smiled against his lips, her hands resting on his chest. "You can't get rid of me, even if you tried." Her lips brushed his again. "Though I don't remember a darn thing right now. Where are we?"

"The ranch I told you about."

Jessica reached for a memory of traveling there but had none. "Everything is fuzzy."

"Marisol said that might happen, but it'll all come back to you. Some of it I wish you could forget. You went through quite an ordeal."

"I don't like not knowing." She stretched a little. "I feel all stiff and groggy." She shoved the covers back. "I need to move around, I think. I want to remember."

"You will. All of this is expected. You've been asleep for two days."

Her eyes went wide. "Two days! Oh good grief. What happened to me?" A flash of memory, of a knife digging into her flesh, made her gasp. She grabbed for the pajama top and yanked it up, touching the entry point, but finding nothing. "What?" she murmured, mostly to herself. Her gaze fixed on that spot, her fingers sliding over the perfectly smooth skin. "I…" She looked at Des. "Was I stabbed?"

"You almost bled to death," he said softly, his gaze turbulent. "Scared the hell out of me."

She shook her head. "But there's not a wound."

"No." He pushed off the bed and held out his hand. "I need to show you something."

She slid her palm against his, eager for anything that meant an answer, willing to go wherever Des led at this point. Already, she felt tension building, the "not knowing" what happened to her freaking her out. She didn't function well in a fog.

She found herself in a small bathroom, positioned so that her back was facing the mirror. Des's fingers brushed the buttons of her silk top, their eyes locking. Intimacy burned between them, sensual yet not sexual.

Once the two buttons were free, Des inched her sleeve off her shoulder. Then he reached behind her and retrieved a hand mirror. He held it in front of her. She accepted it, looking at the image behind her. She gasped at the sight of a beautiful five-pointed star on her shoulder, much like a tattoo.

Her gaze lifted to Des's. "How?"

"I didn't want to do it this way. Please believe that. But you were dying and—"

She cut him off, needing to know only one thing. "Did you do it just to save me, Des?"

"No. You know I wanted this, *mi amor.* You *know* I did."

Relief washed over her and she smiled. "So instead of killing me as you thought you would, you saved me."

"Yes," he said, his hands sliding into her hair. "Now, if it's all right with you, I'd like to make love to my woman the way I should have when I marked you."

"I'd be upset if you didn't." His lips brushed hers, but a memory jolted her out of the moment, her hands going to his wrists. "The box!"

"It's here and it's safe," he said. "And before you ask,

the kidnapped woman is fine. Marisol did something to erase her memories. I'll tell you more, *after* I make love to you."

Her body relaxed, the concern over the box fading into desire. "Hmmm," she said. "I think I can live with that."

At Jessica's request, Des waited on the bed for her. Apparently, two days of sleeping did not undo the female need to perform a beauty routine. Though he didn't know why she needed to do anything to herself. She was beautiful as she was.

Part of him had feared her reaction to their mating, the fears of his past still lingering in the future. But deep down he'd known she wanted him as he did her. Still, digging out of the hole he'd climbed into so many years before would take some time. He barely knew the man anymore, but with Jessica's help, he would rediscover himself.

Even right now, unfamiliar nerves crept through his system. He felt more schoolboy than grown man. Before Jessica, there had been plenty of women, enough to offer confidence in his ability to please his mate. But none had mattered; none had held his heart. Jessica was the one who mattered now. He was going to make love to her as she had never been made love to before.

As eager as he was for her entrance, nothing could have prepared him for the moment when she finally appeared, for the moment when she stepped into the room completely, gloriously naked. His breath hitched in his chest and with a hunger born of passion and love, his eyes slid over her lush curves, her pale skin. High, full breasts and rosy, peaked nipples. Sleek raven hair brushed her creamy shoulders.

But it was not her beauty that stole his breath. It was the message she was sending to him. Because Des knew she was telling him she was his, no barriers, no walls. She was his woman, his mate.

He rose from the bed and undressed, their eyes locked as he tore away all that remained to keep them apart. When his clothes were gone, he stood there for her to view, his body aroused, his own message clear. He was all hers—body and soul, man and Beast.

They stepped forward at the same time, closing the space between them as they had the other barriers. Des took her hands, leading her to the bed and urging her to sit on the edge of the mattress. He wanted to pleasure her, to take his time making love to her.

He went to his knees, parting her legs as he moved forward, between them. His hands caressed her sides and slid up her back; her nipples brushed his chest; her soft skin teased his palms.

Des slanted his mouth above hers, their breath mingling, his chest expanding with emotion. "I love you, Jessica."

She opened her mouth to respond, but he absorbed the words with the brush of his lips. Once, twice, three times. And then he claimed her mouth. It was a gentle kiss, slow strokes of their tongues, passionate and sensual. A kiss of a man reawakened, a man discovering true tenderness. Perhaps experiencing it for the first time ever. Because Des didn't remember anything remotely similar to what Jessica aroused in him.

Slowly, his lips traveled to her cheek, her jaw, her shoulder. She moaned softly as he began an exploration of her body with his mouth. As he kissed her elbows, her fingers, the ripe red peaks of her nipples. He lingered there, molding her breasts with his hands as he licked and suckled.

As he trailed his mouth down her stomach, she leaned back on her hands, arching her spine as he teased her navel with his tongue. He could feel the anticipation and burn in her. Feel her desire for him to kiss her lower, more intimately.

When finally he trailed his tongue along the V of her body, she tensed, waiting, ready. Des pinned her in a stare as his fingers slid along the silky wet center of her core, the proof of just how ready she really was. Her lashes lowered for a moment before she cast him a sensual look. A look that only made Des desire her pleasure all the more.

He took his time, building up the tension, stroking her sensitive flesh with his fingers, long before he gave her what she really wanted. And when he finally drew her swollen nub into his mouth, she shivered and gasped. With only a few caresses of his tongue, she shattered into orgasm. Des vowed it would be the first of many this night. A night that would begin a life of pleasure for Jessica. Because he was devoted to his mate in all ways possible.

After hours of wonderful lovemaking with her new mate, Jessica followed Des into what he told her was Jag's den, promising that a surprise awaited her. To her utter shock, her father was sitting with Jag, smoking a cigar. Judging from their laughter, they were bonding quite successfully.

The minute Senator Montgomery saw his daughter, he

abandoned the smoke and conversation, rushing toward Jessica. She was quickly pulled into one of his bear hugs.

"What are you doing here, Dad?"

"Jag invited me out to see the ranch and talk a little business."

"Business?" she asked. "What kind of business?"

Before he could answer, a beautiful blond female walked into the room holding the magical box. Jessica's heart jumped with excitement as the woman placed the box on a coffee table. Diamonds surrounded gold, the jewels glistening in the sunlight that streamed from the nearby window.

"This is Karen, Jessica," Jag said, motioning to the blonde. "My mate."

"I thought she might be," Jessica said, inclining her head. Only a few people could touch that box, and it made sense Karen would be one of them. "Nice to meet you."

"Nice to meet you, too," Karen said. "I've heard a lot about you." She waved at the jewel-covered box. "It hasn't been opened. We thought both you and your father deserved to be present when it was."

Jessica was surprised and pleased with their actions. "I don't even know what to say."

Des took her hand and pulled her to the brown leather couch in front of the box. They sat down side by side, and everyone gathered around them. In silent support, her mate was there for her, sharing this experience. The way it was supposed to be. She and Des, together.

As she studied the box, Des squeezed her hand. Her eyes narrowed as she noted the keyhole, shaped like a star. Her gaze lifted to find Jag standing directly in front of her, on the opposite side of the table. Ruby and emerald stones lined the solid gold lid. It was a gorgeous box, a treasure holding a treasure.

He squatted down and held up his hand, displaying the ring he'd shown her during their prior meeting. "The key."

"Oh my God," she whispered, her gaze lifting to Jag's. "You weren't supposed to find the box until you found Karen. You wouldn't have been able to touch it."

Jag's lips hinted at a smile, as if he was impressed she'd discovered a secret he'd already been privy to. He reached down and turned the box to face him, inserting the ring. It turned the lock without hesitation, and he lifted the diamond-studded lid. Apparently satisfied with what he saw inside, he turned the box back to Jessica.

"That list holds the bloodlines that offer my men hope," Jag told her. "Will you help us decode them? I suspect you will discover your family is indeed on that list, by the way. Just in case you were wondering." He winked. "I have an excellent informant. Perhaps you'll meet one day."

Her chest swelled at the offer, at the amazing opportunity this was to complete her mother's work. Unbidden, her thoughts went to Max, and she prayed one of those bloodlines indeed held his hope.

"Thank you," Jessica said. "I'd have it no other way." Her own destiny with Des formed a question in her mind, which she presented to Jag. "I assume those bloodlines represent mates to the Knights?"

"They do," he agreed. "And our mates allow us to

defeat the Beast within us so that we can become stronger and more capable of defeating the Beasts. And, thanks to you, their family names are now under our protection."

Jessica's father spoke then, his voice laced with a hint of emotion. "The journal will stay here as well. I believe your mother would want it that way." He glanced at Des. "And she'd be glad to know you, and the journal, have a Knight of White to watch over you."

Jessica took Des's hand in hers, and before he knew her intentions, she placed his palm on top of the box. A small gasp resonated through the room and then a sigh of relief. The box was still intact. Jessica smiled. "He is indeed a Knight of White." She leaned forward and kissed him. "In all ways possible."

"Jessica," Des whispered, his gaze locking with hers. In that moment, they shared a scorching hot stare that had her father clearing his throat and the rest of the room laughing.

Epilogue

A week after their mating, Des sat on the front porch of the ranch, Jessica by his side. Karen and Jag were with them, sitting in matching lounge chairs, telling tales of their recent travels. The feeling of fulfillment that Des felt with Jessica by his side was beyond words. And their love had offered hope to the rest of the Knights.

Karen's soft laugh filled the air as she spoke of visiting Paris. "When the waiter brought us the wrong wine, Jag orbed to the cellar and got it himself. I was a nervous wreck over that."

Jag chuckled and Des's eyes locked with his old friend's. A moment of understanding. Both knew these two women had changed their lives. Before Karen, there was no laughter in Jag. No happiness. Now, here they were, on the porch, changed men. Happy men.

"So Des, my man, any visions of the future you want to share?" Jag asked.

Jag spoke of Des's new power—premonitions. Des laughed and gave Jessica a scorching look that made her blush. His last premonition had been rather intimate.

"Nothing I'd be willing to share," he said, returning his attention to Jag. "So far I'm getting nothing that holds any significance in battle."

"That power will develop as you are ready," Jag assured him. "With time I'm sure your new ability will guide us in invaluable ways."

"My father called, by the way," Jessica offered. There had been concerns her father could be a target for the Beasts, so Jag had offered him protection. "He and Eva are getting along well. She's filled his assistant position quite nicely, and he says she's great with the public."

Karen smiled a bit sadly. "Eva will take good care of your father. I really didn't want her to leave, but she said she needed to do this. And if I didn't let her, she'd be trying to charge the battlefield with the men."

"This seems a good compromise," Jessica offered. "I saw Eva with a sword. She can handle herself, but with my father, most likely she won't have to."

From the side of the house, Max appeared, walking toward his Harley, parked in the driveway. Des's gaze connected with Jag's. "He met with Salvador?"

Jag inclined his head, his expression grim. "He killed a human. There will be consequences."

"But that human was evil," Jessica argued.

Something about Max's vibe wasn't good. Des waved at him. "Where you off to, man?"

Max kicked a leg over his bike. "Nowhere good," he

said, settling onto the seat, offering nothing more. His helmet went on and he started the engine.

The sound of Max's engine was the only noise for long moments. Everyone sat there, watching as he departed. Jessica broke the silence, her attention going to Jag. "What consequences?"

Jag's expression held no emotion, no hint that would give away what would become of Max. "Nothing he can't overcome if he's willing to fight for it."

"But he's already fought so long and hard," Jessica argued.

"He did save Jessica's life," Des added. "That should count for something."

"Saving a human life is his duty," Jag countered. "You know that." Jag glanced up at the sky, Karen taking his hand in hers. "Everything has a purpose," he added softly.

Everything has a purpose. Des took in those words, holding Jessica close, and silently vowing he would never let her go. She melted against him and he knew she felt what he did in that moment. Thankful for what they'd found. Thankful for this gift they'd been given.

* * * * *

Be sure to watch for Max's story,
coming only to Silhouette Nocturne in July 2008.
And now for a sneak preview of
BEAST OF DARKNESS,
please turn the page.

Prologue

He'd broken a rule and now he would pay a price. It was as simple as that. Max had taken the life of a human. His reasons didn't matter.

Pulling his Harley to a halt in front of Jaguar Ranch's west-end training studio, he killed the engine, prepared to face the consequences of his actions. His gaze lifted beyond the wooded terrain, taking in the barely visible main house. To its right was a cluster of extra housing where the Knights in training lived. This was home to the Knights of White. And for a short time he had felt he might finally have found his place here as well. But he'd been wrong.

Dismounting his bike, Max sauntered toward the studio entrance, boots scraping the dirt-and-gravel path, apprehension working him inside out.

He took some comfort in knowing his actions had

saved a woman's life—and not just any woman. He'd saved the mate of one of his fellow Knights. A mate who had healed the stain of the Beast inside that Knight.

But regardless of the reasons for his actions, he'd broken a sacred vow by taking a human life. And for that, he would face consequences. Though Max knew this, even accepted it, he was no more at ease as he stepped inside the air-conditioned studio. He shut the door with a thud that was unintended, that screamed of finality. Of hard actions to come. But then, he didn't expect leniency. Max knew how close to the darkness he walked. Four hundred years of battling the stain on his soul had worn him down.

Max felt the lightly padded floor beneath his feet, barely noticing the weapons lining the walls, weapons that were used in the war against the demon Beasts they fought, the Darkland Beasts. The lights were off; meditation candles flickered in each of the room's four corners.

As he entered the studio, his attention shifted to two men standing in the center of the room. He approached them, in awe of the dominating figures they both were, how similar in so many ways. Long, dark hair touched each of their shoulders, powerful bodies spoke of warriors, of Knights. But more than anything, an inner strength radiated from them both.

Max offered Jag, the new leader of the Knights of White, a nod. Dressed in jeans and a T-shirt as Max himself was, Jag used his role as horse rancher to disguise his true role as demon hunter.

But Max's attention didn't linger on Jag. His gaze strayed to the man dressed all in white, standing beside him, to Salvador—the one who'd created him. The one who could end his existence with a mere wave of a hand.

Max met the light green stare of his maker with directness. If he was to fall this day, he would do it bravely; he would do it with his head held high. And he felt the touch of those eyes as if they moved inside him, as if they reached to the depths of his soul. Perhaps they did. Perhaps that moment, that look, exposed the truth in him; Max was so near the darkness, he could almost taste evil with each breath he drew.

Long seconds passed before Salvador spoke. "Leave us," he said softly, obviously addressing Jag.

Jag hesitated. "Without Max's help, we would have lost Jessica. And without Jessica, I have no doubt Des would have succumbed to his inner Beast."

Max's chest tightened at the protective gesture from Jag, regret biting at his gut. He'd been alone so very long. Finally, he'd felt a sense of belonging at Jaguar Ranch, and now it was in jeopardy.

But that realization didn't change the facts. He had to live with what he had done. All too well, Max knew he couldn't turn back time. Crossing his arms in front of his chest, he widened his stance. "I'm prepared to face the consequences of my actions."

Jag stepped forward then, pausing to lay a hand on Max's shoulder. "Peace be with you, my friend." And with those words, he departed.

Salvador raised his hand, and a sword flew off the wall and into his palm. "On your knees, my son."

Max did as he was told without hesitation, his heart pounding wildly against his chest, his eyes cast to the ground in disgrace. He knew death by beheading would follow and he did not fear it. To take a Knight's head was one of the only ways to kill him. But he wanted the end to be quick. He wanted this to be over.

"Choose now," Salvador said, the blade touching Max's shoulder. "Choose life…" Metal brushed the other shoulder. "Or choose death."

The words shocked Max and his gaze lifted to Salvador. He could barely conceive of what he was hearing. Was he being given another chance? "I don't understand."

"It's a simple question," Salvador proclaimed. "Life…or death?"

Indeed, it was a simple question. Max didn't want to fail the Knights, to fail his duty. And death meant failure. "Life. I choose life."

Salvador pulled the blade away from Max's neck and tossed it in the air. It disappeared as if it had never existed. "To your feet, Knight." Somehow Max obeyed, his knees weak. Once he was standing, Salvador stood toe-to-toe with him. "You will be sent to a place few know of, a place where you will face a great test. There you will need every gift your centuries of life have given you."

Max's response was instant. "I will not fail."

"Make no mistake. This test will punish you to your limits. It will force you to face your greatest fears. And you must face this test on your own, my son." He held out his hand to Max. "But you will not face it alone. You are never alone."

Max understood. He knew the Knights were always there for him. He knew Salvador was as well.

He accepted his creator's hand and repeated his prior words. "I will not fail."

* * * * *

Be sure to look for
BEAST OF DARKNESS,
available July 2008
in Silhouette Nocturne.

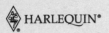

Romantic
SUSPENSE

**Sparked by Danger,
Fueled by Passion.**

The Taken

Tierney Doyle is used to being criticized for
her psychic abilities, yet the tough-as-nails—
and drop-dead-gorgeous—detective has no doubt
about what she has uncovered in the case of a
string of unsolved murders. And Tierney is slowly
discovering that working so close to her partner,
detective Wade Callahan, could be lethal.

Look for

Danger Signals
by Kathleen Creighton

Available in April wherever books are sold.

Silhouette®

nocturne™

COMING NEXT MONTH

#37 MIND GAMES • Merline Lovelace

Mark Wolfson was an expert at influencing women's thoughts. Special Agent Taylor Chase knew the doctor's psychic powers all too well—and she'd had enough of being toyed with. But she'd need his mind and body to complete her vital mission on a forgotten island, where instincts were best kept sharp—and inhibitions let go.

#38 LAST WOLF HUNTING • Rhyannon Byrd

Bloodrunners

The hunt meant more to Jeremy Burns than dominance—it meant facing the woman he'd left behind. Once Jillian Murphy had belonged to Jeremy. Now she was the Spirit Walker to the Silvercrest wolves, and the most desirable female of the pack. It would take more than the rights of nature for Jeremy to renew his claim on her—and she would not go easily once he had.

SNCNM0308